ONIICHAN

BEING THE ADVENTURES OF JEREMY LECLERC, KNIGHT TEMPLAR IN THE ENVIRONS OF CHARLOTTE, NORTH CAROLINA, AGAINST THE FORCES OF EVIL (MOSTLY)

EDWARD MCKEOWN

AD ASTRA BOOKS

PROLOGUE

Report to the Grand Master, subject: Jeremy Leclerc Knight Templar assigned to Charlotte, North Carolina, United States of America.

The Inquisition cleared Leclerc of any impropriety despite his constant violations of the rules of a monastic order. He carries a holy relic that accepts him and is one of the handful of Templars to pair with a guardian angel. Apparently, God still works in mysterious ways when it comes to Leclerc.

This assessment is borne out by his forays into other worlds at the direct behest of the Powers. We know little of what happened there, though rumors of a terrifying nature have reached our ears. The matter of his guardian angel Shadowheart becoming...lost in the role of a succubus during one of these is a matter beyond our jurisdiction. It is our understanding she has been recalled from the Realm of Earth for now. Thank Heaven no more damage or embarrassment was done...

ACT I

CHAPTER ONE

The call for aid came from overseas. A Shinto shrine alerted the Templar network in Scotland, after their priest and a nun were struck down by a mysterious force while blessing the Japanese Legation in Charlotte. The Templar Master assigned: Jeremy Leclerc.

Jeremy left his assistant, Samantha Pelton, to close up their graphic design shop and drove to the Charlotte-Mecklenburg Hospital. The priest was still in unconscious, but the nun, who'd suffered a broken arm the day before, told him in halting English about the attack.

"It was a *Yurei*, a ghost," the Japanese nun had told him from her bed. "The Hara family sensed a disturbance in the *wa* of the house since they arrived last month. It was growing worse: small accidents, disturbances, music playing in odd hours, a feeling of oppression. The restoration work going on in the building was constantly delayed by mishaps, and there is an important diplomatic and social reception to be held soon.

"The Legate, Hara-sama, brought in my priest to bless the house and quell its spirit. We had just arrived from Japan and were met by Hara-sama's son, Kei, who took us there.

"We did not come to do an exorcism and were unprepared. Young master Hara saved me from being flung down the stairs with the priest."

"Did you see anything?" Jeremy asked.

"No," she said, softly. "I was struck from behind but...but I smelled cherry blossoms just before I was struck." She placed a hand on his arm. "The young master did not believe before. Now he does. His father still wishes to cleanse the house. He will need help. The *yurei* is strong and terribly angry. I felt this."

The nun gave him Kei Hara's phone number. A quick and innocuous text sent by her and with his help, set up a meeting with the younger Hara.

"I must remain here with my priest," she said. "If he recovers, I will get him back to Japan. If not, his ashes will go. But the doctors are optimistic, and I will pray."

He wished her well and left.

Jeremy stopped at his South End condo for weapons and to review what little there was in the Templar database on ghosts. He found nothing he did not already know. Most of it consisted of unreliable and ancient accounts. Ghosts were considered a mere story by the Temple.

Soon after, he headed for the Legation and his meeting with Kei Hara. Sunday traffic wasn't bad. He reached the Myers Park area of Charlotte quickly, driving down its streets lined with immense old trees.

He pulled up in his red Mini Cooper in front of the Tudor-style mansion. Hedges surrounded its elaborate gardens of azaleas and thick-boled trees. He had the access code to the gate, but he wanted to study the building. The structure was white, with the heavy-framed dark timbers over stone that reminded him of his childhood in Northern England and Scotland. Steep gables pointed upward to the spring sky. The building had housed a Japanese diplomatic mission since the Russo-Japanese war. It certainly didn't look like a haunted house.

He looked about but did not see Kei Hara. Jeremy punched in the code and drove up the circular driveway. The area was full of worker's materials from the interrupted restoration and repairs. He opened the car door and pulled his long, black-leather duster off the back seat. March was still cool in Charlotte, but the long coat's main use was to conceal the Templar bloodsword in its special scabbard. He also wore a Walther PPK on his belt, and the coat would cover that as well.

It still felt strange to be without the gold and crystal locket Shadowheart often occupied. But after their return from purgatory, where they had lain low for a time, short on Earth but long in other realms, she'd announced she was being recalled. Before he could ask anything further, the angel vanished.

For weeks he'd carried her housing, hoping for some sign. Then he became resigned to soldiering on alone. Given all that had happened during their assignment in Hell, it was too much to hope for no repercussions. But it fed into his fury and resentment of the Templars, religion in general, and a God who was unclear even to him. He began to think the unthinkable—turning his back on it all and walking away.

He reached the personnel gate in the inner hedge and read the plaque beside it, *Kanagawa House,* then keyed the access code he'd been given. The gate clicked open, and he pushed it back to head for the house. Lounging on the front steps of the building sat an unlikely character. Japanese, but his clothes were pure street, a Wu shirt, hoody, do-rag, Vlado sneakers, heavy male jewelry, and sunglasses. He didn't look like the son of a diplomat.

"Yo, yo, yo," he said in unaccented English. "Are you the Templar, Leclerc? The Ghostbuster?"

"Yeah. Who are you, Snoop Dog East?"

The two men eyed each other. Jeremy was tall, slender, with dark-brown hair and gray eyes, in his mid-twenties. The slouching Japanese was nearly as tall as he and about five years younger. For a second, it seemed he might get angry, but then he laughed instead. He stuck out a hand, and Jeremy reached down and pulled him to his feet.

"I'm Kei Hara," he said. "I put that in the order you Yankees use. Call me Kei."

"Yankees as in the Civil War?"

"Yankees as in, 'American Marine, you die,'" he said with a bad movie accent.

"Sorry, I'm a citizen, but I was born in France and trained in Scotland."

Kei shook his head. "Yeah, you have a kinda European accent. So, you're trained to fight ghosts? God, I can't believe I'm even saying this. You've done this before?"

"Not ghosts," Jeremy said. "I can't talk about other cases. The less regular people know about this world, the better, but most of the evil I face, I can cut or shoot."

"Cool, bro," Kei said.

"Less than you think."

"But no ghosts."

"Templar doctrine doesn't embrace ghosts."

"Why the hell not?"

"Come on, Kei," Jeremy scoffed. "Billions of people have died on this planet. We'd be up to our hipbones in ghosts, and the Coliseum and Auschwitz would be the most haunted places on Earth if the tormented dying yielded up ghosts."

"Not a happy thought, that. But you weren't there, bro. You didn't feel the fucking tornado in the stairwell, nor see the bodies flung through the air."

"Did you see what did it?"

He hesitated. "For a second, I thought I saw a girl in a *serafuku*."

"Say what now?"

"Sorry. It's what you *gaijin* call a sailor suit. Something Japanese schoolgirls wear."

"You were attacked by a schoolgirl?"

"No man, it was just an image. Not even sure that I saw it. I was cartwheeling through the air at the time!"

"Okay." Jeremy raised a placating hand. "I believe you, and I've seen stranger things. I'll check the house out."

"Follow me," Kei said.

Jeremy trailed Kei into the mansion. "Where is your family?"

Kei grimaced. "It took a lot of persuasion, especially with the reception around the corner, but I got the old man to agree to take my mother and the brats to a downtown hotel. But the old man is tenacious, seems to feel it's a disgrace to the family not to take up residence in the same home every other family in the Japanese diplomatic corps has used for a hundred years. He hasn't had an idea of his own in his entire life."

"I gather that you're not close to your father?"

"Nah, I came over here years ago to avoid the old man. I never expected that he'd get a posting here. They only arrived a month ago. Japanese families are pretty stiff. Old Japanese samurai families are the worst. I stayed in the States to avoid the mental straitjacket that waited for me in Japan. You have no idea how free you are here."

"I know what you mean. I was raised in Europe, in a very traditional household. We Europeans are still very much prisoners of our history. To Americans, anything longer ago than two weeks *is* history."

Their chuckle of shared amusement was cut off as they passed the threshold of the home, and the temperature plunged at least thirty degrees. Both recoiled, Jeremy clutching his leather duster about him.

"Must be something wrong with the damn thermostat," Kei muttered and walked forward to the house controls, Jeremy on his heels.

"Damn. The heat is on. It's programmed to 68 in here. Why is it so damn cold?" His face was a mix of puzzlement and worry.

Jeremy reached out with his mind. He had no special powers, but more than a decade of working with the occult had sensitized him. He felt heaviness, a sense of malice, but something else seemed to interfere with it, almost another presence, vague, yet totally different from the oppressive shadow.

"Well, homey," Kei said, "you're the ghostbuster. What do we do now?"

"I want to canvass the house—see if there is a paranormal site I can focus on. According to what little reliable information we've found, it's considered best to use the exorcism ritual in the presence of the ghost. I doubt our phantom will be so obliging as to put in an appearance. So, I'll see if there is some place that well, feels weird, and invoke there."

"Dude, I can't even believe I am having this conversation in the twenty-first century."

"Welcome to my life."

"You can keep it, bro."

"Wait here."

"In this cold? No hope, man. I'll be outside where it's spring, kind of."

"Might be best."

CHAPTER TWO

CNN.com: French scientists announced an explosion on the surface of Titan. An errant asteroid is suspected...

Jeremy waited until Kei slipped out through the door. From inside the duster, he pulled the bloodsword—a plain Templar longsword, save for the large stone winking a sullen red in the pommel, as if in warning to the ghostly occupant.

Jeremy walked forward, the sword reversed in his grip, the stone held at the level of his eyes. The grasping cold abated as he scanned the house for signs of the haunt. There was disorder aplenty, water leaks, broken furniture, a charred socket. He headed for the staircase down which the nun had been pushed, sweeping the sword about, but sensing and finding nothing.

He advanced up the stairs with no plan, only a vague feeling. The longer he was in the house, the more he sensed something pacing him, mocking, lurking just out of reach. He shook his head to clear the feeling from his mind, finding that it did indeed fade. Slowly and cautiously, he made his way through room after room of the large building, itself a combination of offices and living spaces.

Hours later, Jeremy stood in the music room, a rotunda at the back of the house, lined with windows, facing the back yard. Kei had told him the family had several times been awakened by the sound of someone playing the large Steinway dominating the lesser instruments in the room. There was no sense of oppression in the room, rather the opposite; the room caught the evening light of the setting sun and seemed somehow cheerful. Still, it had been the scene of paranormal activity and was as good a place as any to start.

He knelt and placed the cold gem against his forehead. As he did so, he felt another presence. It did not seem to threaten, and he swore he could smell cherry blossoms. Drawing a deep breath, he began to speak the ancient words the Jesuits had sent him. The words fit poorly in his mouth, and he felt silly saying them. He'd battled demons of various sorts, yet how could there be ghosts in a world with billions of deaths? Still, he began.

Regna terrae, cantata Deo, psallite Cernunnos
Regna terrae, cantata Deo, psalite Aradia caele Deus, Deus terrae,
Humiliter majestati gloriae tuae supplicamus
U tab omni inrernalium spirtuum potestate,
Laqueo, and deception nequitia,
Omnis fallaciae, libera nos, dominates.

The gem's sullen red glowed more fiercely, and warmth spread in him. As Jeremy cast the remaining lines of the exorcism, a shiver, followed by an unbearable scream, rocketed around him, containing such fear and pain that it brought him up short. The light of the bloodsword faded as his concentration wavered and his head swam. When his vision cleared, he heard sobbing and spun on his heel, bringing up his sword.

Crouching in the corner near the fireplace was a teenage girl, hands over her head as if warding off some blow.

When had she wandered in? he wondered.

"It's okay," he said, extending a hand and tucking the sword behind him. "Nothing to worry about, just a little play-acting."

The arms came down and, to his distress, he saw her face was covered in tears.

"You hurt me," she shrilled.

Jeremy froze under the mistrustful regard of two softly glowing red eyes, seemingly lit from within.

"Why? Why would you do that to me?" she demanded.

Numb shock spread through Jeremy as he gazed down at the ghost. But this was no decaying corpse, no specter of the grave. Her face was a light ivory, flawless, with silky black hair falling to her waist, gathered in an elaborate style, pinned and bowed. She wore a dark-blue dress he recognized as the traditional Japanese "sailor suit" Hara had mentioned.

She's beautiful, he thought, *and about sixteen or seventeen years old.*

"I'm... I'm sorry," he found himself saying, going down on one knee.

Her mistrustful expression did not change. "Why?" she demanded again.

Jeremy felt like he'd been found beating a kitten. "I didn't mean to—"

"Yes, you did! You were trying to exorcise me."

He could only stare. She had him dead to rights. "I wasn't trying to hurt you. I promise. I wanted to send you on—"

"To where?" she sniffled. "What if I didn't want to go? What if it's a bad place?"

"—to the afterlife, where you would be at peace."

"I'm at peace here. I love my music room. At least I was at peace until you did that horrible chant. I've never felt such pain." She wound her arms around herself.

Jeremy stood up in a complete quandary. He'd come to exorcise a malign ghost and found himself face to face with a crying teen. Moved to pity, he asked, "What's your name?"

"Kurita Yukari," she replied.

"Yukari—" he began.

Her eyes flashed. "Kurita-san to you! How dare you use my first name so lightly? Why, we haven't even been introduced."

He nodded. *"Gomen Nasai*, Kurita-san. My name is Jeremy Leclerc. You may call me Jeremy if you wish. We are less…formal than perhaps things were in your day. Whenever that was?"

"A long time ago," she said. "The 1930s." Her arms dropped finally. "You won't hurt me again?"

Jeremy's mouth opened, but nothing came out. How could he promise this spirit safety from his exorcism? But looking down at the pale, earnest face, he doubted he could turn any power on her. *"Evil hath the ability to put on a pleasing face,"* sounded in his mind, something his instructors had drilled into him. But they had never had to look into the tear-stained face of a teen girl. The softly glowing eyes were unnatural, but Jeremy could see no malice in them. Yet, how could he know if this was an honest ghost? Even Hamlet hadn't solved that one.

"A truce," he said slowly. "If you promise not to harm anyone, I will do nothing to harm you."

"Promise?" she asked, her voice uncertain.

"Yes," he said. "I promise. I'm a Knight Templar. My word, once given, is inviolable."

"A Knight Tem… Are you a priest?"

He laughed and then seized control of himself. "No, but I was trained in a holy order. I'm afraid I was not much on the theological aspects though."

They studied each other over.

"Your English is very good," Jeremy ventured.

"It wasn't," she replied. "I seem to understand everyone's speech now that I am dead."

"Oh."

"Your accent," Yukari said, smoothing her dark-blue dress across her thighs, "you're not American."

"I was raised in Europe, so my accent is a bit of a jumble. You have no Japanese accent."

"Another feature of existence in Ghostland."

Jeremy reached a hand down to help her up.

"Don't be silly," she replied with a small smile, swinging her hand at his. "I'm a ghost, you can't touch—"

Her hand smacked against his, and they both froze.

Breaking the tableau, she seized his hand with both of hers. "You... you can touch me! How? How?"

She pressed Jeremy's hands against her chest, rising as she did so, and looked as if she might burst into tears again. Yukari's breath, if she was actually breathing, was coming fast and shallow.

Jeremy's shock was nearly as great as hers.

"What," she finally managed, "do you feel?"

"I feel your hands," he replied, "but they are neither warm nor cold. It's as if my senses can't process the sensation. I feel you... ah... pressing my hand against you, but it doesn't feel like fabric."

"After so long," she said more to herself than to him, "to be touched again after so long."

Carefully keeping the bloodsword away from her, he gently disengaged his hand. He had no sense that he might be "spirited away" but neither did he want to linger in contact with the ghost.

"You're very tall for a Japanese girl," he added.

"My father," she hesitated, and a pained expression stole across her face, "used to call me *Noppo*."

He raised an eyebrow.

"Beanpole."

"Ah well, you would be a very pretty beanpole," he said, then caught himself again.

Yukari seemed to blush and looked away.

"Why have you been attacking people around this house?" he followed, trying to resist his sympathy for the girl.

"What?" she said. "I've never attacked anyone."

"Kurita-san," he said, forcing his voice to sternness. "You asked for my word. I need truth in response."

She shrank away from the harshness of his voice. "I'm not lying. I've hurt no one."

Jeremy was completely at a loss. A ghost was deception itself, an imitation of life, incredibly rare despite billions of deaths. Something in him believed her or wanted to. How could he trust that feeling? Yet, in dealing with things outside of the known, what else could he rely on? Now, more than ever, he felt Shadowheart's absence, but he was here now and had to make decisions.

"You didn't strike down a Shinto priest performing a blessing?"

She shook her head.

"There have been others too, as well as damage to the house, to cars, disappearance of pets."

"I love animals!" Yukari protested. "They can see me, but they're not afraid."

"Something doesn't make sense," Jeremy muttered.

"So, you believe me?"

"I can't commit to that yet, Kurita-san, but I must confess you are not what I expected. I find it hard to believe you are capable of evil."

"Please," she whispered. "Will you touch me again?"

Jeremy blinked at the naïve nature of the request. He knew one did not touch a Japanese on the face, but it was common to place a hand on a child's head, so he slowly reached out and did so. But she anticipated this and took his hand to guide it to her cheek.

"So warm," she said, giving him the brightest smile yet. There was nothing of seduction in her contact with him, just a sweetness and wonder at being able to feel another human's touch. Had she been a living human subjected to such a period of isolation, she would have been driven insane by it, and the reaction to being touched would doubtless be more extreme. Debbie Middleton had told Jeremy that vampirism was not only a change of body, but of mind. The lifestyle of a vampire would also drive a human mad, save that they were no longer human and enjoyed their different existence. Being a ghost must also be different psychologically.

"Would you like me to play for you?" Yukari asked, a shy smile dancing over her lips.

For lack of any better response, he nodded.

Yukari walked over to the piano and pulled back the bench, lifting the keyboard cover. It surprised Jeremy that she could manipulate physical objects like an ordinary person.

She looked up at him in clear invitation to sit with her. To his own surprise, he did so. The girl began to play, her long fingers pressing on the ivory keys. She played Rachmaninov beautifully and sat close to Jeremy, her shoulder touching his.

The music seemed to lift them into another world, a safe world, lit by sunlight and bounded by silvery music. It felt unreal. A memory surfaced, his young cousin, playing her piano when he was in his early teens. He'd been close to his cousin as a child and had taken her death in an auto accident hard. Something he had thought gone stirred in him. They sat quietly while she played to the end.

"Oh," she said, suddenly clutched his arm. "It's so nice to have an audience, one that can see me too."

"The others can't see you?"

"Most people can't. A ghost is alone, unseen, unfelt most of the time. Sometimes, under special circumstances, I can be seen. But usually, it's a scary experience for them, in the dark or when they are alone. I've never been able to touch anyone before. Oh, please let me hold your hand."

Jeremy gave the girl his hand and a small smile, utterly charmed by her despite the bizarre situation. He fought to remember the girl with the glowing red eyes was dead, a fragment of something, a soul? He forced himself to focus.

"Kurita-san," he said gently. "The Hara family who recently moved into this house has been under attack by something. They think it is you."

She shook her head, her eyes wide. "No. Why would I hurt anyone?"

"Do you know why you are a ghost?"

"No," she said. "It's almost as if I have always been here. Which is silly, I was born in Kyoto."

"You don't remember your death?"

"No."

"What do you remember?"

"My family came to the U.S. with a delegation from the Japanese government in 1932. My father believed that the future of Japan lay with the West. It was a controversial position, but he believed if we didn't learn the ways of the West that we would be conquered by it or become just a little backward country. We came to Washington and then here… That's all I recall."

"What happened to your family?"

"I don't know." Her eyes misted over, but only for a second.

"Are you lonely, Kurita-san?" he asked, moved by sudden sympathy.

"No. Not really, it's beautiful here. I love the garden. I enjoy my music. I watch the people who live here."

"Have you seen the Haras?"

"No," she said, puzzled. "No, I have not seen people here recently. There's usually someone around, if only the staff, but not recently."

Jeremy stood, confused and anxious. The sun had slipped down, and the only light in the room was from the girl's glowing eyes. "I have to go now, Kurita-san."

"Oh," she said, grabbing his hand. "Please say you will come back tomorrow. Please."

He could not deny the face looking up at him so earnestly.

"I will. Kurita-san, please be careful meanwhile."

"Careful?" She gave a little bell-like laugh. "But it's always the same here."

"*Oyasuminasai*, Kurita-san."

"Good night, Leclerc-san."

"Jeremy."

A blush stained her cheek. "*Arigato*, well, now that we are friends, please call me Yukari-chan, or just Yukari. I guess that is the Western way."

"Yes."

"Remember your promise to come back."

"I always fulfill my promises." He walked out of the room, looking over his shoulder at the pretty girl by the piano. She raised a pale hand to wave at him, and he slipped through the door. Music began to play behind him.

He made his way outside to the door to find Kei standing just outside the door.

"What up, Dog?" Kei asked. "What did you learn?"

Jeremy stared at him, unable to even begin.

CHAPTER THREE

MSNBC.com: NASA Officials are at a loss to explain the appearance on the camera of Sojourner II *of the so-called "Dust Angel," the mysterious image captured on the probe's cameras. Some scientists think it is just an aberration of light on what is commonly called a dust devil. Others say the ethereal figure must be a Martian...*

Jeremy returned to the house the next day. He'd prevailed on Kei not to allow the family back into the house, at least for now. He again felt the same duality in the building, a sense of foreboding, of being watched, until he reached the music room and found Yukari sitting at the piano. She leapt up at his opening of the door, looking exactly as she had the day before. Her smile was uncertain, shy, and she walked up to him slowly.

"I know that my people do not shake hands," she said, "but, oh, I would so like to."

He smiled at her, despite his resolution to maintain a distance, and held out a hand, which she seized in both of hers. Her smile of pure delight almost physically warmed the room.

"Shall I play for you?" she asked.

"Later," he said. "I am still concerned that there is something in the house, something… unfriendly. Perhaps you could show me the place, even the grounds. Can you go outside?"

"I can. I have wandered around the grounds of the house, even gone up to some of the nearby homes, though I don't go in, of course. Someone would have to open a door."

"What?" he said, bemused.

"Oh," she said, waving a hand. "It's not like the movies and films, at least not for me. I open doors and windows. I pick up things that I use. I feel the cold, dislike the rain, and enjoy the moonlight. I can't walk through walls or anything like that."

"What happens if you try to go farther?"

She shrugged. "I find myself back here. But it's not a burden. I like it here."

"That's good."

Yukari took him on a tour of the mansion, the grounds with their outbuildings, and the folly built in the back under the shade of the pines. She pointed out the paintings she loved, the glass collection in the large upstairs hall, mercifully spared by the tornado that had hurled Kei, the nurse, and priest to the floor below. He watched her draw her favorite books down from the library shelves. She seemed fond of Jane Austen's works. The Japanese ones she showed him, he could neither recognize nor read. Only when he touched her hands while passing the books back and forth did he realize that she was otherworldly.

After the second day, Jeremy let workmen back into the house to handle repairs and prep for the party, but only when he was there. He still felt the other presence, as if it was watching him, waiting. Truth was, he was enjoying his time with Yukari. They ended their visit with her playing the piano for him, locked in the music room so no one would enter and see the piano playing itself.

"You like my playing?" she said, with her big, bright smile. Unlike so many Japanese girls, Yukari did not hide her smile behind her hand or her hair.

"Yes. When I was around your age, I had a younger cousin. Her name was Mary Alice, and I was very fond of her. She wasn't Japanese of course, but she was like you—"

"A beanpole?"

He laughed, then reached up and touched her hair. "She was tall, with long black hair similar to yours. You remind me so much of her."

"I think I like that," she said.

"Me too," he said, knowing it was unwise.

"I have something for you," she said with a sudden shy glance.

"Oh," he replied with an indulgent grin he could not help. "What's this? A present for me? It's not even my birthday."

"It may seem forward on such short acquaintance, but I feel like I have known you for a long time. I am…comfortable with you. Perhaps that is why you can see and touch me."

"Perhaps," he said. "I have no other or better explanation."

She handed him a tiny package, cunningly wrapped in orange-red paper. He took it and unwrapped it, careful not to tear any of the paper. There was a small painting of a tree by a seaside, on rice paper inside a lacquer frame.

"This is beautiful," he said. "You did it yourself?"

"Yes," she said, still shy.

There was a lonely emotion to it that surprised and appealed to him. He smiled at her.

"There have been artists who lived here," Yukari said. "Most have left supplies in the legation. It is something that I did in life, and my skill has not deserted me."

"It must help to pass the time," he responded.

Yukari gave him a curious look, as if what he said made no sense to her. "I cannot say that time hangs my hands. At least I have not been conscious of it."

"Thank you for my present," he said. "A gift from such a pretty lady is to be treasured."

The shy smile broadened, but she would not meet his eyes. "I am so very glad."

"But I feel bad that I have no gift for you."

"Your time with me is the best gift."

"Now you are going to turn my head," he said, with a small laugh.

"Perhaps I will," she said pertly.

A noise broke his attention. He heard a woman's voice raised in argument, then Kei's. They were close by.

He stood. "You may want to hide."

"Jeremy, I am always hidden. Only people who are looking for me can hear or see me, and then only under unusual circumstances."

Jeremy went out through the music room doors to the veranda beyond. Kei was standing facing a very pretty blonde. Her clothes, tan, and hair said old money and refinement.

"Honey," Kei said. "It just may not be safe. I was almost killed here only a few days ago." Curiously, his hip-hop slang had disappeared, even his posture was different.

"Oh Kei, don't be such a wuss. You know how spiritual I am. I can help you! It would be so exciting to meet a real ghost."

"Perhaps too exciting," Jeremy said.

The pair took notice of him for the first time. Jeremy had left his coat inside and wore only a light red sweater and jeans. The girl gave him an appraising look as Kei gave a guilty start.

"Ah, Jeremy, this is my fiancée, Sarah Roshal."

"And this must be the spiritualist," Sarah said, advancing on him and sticking out a hand. He shook hers. "We have a lot in common."

"I'm not sure that spiritualist describes what I do," he replied, wondering what Kei had told her, despite his being sworn to secrecy. He'd probably felt it didn't apply to his fiancée.

"I've been telling Kei that I could help," she added. "I've read extensively on hauntings and ghosts. Studied spells...."

Jeremy groaned inside. Born-again wiccans were the bane of his existence, traipsing around with no actual knowledge, on the borders of things that could consume them in an unguarded instant.

"For now," he said, raising a hand, "I think it best that we keep the number of people in the house to a necessary minimum. The workmen have to be here, but I am watching over them. I don't feel that the house is clear—"

"Then you could use more help," Sarah said.

Before he could stop her, Sarah swept past him into the music room.

"It's daylight," Sarah said, over her shoulder, as Jeremy and Kei quickly followed her. "Ghosts aren't active during daylight."

Jeremy looked past her at Yukari, who stood up from the piano glaring at Sarah. She stuck out her tongue at the blond girl. "Bleah!"

"No, you would never see a ghost this early," Sarah announced. "I'm sensitive, and I can tell you here is nothing going on in this room."

Yukari, standing right behind her, lifted a lock of Sarah's hair.

"Insect antenna," Yukari said with a grin.

Jeremy waved frantically at her. Sarah caught the motion from the corner of her eye and turned, while Yukari twisted Sarah's hair into cat ears.

"Uh, Kei, close those doors," Jeremy said before the young man could notice his fiancée's bizarre hair.

Sarah moved around the room, touching the instruments, with Yukari behind her watching in apparent annoyance.

"Kei," Jeremy whispered, as his fiancée picked up a harp. "Do you see anything?"

"My fiancée being headstrong as usual?"

"Beside that?"

Kei hesitated. "It seems like the light is weird in here. It's like Sarah has two shadows."

"Do you hear anything?"

"No."

"Kei, I don't think she should be here, and I'm not so sure you should be in the house either."

"It hasn't gotten cold."

"Yes, but I have a bad feeling."

"She really wanted to bring some of her girlfriends over. They have, like, a club for this supernatural shit."

"No way."

"Dude, she ain't easy to stop."

"Kei, grow a pair. This could be dangerous for them."

Sarah took advantage of their distraction to open the door to the main part of the house and slip inside, which judging by Yukari's now stormy expression, had happened none too soon. The sanctity of her music room restored, she seated herself at the piano. Jeremy gave her a frantic but surreptitious wave not to start playing. While she returned a mutinous look, she folded her hands in her lap.

Meanwhile Kei chased Sarah in the main part of the house, in what turned out to be a largely futile attempt to corral her. Jeremy didn't like having a Hara in the house before he had figured out the mystery of Yukari.

Yukari, where was she? he wondered. A minute ago, she'd been by the piano. Now she was gone. Disturbed, he gathered up his duster with its hidden blade before following them into the house proper.

He caught up to the pair, just as the contractors left by the front door for lunch. Now, the three of them were alone in the house. Though it was bright outside, the house suddenly seemed full of shadows.

"Kei, you need to get out of here," Jeremy said. His breath smoked in the air that had grown cold impossibly fast. He threw his duster on.

Sarah clutched her thin jacket around her. "Is the A/C broken? What's going on?"

"It's not," Kei said grimly.

Something crashed upstairs, and Jeremy grabbed Kei by the arm. "Take her and get out. Now."

"Oh, don't be silly," Sarah began. "The contractors knocked something over, that's all."

Jeremy shook his head. "They left for lunch, all of them."

"Honey," Kei said, a note of desperation. "Come on, let's go. I'll buy you lunch at Amelie's."

"Yes," Jeremy said. "Go. Go now."

Sarah looked askance at Jeremy. Clearly, she was used to getting her way with the hired help. "All right. Think on my offer though. My girls and I can really help you."

"Maybe later," he said, ushering them to the door the contractors had left by.

Kei, sensing victory, piled on, and in seconds, he and Sarah were out the door.

With a sigh of relief, Jeremy shut the door and headed for the stairs, determined to investigate the sound. A wind slapped at his face as he gripped the banister, indoors where there couldn't be any wind. He looked up the large staircase to see Yukari standing in the shadows at the top of the stairs.

"Yukari," he called.

She took a step forward.

Jeremy froze.

The girl at the top of the stairs wasn't Yukari. The shadow wasn't on her; it was part of her. Her face was empty of animation, corpse-like.

Then, it wasn't the face of the young girl, but of an older Japanese man with an anguished expression, then a woman, tears streaming down her face, a little girl, eyes open and unseeing, and finally the rotting skull of a long dead body.

"Who are you?" he called, slipping his hand into the duster to find the hilt of his sword, the gem pulsed with heat, warning of the presence of evil. He gripped it but did not draw.

"You know," the voice hissed and slithered.

"You're not Yukari," he said.

"So you prefer my creation, my little doll in her doll house?"

"I like her."

"Thank you. She deserves to be cared about."

This stopped Jeremy cold. Sympathy was the last thing he expected out of the shape-shifting horror at the top of the stairs.

"And you don't?"

There was no answer from the figure.

"What do you want?" he called.

"Justice. I have lingered in this shadowland for that reason."

"Justice?"

The figure wavered and became indistinct save for the changing faces.

"The Haras destroyed my family. They will pay with their blood."

26

"I will stop you," Jeremy said. The ghost's face stabilized as Yukari's, only with eyes black from lid to lid.

"You cannot," the ghost replied, its voice cold and lifeless. "Destroy me, destroy my little doll."

"Then you are part of each other?"

"She doesn't know me and would deny me if she did, preferring her music room, her endless hours of the garden, her aimless existence, while her family wanders in Hell, unavenged. We are sisters of the grave, but she will not see or heed me."

"And you?"

"I am my father's sword. I am the vengeance of my slaughtered family. I slept while she played, remembering nothing, thinking nothing. I bore it all."

"Bore what, Ghost?"

Now the black pits of her eyes bore a hot golden point and the temperature plunged with a cold so intense, Jeremy could barely breathe.

"Bore blades slicing a belly, slicing a throat, the rush of blood, the tightness of rope, the cold of water filling lungs. Bore the deaths of a sister, a mother, a father, all dead of shame for being blamed for my murder!"

The impossible wind raced around the room, tearing pictures from the wall.

"Your family," he called over the rising wind. "Yukari's family?" He raised his left arm to protect his face.

"Yes," the ghost shrieked. "All dead. My father blamed for my murder. Sent home in disgrace."

The blackness of the eyes spread to the rest of the face, and her long hair writhed like striking snakes.

"Death!" she screamed, and suddenly the wind was a fist hurling him across the room. The cold clawed into his bones, the air full of razors.

The sword flashed into his hand, and he sank to his knees, bending his fading will into the weapon. Its gem glowed to life and drove back the cold. He raised the glowing stone against the rage of his enemy's eyes. Even as he did so, he wondered why the glow of her eyes seemed similar to the stone's.

But the Dark Yukari faded away from the glowing stone. Jeremy regained his feet and switched to a fighting grip. The stairs were now merely stairs, with no shadowy figure above them. Dark Yukari was gone, but not banished.

She was back between the walls, between the seconds, between the blinks of an eye, and he could not reach her.

CHAPTER FOUR

NASA announced that Palomar Observatory reports an unusual and unexplained shadow on the moon near the Moltke crater. There is no known reason for the shadow. Plans to alter the course of a Chinese probe to inspect the crater are being considered.

Jeremy knew better than to call Debbie Middleton in daytime. Without Shadowheart's help, he needed to talk to Debbie, to somehow process what he had learned, because it had led him nowhere. He had no idea what he was to fight, or how to do it without harming Yukari.

Toward sunset, a text reply hit his phone. He gathered his coat and weapons and hopped in his car. Twenty minutes later, he parked his Mini Cooper in the Landmark Diner lot, his usual "holy ground" for meeting Debbie. The vampire favored the less wealthy side of Charlotte, despite her immense portfolio assembled over 180 years. "My needs are simple," she'd told him, "sex, blood, and anonymity."

He paused at the door until he spotted Debbie, which didn't take long. Debbie was short, busty, with blond hair piled up like a country singer. Tonight, her makeup and clothes were more conservative than usual, though she always filled out any top she wore to bursting. His body twinged at the sight of her. "Twenty-something forever," he murmured.

Debbie had a truce with the forces of light, in token of which she wore a ring with a white stone set in it. Truth was, there was no need to battle the vampire. Debbie hadn't killed or turned humans since the First World War, well, unless attacked. She traded her encyclopedic knowledge of sex for a little blood and the life-force that came with it.

Her eyes met his with a force he felt deep in his body. When she wished to be, the vampire was sex incarnate. They'd occasionally found themselves in bed together. It wasn't a good idea, but it still happened.

"Hey, sweetie," she said with an Alabama accent and a country twang.

"Hello, Debbie."

She crooked a finger at him as if she wanted to whisper something, but as he bent down, she pulled him into a kiss, her tongue flicking over his lips, so quickly he wasn't sure it had happened.

He slid into the seat opposite her. An Indian waiter forestalled any questions by appearing at his elbow. Jeremy ordered his usual pasta and then watched in amusement as Debbie ordered enough dinner to fill up two men and enough wine to wash it all down.

"Nice to see you again, handsome," she said, mischief dancing in the cornflower blue eyes.

"And you. Still loving the night life?"

"Do I have a choice?"

"Guess not." The waiter returned with a bottle of wine and some bread and poured for them. They were known here, and the waiter didn't indulge in idle chit-chat.

"Vamp life isn't about change. Rise with the moon, shag my ass off, bite people, watch the latest movies, read the latest books."

"Hmm, doesn't sound that different from mine. Well, apart from shagging my ass off."

"I've offered to help you with that," she said, snagging a glass of wine.

"That would be hard to explain to my guardian angel."

Debbie chuckled. "So, what can Sexy Evil do for you?"

"What do you know about ghosts?"

Her eyebrows shot up. "Ghosts? Enough to know that they are rarer than hen's teeth for all that you humans blame every bump in the night on them. Never met one myself, though I've heard of others who have. But them's just stories. Anyway, didn't they cover this in Templar School?"

Jeremy sipped his own wine. "Officially, the Temple doesn't believe ghosts exist, but there's a lot of disputes about that. They quote the stories of an entire Russian village lost to a Rusalka in Siberia."

"Rusalka?" Debbie asked, as the first part of her epic meal began to arrive.

"It's a form of Russian ghost, a young girl that has drowned. The Rusalka sucks the life out of people, even entire forests. Kind of a psychic vampire."

"Wow, them Russians are a grim bunch."

"True."

"Why the sudden interest?" she asked, buttering some bread and handing him a piece.

"New client. Son of a Japanese diplomat. He says his family is being haunted out of their diplomatic mission."

"How so?"

"It's confusing; there is a ghost there, or perhaps two. Her name is Yukari Kurita, she seems to be sixteen or so. She's sweet and... hell, I don't know... she's just a cute kid. Her haunting is just wandering around the building and occasionally playing piano at night. She has to open doors, pick up objects. She's not very ghostly.

"But there seem to be two versions. The second looks like her, but its appearance wavers between images of what I think are her father, mother, and perhaps a sister. It has supernatural powers. It sent a Shinto priest and nun who were blessing the house to the hospital."

"I don't know much, Jeremy. No weapon I know of will affect a ghost. I bet that bloodsword of yours could though."

"How can I cut something I can't see or can't reach? She disappears in an eye blink."

Debbie shrugged. "Tell me more."

Jeremy stroked his chin. "I swear there is no deception in Yukari. She seems as sweet and innocent as anyone I've ever met."

Light bounced off Debbie's blond hair as she shook her head. "Jeremy, she's a ghost, a being that gives a lie to life itself. There's no dealing with the dead. Pass the ketchup."

Jeremy handed her a bottle of ketchup and held onto it, a smile playing over his lips as she tugged at the bottle in his hand. She looked over at him for a beat.

"Oh, all right," she snapped. "I get the irony, but honey, I am the living dead, a ghost is the dead-dead. Even we don't fool around with them. Their powers are unpredictable and far less bounded by space-time than mine. Besides, why are you asking me about this? Isn't this Shadowheart's territory?"

Jeremy hid his embarrassment behind a sip of tea. "Well, we both got called on the carpet for a recent...er..."

"Assault on Hell itself?" Debbie said sweetly.

"Ah, so you heard about that?"

"Oh, honey, that is the best story to come out in an age of the world. Did she really pose as a succubus—"

Jeremy jumped in. "The less said about that the better. Shadow-heart had to return to... You know I still can't quite get myself to believe in a heaven—"

"Despite your having been to Hell? You really are a human, ain'tcha?"

"Anyway, I don't know when she will return, or if she will be quite the same."

"Problem for another day," Debbie returned, her fangs briefly visible as she bit into her steak.

"So anyway, I could use some top cover when it comes to dealing with something so incredibly rare and unpredictable."

"Oh honey, is this more pro bono work for the powers of light?"

"Something like that. Doesn't it pay to have a favor or two banked with us?"

"Don't you give me those big gray eyes of yours. I keep telling you that you are too damn comfortable with me. We may have a truce, but dammit, I am evil with a big E. I could lie to you, take advantage, bite you on the ass or something,"

Jeremy laughed and almost spilled his drink.

"Dammit, boy, I'm serious. I'm 184 years of evil sitting right here—"

"Resting your Double-Ds on the table as usual."

"Gotta put them somewhere, and your mouth seems busy at the moment."

"So will you help me or not?"

She sighed. "Yeah, I will. I like you, and you'll just do something dumb without me." She bit her steak again as if it was a personal enemy. "Just you remember what I said."

CHAPTER FIVE

Communist officials have refused to confirm or deny the escalation of the so-called Happiness Sect of Buddhism, which has reportedly taken hold of several Buddhist districts in the Tibetan mountains. The inhabitants claim to have met a "living Buddha." They now recognize no earthly authority, reportedly leading to clashes with Party officials and police.

Jeremy met Debbie the next day after sunset at the mansion. He'd spent the day guarding the workmen finishing the house. He'd tried to persuade the elder Hara to move the upcoming reception, but neither he nor Kei had any success moving his father. "Nonsense. What am I to tell all these important people? That we cannot use the official residence for fear of ghosts? I will be locked away!"

Kei and his father did not see eye to eye about much, and that conversation had not ended well. Even the son's story about being attacked with the priest did not move the elder Hara, who seemed to fear a diplomatic or social embarrassment more than any haunting.

So, all he could do was guard the workers as they rushed to finish. They, in turn, stared at him resentfully, as if they'd been suspected of threatening the diplomatic silverware. The Dark Yukari had put in no appearance, but neither had he seen her less threatening manifestation. He'd heard music playing, but when he'd gotten to the music room, she wasn't there.

Debbie pulled her pink VW behind his Mini Cooper, where he sat on the hood watching the twilight fade. She wore a red top under a black leather jacket and a short skirt over boots. He smiled at her, but she didn't indulge in a kiss this time. "Hey, honey. All quiet on the ghostly front?"

"Too quiet. I can't even find Yukari, much less the dark and awful sister."

She looked up at the house, a vampiric shimmer in her eyes. "There's a lot of dark energy about the place. You sure you want to do this?"

"Like you said about your own life, not a lot of choices."

"Well, while you were running around under the sun, I spent some time doing research. There's not a lot on the net—"

"You googled Yukari?"

Debbie sighed. "Yes, I know how to use a MacBook. Listen, I found out about your friend's death. It wasn't happy reading."

"Tell me," he said, as they started toward the house.

"Yukari Kurita was the daughter of a Japanese diplomat. The family was in Charlotte, in 1933, when she was raped and murdered, allegedly by her father, in this very house."

"God." Jeremy raised a hand to his mouth.

"Her father was found by her strangled body, passed out drunk. He was accused by the number two in the delegation, Shoji Hara, of having spent the night drinking, acting bizarrely, and inappropriately with his daughter."

"He was arrested?"

"No, they were diplomats, so they were briefly detained before being released to their own authorities. The father protested his innocence and was supported by his wife, but he was sent back to Japan in disgrace. He and his wife committed suicide in the traditional samurai ways. He slit his belly. She stabbed herself in the throat. The younger daughter, Ayane, was sent to live with her grandmother, but both drowned themselves jumping off a ferry. That was the end of the family."

"How horrible, poor Yukari. What a fate for such a sweet girl." Jeremy stopped in his tracks. "Wait, you said Shoji Hara?"

Debbie's eyes had narrowed at his description of Yukari as sweet, but her voice was cool and even as she spoke. "I think there's more going on here than meets the eye."

"What do you mean?"

"Yukari's father was part of *Rikken Seiyukai*, the civilian democratic party that opposed the Japanese military's grasp for power. He was also in the Japanese delegation that accepted the London Treaty, which slighted the Japanese Navy. The militarists hated his party for that."

"What does that have to do with a murder here in Charlotte?" he asked. They paused by the ornate doorway.

"Shoji Hara testified against the father. He was part of the militarist party and a rabid fascist. Yukari's mother, Lady Mitsuko, claimed that Shoji desired Yukari, and was furious when the father disapproved of the union."

"Shoji Hara," Jeremy murmured.

"Yeah," she replied, "the grandfather of your hippity-hop pal, Kei."

"So you think Shoji Hara raped and murdered Yukari, set up her father for it and—"

"—rose to prominence with the government that led Japan to war. Shoji was hanged as a war criminal after the surrender. He ran a POW mining camp using slave labor."

Jeremy shook his head. "Amazing. You're a hell of a researcher."

"Some of it was research; some of it was memory. I lived through the Second World War. I remember what they don't bother teaching in the history books."

"That explains the Dark Yukari's hate of the Haras," he replied with a shrug. "Shoji destroyed her family, but he's dust now."

"Japanese culture is different, Jeremy, and was way different back then. *Katakiuchi* is the word for revenge on the family of an enemy.

The fact that the individual family member may have done nothing to you is irrelevant."

They entered through the main door. No wave of cold greeted them, and the hallway was well lit, freshly painted, and looking as unhaunted as a Holiday Inn. Jeremy led Debbie to the music room, but Yukari wasn't there.

As they made their way to the second floor, Jeremy heard a car pulling up. A quick glance from the window confirmed his fears. "Trouble."

Debbie glanced out the window. "All I see is three rich bitches."

"That is Sarah, Kei's fiancée, and her group of amateur ghost hunters. This, I don't need."

"Maybe they won't come in?"

"No such luck. She has a key, and she knows my car. At least she isn't a Hara, yet."

"So, are we going to do the adult thing and confront her and tell her to stay out of it?"

"No. We tried that. We're going to hide until they leave. It's a big house."

"Great," Debbie said. "I feel like I'm at a twelve-year-old girl's birthday party ducking the unpopular girl."

"Jeremy," Sarah's voice called from downstairs. "Are you here?"

"Maybe the ghost got him," giggled one of her minions.

"Or he's upstairs banging whatever skank drove the pink VW."

Debbie's eyebrows shot up, and she turned toward the stairs. Jeremy grabbed her arm and after a moment of struggle and an imploring glance, managed to drag her away. But huge as the house was, it proved impossible to avoid the amateurs following Sarah's divining of "auras" around the house. They'd duck out of one room a second ahead of Sarah's pack, or pull up short, finding them in the room ahead. Finally, they were cornered in an upstairs bedroom.

Jeremy looked around. They were too high for him to jump out the window, though Debbie could doubtless manage it. The only option was a large, free-standing wardrobe.

"Come on," he said to her, opening the door.

"Why, are we going to Narnia?"

"Very funny, get in here."

She piled in next to him. Between coats and boxes, there wasn't much room, and they were pressed close together.

"Hell of a way to treat an antique," he said, closing the door.

"You'd better not be talking about me."

"Shush. They're at the door."

Sarah and crew walked into the room.

"Wow, look at this place," said one of the girls.

"Yeah, I thought the Japanese were into everything modern."

"Not Kei's family," Sarah said. "This is just their style. I can't believe he came from these people."

He heard a bed creak and realized the girls were settling in on the bed and chairs. *Oh no*, he thought, *not a yakfest*. But his worse fears were realized. The girls had brought a Ouija board with them and were calling out to the ghost, in between critiquing the decorations and gossiping about Kei.

In the wardrobe, Jeremy shifted slightly. Debbie was pressed against him, and he was very conscious of her breasts against his front. The air filled with the scent of her. Her thighs were on either side of his and, slowly, she raised one. An electric jolt went through him.

He looked down into her shimmering eyes.

"Jeremy, honey," she whispered, "I'm getting kinda hot and bothered in here."

He wanted to tell her to think of something else, but he was filled with the memory of her parted lips, how her body could move against his, and what she could do with it. He wanted to say something; instead, he found his mouth on hers and his hands on her body. The kiss was like inhaling champagne. They tried, at first, to keep quiet, to not move together like teens making out under the stands. But she felt so good, soft and firm, the scent of her was pure intoxication.

Debbie opened her blouse and hiked her skirt and climbed him like a tree. Her legs wrapped around him with their vampiric strength and there was no denying her, even if he had mustered the will to think it. At first, she moved slowly. He kissed her, quietly aware of Sarah's gang still critiquing the furniture and decorations, but in the heat and closeness of the wardrobe, he could not contain a moan of lust.

"Oh my god," exclaimed a female voice. "The wardrobe. It's rocking."

"It's the ghost!" cried a younger voice.

At that second, Debbie's back arched and she gave an unearthly howl of satisfaction to which he answered as his climax rocked him.

"Run," Sarah screamed. "It's after us!"

Debbie added the snarl of a hunting animal to her inventory as the doors sprang open and they tumbled out. But Sarah's wiccans had already had enough, and only their trailing screams remained.

Jeremy gasped from the strength of what she had coaxed out of his body. "Well, that could have gone better."

Debbie's teeth flashed as she pressed his arms to the ground and locked her legs around him. She buried her fangs in his upper chest.

He couldn't even struggle. The bite plunged him back into her pheromone-soaked sexuality and he was instantly ready for her again. Her hips moved as she growled; her teeth deep in him.

What if she doesn't stop, he thought, with what little reason he still had. *What if this time she goes back to what she was?* He'd been with her before, but it had never been this dark, raw, and animalistic. His vision blurred even as he climaxed in her a second time, and she drew blood, and the life-force behind it, out of him.

I may have made a terrible mistake, he thought, as his eyes closed and it all grew distant, dark and warm...

CHAPTER SIX

The Indian government spokesperson was unable to explain the reappearance of a new suicide cult below the headwaters of the Ganges. Thousands of corpses are reportedly clogging the river downstream. A few survivors describe the appearance of the goddess Kali in their villages and a sudden madness that swept over the populations.
Others claim to have consorted with devils and demons driven before the goddess.
Indian Army units are moving in to pacify the region.

His eyes opened slowly, and he realized that he was in a chair, with his feet propped up and under a blanket. He turned his head to see Debbie walking out of the bathroom, with only her miniskirt on and a tumbler of water.

"Don't move," she said. "My bites coagulate, but if you move, you'll bleed. Drink all of this."

He realized he was incredibly thirsty and drained the glass. She raced back to the bathroom to refill it, and in a distant way, he marveled at the movements of her chest as she ran.

"Here," she said. "Tylenol and more water."

He took them both.

"Does it hurt?" she asked.

"No," he lied.

"This is all your damn fault," she swore.

This time it was his eyebrows that shot up. "Umm, who bit who?"

"You jumped into a small dark space with a vampire, dumbass. Did it occur to you ask when I last ate and who? Dammit, I'm as into sex as a succubus, and you just decided to put your nice, young, well-hung body next to me. What the hell did you think would happen? Huh? You do remember I eat people."

"Well, you don't actually eat—"

"Don't get technical on me, boy! Oh, I am so damn mad I could just spit."

"Sorry." He'd never seen her so angry.

"I'm going to the nearest CVS and get some vitamins, energy bars, and Gatorade. Now you sit on your pretty ass and do not move, or I will beat it black and blue. Do you understand?"

He nodded.

She tucked the blanket around his feet and put a hand on his forehead. It was warm.

Of course, he thought, *warm with my life force.*

"And quit getting erections," she snapped. "You don't have the blood to spare."

"Perhaps if you covered up your magnificent breasts..." he said. "Actually, you'd probably be best throwing a blanket over everything."

She stared at him for a second, then laughed. "Damn you. Pretty, young, and too damn confident. I ought to suck you dry and not in a way you'd like either." She grabbed her clothes and ran out of the room.

Jeremy lay in the chair, wondering about life, the universe, and everything. He must have drowsed, because next thing he knew he was gazing into Yukari's softly glowing eyes.

"Where have you been?" he asked.

She gave him a surprised look. "Why here, of course, as always."

"We searched. We couldn't find you. Not yesterday or today."

"How odd," she said. "I have been here so far as I know. I don't

41

remember seeing you earlier. Well before you and your blond friend with the enormous chest ran into the wardrobe. I thought it...rude to bother you. Honestly, how does she walk upright?"

"Um, I'm not sure that this is a subject we should—"

"Jeremy-kun, I am not actually sixteen." Yukari giggled. "Well, my body is, but I have been here for over eighty years, and people have made love before in this house. I... ahem... have seen things."

Jeremy's face burned, and he wondered how much of Debbie and he Yukari had seen.

"Yukari," he said. "Do you know... Are you alone in the house? I mean apart from the living, have you seen or heard anyone else?"

"What a peculiar question," she said. "No, there's just me."

He searched her eyes for the truth. She was as guileless as ever.

"Something has changed." This time she seemed to be searching his eyes.

"Yes," he replied. "I have learned some things. Things from the past."

She glanced away. "You know how I died, don't you?"

He nodded.

She bit her lip. "Jeremy-kun, please don't tell me. I remember very little and don't wish to know more."

"As you wish, Yukari-chan. For now."

She came forward and put a gentle hand on his forehead. "Much as I wish for your company, perhaps it would be best if you went home and not with Miss Melons. I think you need to rest." She giggled and leaned forward to kiss him on the forehead. Then, as if startled by her own action, blushed a bright crimson.

Jeremy heard the door downstairs open, and when his eyes flicked back to Yukari, she was gone. He heard Debbie come running back up the stairs and decided that Yukari's advice was probably best for tonight. He was running out of time. Saturday was the night of Kurita-sama's reception. The house would be full of Haras.

After a little more first aid from the source of his anemia and some help getting down the stairs, he headed home after a quick kiss with

Debbie, who seemed to want to say something but suddenly turned reticent and strode back to her pink VW.

Jeremy slept the rest of the night, but woke midday, embarrassed and rueful over his actions last night. The Templar Order would melt down if they knew. His phone showed a message, and he picked it up. Debbie had called several times and texted. He hit call back.

"Oh, thank God," she said, answering.

Irony abounds in my existence, he thought, *a vampire thanking God that her last victim can still use an iPhone.*

"I'm fine," he assured.

"Good, then I can continue chewing you out for taking stupid chances."

"I think you chewed on me enough last night," he said, trying to head off another lecture.

There was a second of quiet then she burst out laughing. "Damn you," she said. "You keep making me like you too much. Okay, funny man. Are you sure you're okay?"

"Yes, and I guess I have to admit it was worth it, so long as we keep this little incident to ourselves. You are incredible, both vertically and horizontally."

"More things we don't tell your guardian angel when she comes back."

Jeremy fought off a stab of depression. For all his protestations about Shadowheart's interference in his life, he'd only been separated from his guardian angel for brief periods until now.

"A list that keeps expanding," he replied. "I have to fight off my recollections of all those colorful little books they gave us as children, *Your guardian angel,* showing them always at our elbow, unseen."

"If she was there, she would have blasted my pert butt right off your body."

"Probably would."

"You sure you're alright?"

"Do you want to get back in my good book?" he asked.

"Ah, depends handsome, what is it going to cost me?"

"All you have to do is hang on my arm at the reception tonight."

"Is that a good idea, honey?"

"I'm still flying solo, and I don't know what I am up against. The whole Hara family will be there tonight, and the place will be crawling with VIPs and diplomats. I need the help."

"Well, I suppose I owe you for the chomp on the chest."

"Pick you up?"

"No, I'll meet you in my skankmobile."

"Don't bite Sarah or any of her friends."

"No guarantees," Debbie said and clicked off.

CHAPTER SEVEN

Chapter 27 Verses 38-40 Translation: Yusuf Ali said an Ifrit of the Jinns: "I will bring it to thee before thou rise from thy Council: indeed I have full strength for the purpose and may be trusted."

The house was brilliantly lit as Jeremy approached, just as the sun set in the west. Jeremy waited for Debbie to drive up in her VW. The car was more than just a statement. The tinted glass protected her enough from the UV rays, so she could drive it in the late afternoon. As the door opened, Jeremy got an eyeful, not in itself unusual with Debbie, but she'd forsaken her usual hooker wear for a red, formal gown that was enough to stop the valet in his tracks. Her hair was coiffed in a sophisticated but simple shape. Debbie gave the valet a brilliant smile and her keys.

"Wow," Jeremy said, as she walked up. "This is different."

"This is Vera Wang," she replied in a voice devoid of anything but the hint of a delicate Southern accent.

His eyebrows shot up.

"Something?" she said.

"Nope," he replied and offered her his arm, wincing slightly as he did so.

Her smile dimmed for a second.

"You smell as good as you look," he said, to drive away the remembrance, as he draped the duster holding the sword over his other arm.

"Thank you," she added. "Chanel never goes out of style."

Arm in arm, they went up to the door where they were greeted by a butler who took Debbie's wrap. Jeremy held onto his coat with his weapon. "I may be going outside in a little bit."

As they moved on, Debbie reminded him of the figurines that graced the bows of ships as she launched into the party, both from her stately carriage, impressive bustline, and the way people parted in front of her. Debbie had obviously decided that as she could not escape attention, she would capitalize on it. So, she was the subject of furtive glances, honest admiration, jealous and speculative looks, all at the same time.

Kei Hara came toward them, trailed by an older Japanese male and Sarah, resplendent in a blue gown. It took Jeremy a second to recognize his client. Gone were all the signs of his hip-hop lifestyle, though the tuxedo he wore was clearly a rental, unlike his father, who wore tails in a tuxedo of classic style. Kei had a finger down the throat of his starched white collar and looked about as comfortable as Debbie in a cathedral.

"Well, son," Debbie whispered in her newly unaccented voice, "introduce me to our hosts."

Jeremy nodded but waited for Kei.

"Father," Kei said, speaking carefully. "You remember Jeremy, the specialist sent to deal with the difficulty."

Kei's father, his face impassive, nodded.

"And who is this statuesque beauty?" Sarah asked, eyeing Debbie, who returned a slight smile. "A friend of yours, Kei?"

He gulped and shook his head.

"An associate of mine," Jeremy said. "Ms. Deborah Middleton of New Orleans."

"I'm Kei Hara. This is my fiancée, Sarah Roshan, and my father, Kentaro Hara."

The elder Hara again bowed.

Debbie did a small curtsy and then spoke fluidly in Japanese. Even the stoic Kentaro Hara looked surprised. He nodded and smiled briefly and spoke back.

"You're quite accomplished in language," Sarah said. "I've been at it for two years and I could hardly follow you."

"Yes," Kentaro said, "your accent is Tokyo, but the Tokyo of my youth."

"My teacher was an older lady," Debbie replied. "She lived in Tokyo long ago."

"And what is your profession, Ms. Middleton?" Sarah asked.

"Why call me Debbie, please," she replied. "My work is in a medical line. You might say I'm in international blood work."

"How interesting," Sarah said. "I'm in international law myself. We might have some things in common."

"As a hobby," Debbie continued, "I studied architecture. I love older Southern homes. I've been in so many and now I have a chance to look over this one."

"Please," Kentaro said. "You are my guest, and I would be delighted to have you see our home, though we have only arrived and are not quite moved in. My son Kei will conduct you."

"Oh, I will help," Sarah said.

"Actually," Kei said, "until my mother arrives, I'd appreciate you helping my father greet the guests."

Sensing that Sarah had reservations about Kei disappearing into the huge house with Debbie, Jeremy again took her arm. "I too, need to inspect the house as part of my work."

"Very well," Kentaro said.

More people arrived behind them, and Jeremy and Debbie stepped past. Sarah released her hold on Kei's arm to stand alongside Kentaro.

Jeremy aimed the three of them toward the music room, where he had most often found Yukari.

As soon as they left the ballroom of the house and headed down the long corridor to the back, Jeremy heard the gentle tinkling of piano keys. He glanced at the others, who nodded. Jeremy took a deep breath and opened the door.

Yukari looked up from the piano as they entered the room. Her usual bright smile flitted over her face. "Jeremy, at last you are back! And you have brought friends. Well, they will not be able to see me—"

"I see you fine," Debbie said, in her usual twang. "You're as pretty as Jeremy said you would be."

"Ah, I remember you." Yukari giggled. "You're the one with the big boobs and sharp teeth. You're like me, one of the dead."

"Just so, little girl, but of a very different type, a different fate."

"Who are you talking to.... wait... is that a girl?" Kei said, squinting.

"You can see her now?" Jeremy said.

"Yes... yeah, Jesus Christ, I can!"

"Are you a Christian?" Yukari asked, standing.

"Ah, no," he said, shock on his face. "I can see her more clearly every second and hear her too."

"Can they touch me too?" Yukari almost skipped toward Debbie, who put her hand up.

"Close enough, honeychile. I don't know you that well. Frankly, we just don't know what would happen."

Jeremy walked over and took the disappointed girl's hands in his. "How are you, Yukari? Has everything been okay? Have you seen or heard anything unusual?"

"No," she replied, with a puzzled expression. "I mean, there is a party. I was going to go in and watch for a little while, but for some reason, I didn't feel like going anywhere near everyone earlier."

"This is Kei Hara," Jeremy said. "It's his family hosting the party. It is their home now."

At the mention of the name Hara, Yukari shrank back against Jeremy, her face clouded.

"Do you feel anything when you look at him?" he asked.

"Afraid," she whispered.

"Jeremy, what's going on here?" Kei demanded.

Jeremy felt a terrible weight fall onto his shoulders. "Yukari, I am sorry, but I have to tell you something about your past. Something that I wish I did not have to."

"I will tell her," a voice sounded from by the windows.

They all spun to face the Dark Yukari hovering in the air in front of the music room windows. Yukari looked up and gasped, seeing her dreadful other self. But the dark one gazed down at her as if in pity, her shadowed face saddened. The look faded when her eyes fell on Kei. Her eyes grew hard and glowed.

"I will tell her," Dark Yukari said, "for all that I never wanted her to know. For all that I wanted some part of me to remain pure, unraped, unsullied by a hatred that has burned undimmed for all the decades."

Yukari shivered next to him.

"Will someone tell me," Kei said, "what the hell is going on? I've never seen either of these girls before, and I've never done anything to either of them."

"We are one," Dark Yukari said. "We are what your family made us. What Shoji Hara your grandfather made of me, a rotting corpse in a dead family. Your grandfather got my father drunk on sake, then raped and strangled me. My father was blamed when Shoji testified against him, so he slit his belly, my mother stabbed herself, my sweet little sister, Ayane, only ten years old, drowned herself for shame with her grandmother. My whole family died for a man who wanted my body and my father's ruin."

Kei folded to the ground, his face open and slack. "No," he whispered.

"All true," Dark Yukari spat. "You cannot deny me. I am the creation of that wrong."

Beside Jeremy, half-hidden behind him, Yukari wept.

"I am sorry," the Dark said to the Light. "You are just a little part of me, a dream of what I might have been once. When you wandered about, so childishly happy, I could forget my sorrows for a while. I could sleep, for until the Haras came within these grounds, I could not reach them."

"Is this all I am?" Yukari whispered.

"No, Yukari," Jeremy said, grabbing the girl by both arms, her shocked face turning toward him. "It's not. You're gentle. You're kind. You love beauty. You're *not* the lesser part." He spun back to the

49

floating darkness and leveled a finger. "That is. It's just hate and dark dreams."

The Dark Yukari shook her head. "Would that you were right."

She looked down at her other self. "Come, sister. I have caused the guests to fall into a deep sleep. Our enemies are all here now, they wander the garden, seeking to escape, but oh, I hedge them, I play with them, they see my bones, my father's blood, mother's body and Ayane's sightless eyes. They wander in terror now, and soon in death. They will join us all in Hell."

"They did nothing to you," Jeremy threw at her. "What good will any of this do? It's so pointless!"

The dark one looked at him in infinite weariness. "*Gaijin.*"

Jeremy felt himself shoved to the floor. His duster fell from his hands. Next to him, Kei gave a strangled yell, then froze, arms outstretched, as he was lifted to hang in the air.

"Yukari," Jeremy shouted. "Stop her."

"Jeremy," she sobbed. "I can't. I have no power over her. She made me. I'm just a daydream."

"I don't believe it," he gasped. "You're more. I know it."

"Come, sister of the grave," the Dark Yukari said. "Come and let us revenge our family, then we can rest quiet, or at least leave this world."

"No," Yukari screamed. "I won't. Maybe I can't stop you. Maybe I am nothing more than bits of your dreams and memories or your hopes. But if that is all I am, I will still say no!"

"Good for you," Dark Yukari said. "Maybe you are more of what I once hoped to be than I am. But no matter. Stay then, but it will end for you when it ends for me."

"I had hoped," Debbie said, "that it would not come to this, for Jeremy's sake. He's a real nice boy, very sweet even."

The Dark Yukari stared down silently, but her face wavered, once Yukari, once rotting, once bone.

"Last chance, sister," Debbie said. "These boys don't want to hurt you, but I am too old and too much of a realist for such qualms." Debbie's fangs slid out farther than Jeremy had ever seen, the shimmer of her eyes made them seem silver, even the lines of her face no longer appeared human.

"Down," said Dark Yukari, with a wave of her hand.

Debbie staggered as if an immense weight had landed on her. The muscles of her body stood out like cables as her gown tore and split around her, even her high-heeled shoes collapsed. Debbie gave a savage growl and advanced a step, then two, and finally fell at Dark Yukari's feet, silent and unmoving, wrapped in the shreds of her gown. The silver glimmer faded from Debbie's eyes, and she looked like a corpse.

Dark Yukari leveled a figure at Jeremy. "Remain." She turned and with Kei, his body wrapped in a faint blue shine, floating behind her, flew through the huge glass doors that opened at the wave of her hand. They were gone.

CHAPTER EIGHT

Authorities report the mysterious disappearance of all 10,000 inhabitants of the city of Gakuch. ISIS terrorists are believed to be involved.

Jeremy threw himself at the invisible forces holding him down, but if Debbie, with her immense vampiric strength, could not stand, what chance had he? He stopped and became aware of the Yukari kneeling on the floor, bent over, crying.

"Yukari," he said. "Help me."

"I can't do anything," she wailed. "I'm nothing. I'm not even a ghost. I'm a dream a ghost had."

He schooled himself to calmness. "Yes, you are something, Yukari. You're a dream she had of a better self she wanted to be. We all have that dream, but you, you are that dream. You're Yukari's dream, come save Yukari."

She looked up, her eyes brilliant with tears. "What can I do? Tell me!"

"Bring my coat to me, quickly. Don't touch the gemmed sword inside."

She scrambled up and grabbed the duster.

Jeremy knew she could not touch the sword with its deadly red gem, but perhaps its nearness could help him. "Throw it over my shoulders."

As the leather coat settled around him, he felt the binding loosen. He concentrated on his right hand, moving it to where he could touch the gem. The invocation shattered when his flesh touched the gem, and he leapt to his feet.

"It worked," Yukari said, also jumping up and embracing him. He slipped the coat on so she would not touch the jewel.

A deep groan distracted them. Debbie rose from the wreckage of her gown, down to a bra and panties. "Bitch owes me for a Vera Wang and some Blahniks."

"I thought you were dead," Jeremy exclaimed.

"Honey, everyone but you in this room *is* dead."

Screams sounded from the garden. They raced out the door, Yukari holding fast to Jeremy's hand. Only yards away, Kei was pressed up against the outside of the building, as if nailed there, staring, his face contorted, into the garden below the terrace on which they stood.

Yukari pushed past him. They were two levels up and about a hundred feet from where Kei's family and Sarah stood at bay in a circle of blue flame. On the far side of them, Dark Yukari floated well above them, her eyes glowing pinpoints, her mouth in a rictus of hate.

"No," Yukari screamed. "Don't do this."

The blue flames surrounded Kei's family, snapped at them like snakes, mounting higher about them.

"Oh God, Jeremy," Kei said, "my whole family. Do something!"

"I can't stop her," Yukari sobbed.

The flames beat higher. There was no time to reach the Dark Yukari.

No, Jeremy thought. *No, not this way. Please. It's not for me to decide.*

But it was—the choice was stark, merciless, savage—and this time there was no Shadowheart to save him from it.

Sarah shrieked, beating at her sleeve as a snake of blue flame wrapped around her arm.

"Jeremy!" Kei screamed.

As if imbued with a malign life of its own, the bloodsword flashed into his hand, and he swung.

Cutting through Yukari's middle.

She hung there for a moment twisting in the air like a sheet on a line. Her head turned toward him, the mouth open in shock, the eyes wide in terror and pain.

"*Doshte?*" she breathed, and then the wind made rags of her, and she was gone.

The flames surrounding Kei's family disappeared as if blown out in the same instant. Dark Yukari gave a chilling wail, and she, too, became rags on the wind and faded from the world.

Kei fell from the wall, then staggered up to run for his family, leaving Jeremy and Debbie behind.

"It's too much," Jeremy said, quietly. "It's all too much." He went to his knees very deliberately and placed the sword hilt against the ground, jamming the gem into a space between pavers, its point toward him. He reached for the crosshilts to hold it steady and pull himself onto the blade.

"No, Jeremy," Debbie shouted. The vampire's grip closed on his forearms with paralyzing strength before he could reach the quillons.

"I've murdered an innocent, you see." Jeremy's voice seemed to come from somewhere far away, calm and reasoned, even as the muscles in his forearms stood out against her grip. "I promised her I wouldn't hurt her. She was just a little girl. A Templar's word is inviolable. Only death can answer for breaking a sacred oath."

But the vampire's strength was too great, and she pulled him back. The sword fell free of where he had wedged it, striking the pavement with a ringing sound.

"Jeremy, honey," she whispered in his ear, pulling him back against her. "Baby, listen to Debbie. There was nothing else you could do. You had to save the living over the dead. It's not your fault."

He shook his head slowly. "I'll never forget her eyes. How she looked at me when I murdered her."

"Listen to me. You had to."

He could only shake his head, overwhelmed with a sickness of body and soul.

I will not throw up, he thought. *I will not dishonor Yukari with a disgusting display*. But neither could he rise. There was no strength in his body.

"I'm sorry, baby," Debbie said holding tight to him. "It ain't fair, it ain't right, and it's a crying shame, but it had to get done."

Kei's running footfalls sounded dully in his ears. He didn't bother to raise his head.

"Oh my god," he said. "Is he alright? Did he try to—"

"Hush," Debbie said.

"Jeremy, man. You saved my whole family. You can't throw your life away." Kei knelt next to him a hand on his shoulder.

"I murdered Yukari," he replied, it was such an effort to speak. "Little Yukari, whose only sin was to be killed by a bunch of power-hungry bastards who didn't care that they destroyed her whole family."

The sound of the sword scraping across the stone flags, and Debbie's gasp, finally made him raise his eyes. He froze along with Debbie and Kei.

Yukari knelt next to them and reached out, taking hold of the sword by its cross hilt and dragging it away from them with one arm. The other was pressed across her breasts. She was naked, and her body shimmered under the moonlight. The sword, which should have reacted to the ghost, lay quiescent.

I've gone mad, Jeremy thought, looking into her eyes, still red-irised, but no longer lit from within.

"No, Jeremy," she said, her voice gentle.

"I struck you down," he managed.

She shook her head, the silk hair flowing down her shoulders. "You had to. I couldn't stop my other self, couldn't control her hatred." Tears rolled down her face. "She's back with me. We're one now. We mourn our family, but we no longer wish the death of the Haras."

A million thoughts fought for possession of his tongue. None won.

He ignored the sword, hating even the sight of it, and reached for the girl.

"Jeremy," Debbie said. "Prepare yourself."

"For what?" he said, still vague and distracted. "Death? I don't care. I'll go with her if it takes her to peace."

Debbie sighed. "No, dumbass. She's real. She's alive again."

"What!" Jeremy and Kei said, staring in shock.

"Are you sure?" Kei asked.

"Oh, hell," Debbie returned, turning loose of Jeremy and standing. "I can smell a damn virgin at a hundred yards. She's alive."

"Hey!" Yukari protested, her furious blush visible even in moonlight. "That's personal."

Jeremy, his hand shaking, reached for her. Yukari's hand met his and their fingers interlaced. Her hand was cold. He realized that she was shivering, but there was no question that the hand was that of a living human.

"Yukari," he breathed. Suddenly he embraced the girl, fighting emotions that threatened to overwhelm him. He could not forget what he'd done, but here was the possibility for redemption. The delicate strands of her hair lay against his face. She gave a little sob.

"I broke my sworn word—"

She released his hand and put hers against his lips. "I forgive you. I would rather you struck me down then allow me...me, to burn a family to death for something done by their ancestors."

He hugged her close.

"How is this possible?" Kei asked.

"I don't know," Yukari said, her voice muffled as her face was against his chest. "I felt the cold of the sword go through me. I felt my other self come back to me. Oh, the poor thing, how she has suffered, knowing all I had forgotten!

"Then it felt like I was falling, falling forever. I saw Jeremy reach for his sword and knew that he was going to kill himself for doing what he had to do. What I would have had him do. And I had to reach him, to tell him it was alright. Then I was here kneeling beside you."

Jeremy could only shake his head. "I don't understand."

"You got me hanging," Debbie said from behind them.

Yukari shivered, and it struck Jeremy that he had his arms around a naked sixteen-year-old girl. He released her and whipped off his leather duster.

"Turn around," he said to Kei.

Kei looked at him, but his reply died on meeting Jeremy's eyes, and he turned.

"Well, I guess I can peek at her," Debbie said, amusement in her voice.

Jeremy ignored that and held the coat out for Yukari, closing his own eyes while she slipped into it.

"How overwhelming," Yukari said, as he opened his eyes. "The smell of leather, the cold of stone on my feet, it's rough, and oh, my feet are sore."

"Welcome back to human life," Debbie said, but there was a clear note of envy in her voice.

Yukari walked over to Debbie and kissed her on the cheek, to the vampire's evident surprise.

"Ah, honey, lovely gesture and thank you, but you being so fresh and all, I'd suggest we just wave hello from now on."

Yukari turned to Kei. To Jeremy's surprise, the young man knelt in front of her and placed his forehead against the stone. "Kurita-san, I have no words to express my shame and sorrow over the wrong my family has done you. I must apologize for the disgraceful actions of my grandfather. I beg your forgiveness."

"Perhaps," Jeremy said, "we should all take responsibility only for our own actions."

Kei shook his head. "We are Japanese. Even for me, raised here in the U.S., my soul is Japanese, and it does not work that way for us."

Yukari wrapped her arms around herself. For a moment, Jeremy felt he was in the presence of her dark self, but the moment passed. "For my part, I forgive. I have regrets for all that I have done as well. We must leave judgment to Heaven. We have done too poorly here on Earth."

Yukari turned to Jeremy. "But now that I live, where am I to go and what am I to do? My family is gone."

Kei face was grim. "My own family can be made to understand, in time. We could offer you a home in Japan—"

"No," Yukari said. "My forgiveness cannot extend so far."

Kei bowed again his head, touching the stone. "Then, at the least, we must make sure that you never lack for a means of life."

"But alone..." She shivered, and her eyes were frightened.

"Kei! Where are you?" a voice called.

Kei's head snapped up. "Oh God, Sarah. If she finds me up here with a naked Japanese girl in only a coat and the queen of the D-cups in her underwear, I'm a dead man."

"What do I—" Yukari asked.

"Jeremy, dude," Kei implored, "help a brother out."

"Kei!" Sarah's voice came again.

"Yukari," Jeremy said, filled with a certainty that had so often eluded him, "will you come with me? I'll take care of you, and we will find a place for you in this world."

"You will?" she whispered.

A smile slipped onto his face. "I guess I always wanted a little sister."

Tears filled her eyes. "Oniichan."

"Guys," Kei said. "More later. I gotta go."

Jeremy nodded. "We'll slip out the back."

Kei smiled and ran back to Sarah and his family.

"Let's go," Jeremy said. "It's a walk through some woods. I'll carry you."

"Your sword," Debbie said quietly.

He glared at it with utter loathing. "Let it lie."

"Jeremy," Debbie said. "I know it hurts, boy, but you can't leave something that deadly around. It has powers for good or evil depending on the wielder."

"I will not touch it," he said, rejection in every line of his body.

"I cannot," Debbie returned.

Yukari stooped and picked up the sword, she turned around, opened the duster, and slid the weapon into its special scabbard.

Jeremy picked the girl up. Yukari was not small, but he felt that he could carry her over a mountain if he needed to.

"I will not fail you a second time," he said.

"Oniichan," she whispered back. "You did not fail me the first time."

Vampire, returned ghost, and Templar faded into the shadows behind the house.

ACT II

CHAPTER NINE

Desert winds in the Northern Sahara were clocked at 225 mph today.

Yukari Kurita, now whole and entire and alive, lay on the bed of a man she had met only a week ago, overwhelmed with the sensations of being alive again. The cool crispness of sheets, the hum of something she recognized as a heater, the soft pillow that her head rested on. So different than her childhood of futons and a wooden *kimakura* to rest one's head on. She felt the breath run in and out of her body and was both aware and fatigued.

But another sensation was chiefly responsible for her sleeplessness. The boy, no he was a man by any standard, Jeremy had carried her to his car as if she weighed nothing. She remembered his strength, the kind, concerned look on his face as he did so. The idea that a man had seen her naked, and even carried her wrapped in his coat, once would have shamed her and her family. Now that thought seemed irrelevant.

When I was only half myself...no, she forced herself to admit, *not even half. I was the lesser part of a dream the ghost had. The ghost of a ghost. But when I was the innocent Yukari, I enjoyed the touch of Jeremy's hand and his presence. Last night, when he lifted me and I was myself again, I felt some-thing more.*

But with that realization came something hideous, the memories Dark Yukari had held her safe from. For over eighty years, Dark Yukari had born the remembrance of being violated and kept it away from her. There was no such protection now. When her heart had sped up last night, it had also flinched away.

I am such a late bloomer, she thought bitterly. *My father wanted to keep me by his side, finding no suitable match for me, especially among the militarist samurai families that hated his Western influences. All my class-mates were married by my age, but I was still home. Now, I am returned to the world. What am I to do with myself?*

She sighed. Jeremy had promised her protection and a home. She knew that he meant it from the bottom of his soul. *There is some karma between us,* she thought, *or this miracle could not have happened. I must be very clever and go slowly. I have a second chance; I must use it carefully.*

Her knowledge of the world was spotty at best. She had heard much in her years of haunting the embassy. But in the distant, dream-like dusk world she'd inhabited, it had meant little to her. Now she reviewed the bits and pieces she had learned or overheard. In this time, women married later and had much more say about their lives. With that realization came a relief that she need not think about these things just now. She could be sixteen in this modern world where the decisions of adulthood could be delayed or avoided. A happy sigh escaped her, and she snuggled down in the soft Western bed and let sleep overcome her.

The sun slanted through the windows of Jeremy's bedroom, finding him awake, as he had spent much of the early morning hours after a brief, exhausted sleep. In the bedroom opposite him, a sixteen-year-old girl wearing one of his shirts, lay sleeping. That is if Yukari, only last night resurrected from being a ghost, had been able to sleep either.

What the hell am I going to do now? he thought for the hundredth time. Nothing in his life, or training, had prepared him to be the guardian for a Japanese teenager murdered in 1932.

"Food," he said, "living teenagers need food. What am I doing in bed?" He leapt up—brushed his teeth, shaved, and showered in record time. Then he raced downstairs to his small kitchen and slid to a halt.

What do Japanese girls from 1932 eat? he thought frantically, and then realized he had no idea what modern Japanese girls ate for breakfast either. *Tea,* he realized, *tea is needed.* He put on a kettle, recollected that he had rice, and while it seemed a stereotype, he figured he would make rice. He was so preoccupied with his attempt at breakfast that he didn't notice Yukari until she spoke.

"Jeremy-san, what are you doing?"

He turned to find Yukari dressed in his spare robe, her long hair hanging well below her waist. Only her eyes, the pupils of which were red, but no longer glowing, betrayed anything unusual.

"Yukari," he said. "How are you? Do you feel alright?"

"I am very well," Yukari said with a shy smile.

"I was making, well, trying to make breakfast for you, then realized I have no idea what you like."

"I like," she said, sweeping past him into the kitchen, "being alive, feeling cold and warm, seeing the sun. And," she added with an impish tone, "I like the idea of taking over the preparation of breakfast."

"Oh, but all this modern stuff." He gestured at the ranks of devices with their blinking lights.

"I believe the modern stuff is burning the rice." She slipped past him and removed the pot. She then turned to the refrigerator and opened it, tsked at the paucity of the contents, and made her selections.

"Please sit, Jeremy-kun," she said with a slight blush, the *kun* was honorific for someone in her age group, a close friend.

He sat at the table as Yukari, surprisingly apt with the modern kitchen, though avoiding the microwave, took charge. She spooned out the rice, broke an egg over each bowl and placed two cups of regular tea on the table.

She sat opposite him. "Ah, my first meal in my new…"

"You can say home," Jeremy replied, his voice grave. "Wherever I am, I will always make a home for you."

"Your friendship is more than enough for me," Yukari returned, a shadow over her face. "Jeremy-kun, please do not think so much on the events of last night. I am alive again, thanks to you and saved from the horrible sin of murder."

Jeremy looked down at the rice and egg on his plate but did not see it. He saw the face of Yukari, turned to him in shock as the blood-sword sheared through her, felt the dreadful resistance as the weapon cut through her ghostly form. Heard her cry, "Doshte?" as she disappeared into rags of ectoplasm.

"Jeremy, no!" she said, reaching a hand across to seize one of his. "Come back to me."

With a great effort, he pulled himself back to the present. His breathing slowed; his heart ceased trying to tear out of his chest. "What a lucky man I am," he said, "to have such a fine breakfast prepared by such a pretty young lady."

She gave a quick and nervous smile. They spent the next few minutes quietly eating their breakfast.

"There are a thousand things to do today," he said, fighting off a feeling of being overwhelmed. "Fortunately, some will be done by others. The Haras and Templars will be working on all the legal documents to give you a legal identity in the world."

"I leave all those matters to you, Oniichan."

Oniichan, he thought, *very well then, that is my part to play.*

"For today, we will start slowly," he added. "You need clothes, shoes, and probably a hundred other things I can't think of."

"Jeremy-kun, I have no desire to be a trouble to you."

"Please never say that again," he said. "Anything I can ever do for you will be the smallest payment on what I owe."

Yukari pressed her lips together, then her face smoothed. "Well, a day shopping, how lucky for me."

"I have a friend named Samantha Pelton," Jeremy said. "She works with me both in the graphic design cover business and as a Templar. She'll help us out."

"Oh?" Yukari said, one delicate eyebrow raised. "Tell me more about this lady friend."

Uh-oh, Jeremy thought. "Sam was one of the first friends I made here. She's a few years older than me."

"Is she pretty?" Yukari asked. "Tall? What color is her hair?"

Jeremy smiled. "Sam is pretty. Her hair is brown, eyes green, but she is not tall."

"And is she married? Does she have a boyfriend?"

"Ah, Sam's not interested in men that way."

"Oh, she is *yuri* then?"

It took a second for Jeremy to remember that *yuri* was a Japanese euphemism for lesbian. He nodded.

"It will be interesting to meet her. Perhaps she will be my friend. She certainly seems a more appropriate friend than Miss Melons," Yukari said with an audible sniff.

"Yes," Jeremy said, fighting the desire to laugh for the first time since he'd struck at Yukari with the bloodsword.

Yukari stood and reached for the bowls.

"Oh, no," he said, forestalling her. "If you cook, you do not have to clean." Over her continued objections, he cleaned up breakfast.

"Jeremy," she said, as he loaded the dishwasher. "Your coat and the sword are still in my room."

He froze. "Please bring me the coat when you feel like it," he said, slowly, not facing her. "I do not want to see the filthy sword again."

"Jeremy-kun," Yukari said, "the sword was only a tool—"

"Please," he interrupted, "just tuck it out of sight somewhere, the closet, under the bed."

Again, Yukari's lips pressed together, but she realized now was not the time press the issue.

"You did say something about shopping," she continued, smoothly changing topics, "but it would be hard to go out in…" She gestured at the robe she was wearing.

"I'll call Sam," he said. "She'll know what to do."

CHAPTER TEN

A herd of African elephants has been found dead all in a perfect circle in Kenya. While poachers are suspected, it has been noted that the elephants were unmarked by gunfire and their tusks were not removed. A mass poisoning is suspected.

Samantha Pelton took the phone from her ear and stared at it as if it had become something unnatural, then put it back. "Say what now?"

"I realize that it's a lot to take in, but it's the truth. I now have a ward, she's sixteen, Japanese and yes, you heard correctly she used to be a ghost. I'll give you the full story after we meet. Meanwhile, I need help with a major shopping expedition for everything from socks to hair bows. All the things a teen girl needs to survive."

"Jeremy, I haven't been a teen girl in more than a decade, and I was never Japanese."

"Sam, I need you."

"All right, all right. I'm on my way."

"Umm, would it be possible for you to stop on the way and get like one outfit somewhere so she can come out with us?"

"Jeremy, did you inherit a naked sixteen-year-old?"

"I'll explain later."

"That will be good. What are her sizes?"

There was a quick conference at the other end. "Well, she's five feet-nine inches tall, weight 110, slim built."

"Does she need a bra and panties?"

"Ah, yes,"

"What's her cup size?"

"I can't ask her that!"

"Well, let me put it this way, when you inherited Miss Naked Japan, did she show signs of needing a bra?"

"Not a lot."

"Okay. I'll stop at a Target, get the necessary, and be there in about two hours."

Two hours later, Samantha parked her Land Rover in the usual spot outside Jeremy's condo, contemplating all the recent changes and how little she actually knew of what was going on. Jeremy and Shadowheart had disappeared for the better part of two months. Fortunately, he had the foresight to warn her that he might be gone for an extended period and to arrange for Templar brothers overseas to cover much of the design work. They hadn't lost any jobs as a result, but she'd demurred on new work as he was not there to meet with clients.

When he'd come back, his angelic companion did not. Samantha wasn't close to the angel—only Jeremy was—but her absence unnerved her. Privately, she found the teenage bubblegum-popping version of Shadowheart rather annoying and the Warrior Princess version scarier than, well, not Hell, but pretty scary. Jeremy had only said that Shadowheart was gone "northwards" for an indefinite period.

Now a Japanese girl had popped into their life, and Jeremy had indicated that it was related to the job that took him away for the last week. She hopped out of the Range Rover and decided to take her jacket; it was still cool in the mornings and had rained in the early hours. She pulled two bags out of the back seat then bounded up the stairs, took a deep breath, and rang the bell.

Jeremy opened it moments later, and her usual, "Hi, handsome," died on her lips. "You look awful," she blurted out. *Oh great, Sam, tactful as always,* she thought. But it was true. He was pale, even for him, and there was a haunted expression to his eyes that she had not seen before.

"Hi, Sam. Yeah, rough night. Details later. Come on in—there's coffee ready, and I want you to meet someone."

She followed him into the kitchen. "Yukari Kurita-san, this is Samantha Pelton."

The girl who rose from the kitchen chair was beautiful and willowy, with black hair that fell below her waist and towered over Samantha by a good six inches. Her face was symmetrical and heart-shaped, but it was the eyes that compelled her. They were red-irised, matching the robe that she wore, a Christmas present to Jeremy from Samantha. She'd expected brown, or black, but not an unearthly red.

"*Hajimemashte*, Pelton-san. Oh, sorry, I mean, it is nice to meet you."

"A pleasure, please call me Samantha."

"Then you should call me Yukari, as is the custom here." She gave a small bow. She didn't seem to be embarrassed by being clad only in a robe in the house of an older, single male.

Sam felt she was hiding the fact that she was amused by it all.

"Well, I guessed right on your sizes. I went for extra slim on every-thing." She lifted the two bags.

"*Arigato*, Samantha-chan," Yukari smiled, excited by the thought of new clothes.

Jeremy sat down as the two girls disappeared upstairs. He felt suddenly drained of energy and knew it was a sign of a depression that he dared not allow to take hold. So, he got up and paced. Fortu-nately, the girls were not long. Samantha came down first and pointed behind her. "Ta-da."

Jeremy looked up as Yukari came down the stairs. She wore flat sneakers, leggings, and a dark-green tunic that came down to mid-thigh. She held a denim jacket in one hand and looked like she's been born in twenty-first century. He could feel the depression fade.

Sam walked past him, poured herself a coffee, and leaned against the counter. "So, Jeremy," Sam said, "how is it that you ended up with a Japanese girl with no clothes?"

"Well," Jeremy said, scratching his head. "It's kinda hard to explain but, well, Yukari was a ghost, haunting the Japanese Legation here. She was the daughter of one of the diplomats stationed here once."

"Really?" Sam said. "Wow, a ghost, we've never run into one of those before."

"Yurei," the girl said in her delicate accent, "are the rarest of supernatural beings."

"And given that I can both see and touch her..." Sam continued.

"She is no longer a ghost, no longer..."

"You may say dead, Oniichan," Yukari said. "I was dead for eighty-five years."

"Oniichan?" Sam asked.

"It kind-of means older brother," he said. "The more important point being that Yukari is the only person we actually know who has returned from the dead."

"In a way," Yukari said with a nod of her head. "I never actually crossed over to the land of the dead. While I did die, I lingered in this world."

"Rather still the accomplishment," Samantha said, alternating between shock and bewilderment.

"I'll talk about the whole story another time. Here are the essentials: Yukari is alive, but she has no living relatives, at least none we could trust with the reality of who and what she is. She...passed away in 1932. Another Japanese family, the Haras, are involved as well, and they owe Yukari a great debt. Part of which they will discharge by coming up with the paperwork that will make her a citizen of Japan with legal residence in the USA. The Temple will be cooperating in this effort supplying the U.S. end of the documents that we need. I'm going to be Yukari's legal guardian. From today, I have no greater responsibility than ensuring her happiness and safety."

Sam's eyebrows almost crawled off her forehead. Jeremy's face was grim and determined. As for the girl, she watched him with now literally shining eyes.

Way more, she thought, *is going on here than I am being told.* "Well," she said aloud. "You won't find a better guy to look out for you than Jeremy."

"This I know," Yukari said. "But I must not become a burden to Oniichan. I must learn to fit into this new world. There is much that I can do for him and wish to."

Jeremy gave a sad smile. "Well, for today, I was hoping that we could take Yukari shopping. She literally has nothing."

"Yeah," Samantha concurred, "and I would suggest a pair of contact lenses to tone down the eyes. They almost glow."

"I think," Yukari said with a determined voice, "that I can do something about that." She concentrated for a few seconds, and the light in her eyes dimmed and went out, though they remained red. "It will be something I must be aware of. Perhaps it happens when I am excited."

They piled into Jeremy's Mini and pulled away from the curb into the usual death-defying Charlotte traffic. Yukari did not appear to notice the random lane changes, lack of signaling, tailgating, and other traffic sins and just enjoyed the sunshine and high-scudding clouds. They opted for Park Road shopping center due to accidents, construction, and the generally hellish traffic around South Park Mall. The trip from his condo was not long.

They spent the rest of the day working their way through the quaint strip mall with the tall Japanese girl in tow and Jeremy hovering over her like a protective cloud. Yukari was both beautiful and distinctive, being tall for a Japanese even in the twenty-first century. If boys gave her the eye, Jeremy gave them a glare. There was something in the regard of a man who had killed, not present in the gaze of a man who hadn't, and the boys instinctively recognized it. They sidled off, but Samantha wondered at the reason behind it. Jeremy was protective, even old-fashioned toward women, but this was something else.

For her part, Yukari regarded the world with wide-eyed wonder and an un-Japanese lack of reserve. She was rather like a puppy, happy with her whole body and smiling at everything. Occasionally, she would clutch Jeremy's arm if she was surprised or uncertain. Then she would blush or smile shyly. Jeremy's expression was fond, even indulgent, but when Yukari wasn't looking, Sam saw something in her friend that was unusual: suppressed rage, grief, a cloud of negative emotion that he would either cloak, or momentarily escape from, when he engaged with either her or Yukari.

Sam checked with Jeremy several times about money only to have it waved off.

"Buy her anything she wants, anything she needs," he stated. "Don't check price tags; it's not a consideration."

This flew into opposition from Yukari, who found everything too expensive and insisted that she needed only the bare essentials. Finally, Jeremy insisted, stating it was his decision and his responsibility to provide for her.

"I cannot have you go into debt for me," she protested.

"The debt I have to you," he replied, turning grim, "is already great. This is money and nothing. The Haras have supplied considerable funds for your use, with more on tap as needed. Please have no concerns about money. That is my obligation."

Sam sensed that Yukari's concerns were not alleviated, but she let the matter drop and accepted all the purchases as gifts from her "older brother" graciously.

They stopped for gelato at a small shop and sat outside, people watching and enjoying the sun. Yukari reviewed her purchases, tsking at the prices despite Jeremy's assurances. The girl's taste was very modest for a sixteen-year-old until one recalled she had been born in 1918. She stared around in surprise and embarrassment at some of the outfits girls wore in early spring.

"I knew that dress had changed much," she whispered to Samantha, "but how much!"

"Didn't people dress this way...er...around you?"

"I was haunting a legation home," she replied matter-of-factly, "people apparently dressed more conservatively there than..." Her eyes drifted to a girl whose chest was displayed like a public offering, bouncing around as she bopped through the parking lot.

"Well, what sort of thing did you wear?"

"Often a yukata in spring and summer, sometimes a kimono, but as often as anything, a serafuku."

"Ah," Sam said, "don't know that one."

"You would call it a sailor suit," Jeremy said. "One sees them all the time in anime."

"Yeah, don't watch that."

"A dark-blue dress, with a sailor's collar, tapered in the middle," Yukari added. "They are worn for school even now. We are a very traditional people."

"No doubt," Sam said.

Hours later, Jeremy was loaded with bags of jeans, blouses, and dresses. Other bags held camisoles and panties, but a scandalized Yukari would not allow Jeremy to carry those. Sam found it very cute but puzzling.

After the plunder was deposited in Jeremy's studio, he took them both out to dinner at a Japanese family restaurant. The staff was delighted with Yukari, crowding around to ask her about herself. While Jeremy looked concerned, Yukari handled the interest calmly and appeared to enjoy the attention.

Sam had intended to grill both of them about the situation but found herself forestalled by a combination of Jeremy's reticence on the subject and Yukari's adroit turns of conversation.

Well, she thought, *she was the daughter of a diplomat.* At the end of the evening, she started her probing again, only to freeze at the site of a tear running down the girl's face.

Jeremy snapped upright in his seat. "Yukari, what's wrong?"

"I have not had a night like this," she said, voice trembling, "with the taste of good food on my lips, in the company of those who care for me...in such a long while."

"Life will be like this from now on," he said, "I swear it, and this time there will be no failing in that."

She gave a small silver laugh. "Oniichan, you are taking a silly girl's speech too seriously. Please do not worry so. I am grateful for all you do for me."

She turned to Sam. "*Gomen nasai*, Samantha-chan."

Sam patted the girl's hand and was surprised when Yukari's hand closed almost convulsively on hers. "Nothing to apologize about. I'm amazed at how well you are functioning in a world so different from the one you were born into, and after all you have gone through."

Yukari did not release Sam's hand, nor did she meet her eyes, but she said, "Though I was not of the world of the living, I did see and learn much of what transpired. The Great Pacific War, men on the moon, the internet, these things made their way into the Legation, though I confess that as I dreamed my days away, I was not terribly interested. To be *yurei*, a ghost, is different. Time has no meaning. I was never bored, yet rarely excited. I might spend weeks in front of a single flower. I did not hunger or thirst, for all I would occasionally sneak a tea, or a bean mochi away, that was more for a familiar sensation than a need."

"Jeremy has said as much, mostly about Debbie Middleton. Vampire isn't just a physical change of a dead human; it's a change of soul, of mind."

He nodded. "She enjoys her life. It would drive a normal human mad, but for her, it's as natural as eating three squares a day and catching eight-hours shut-eye."

Yukari released Sam's hand. "Yes," Yukari said with a prim sniff. "I have seen her enjoying her life very much."

"Ah," said Jeremy, embarrassed.

"And how did this come about?" Samantha asked, sensing an advantage.

"There was a wardrobe—" Yukari began with a conspiratorial tone.

"No need to go into that now," he said hastily. "I should get the check."

Yukari yawned, then put both her hands over her face in embarrassment. "Oh! Apparently, another difference, suddenly I am very weary."

"It has been a long day full of sensations," Jeremy said, "perhaps it's time to call it a night."

"What about tomorrow?" Samantha asked.

"For the next few days, keep pumping the design work to the Templars. I have so much to do with Yukari—"

"Oniichan," Yukari, looking more heavy-lidded by the second, managed. "You must not neglect your work."

"It's only for a few days, and I have not had a vacation since I got here," Jeremy said, "but we have to get you into a school. There's all sort of paperwork."

"As you wish," she whispered, nodding.

"I can handle the office," Samantha said, leaving far more unsaid to his obvious relief.

Jeremy quickly paid the tab. The two of them managed the sleepy girl into the car, and when they got to his home, Jeremy carried her into the house, laying her in her bed and asking Sam to slide her out of her clothes.

"First couple of days with the new body," he said, after she came out of Yukari's room.

"You look kinda done in yourself," she said.

"I am. You want to stay over? I'll take the couch; you can have my bed."

"Hah," she replied, "the dogs will eat the house. I'm for home."

"I'll call you at the office tomorrow. I am going to be out of circulation for a few days at least."

"And if something monstrous and hairy attacks?" she asked.

"Not my issue at the moment. Yukari is. If the Temple wants to send somebody to take my place, the sword is under Yukari's bed. They can have it. I'd have thrown the filthy thing away if there was a safe way to do it." The last came out with a vehemence that surprised Sam.

Not the time, she thought, *I'm tired, he's tired, and it's late.* She reached up, pulled him down for a goodnight kiss, and said, "Call ya tomorrow."

As she walked down the steps, Jeremy closing the door behind her, she knew something was very, very wrong.

CHAPTER ELEVEN

Sudden wildfires have raged through Madagascar, killing hundreds. Bizarre reports of a burning woman walking calmly through the fires have surfaced in multiple locations.

The difficulties in establishing Yukari in a new life were many and varied as Jeremy found out over the following weeks. The Haras worked overtime with the assistance of the Templar network, creating a back story for Yukari, visas, passports, school and health records, so that she might have a legal existence in the U.S. Money flowed freely, both from the shame of their ancestor's actions, Kei's demands, and the family's lingering fear of the ghost become mortal. No one really knew if Yukari was merely a teen girl, or if some power still resided in her. She professed ignorance, and Jeremy believed her.

The Templar network was glad for ridding the world of an angry ghost. Otherwise, they were held at bay by Jeremy. As yet, the Templars did not know of his estrangement from the bloodsword. So, Jeremy remained too valuable a resource to be trifled with, and his adamant refusal to allow Yukari to be examined, or inquisited, stood. His implicit threat to deal with any interloper harshly, raised eyebrows on the Marshall he spoke to. That Marshall knew Jeremy was a favorite of the Grandmaster, despite his near total disregard of Temple rules. He did not understand it, any more than he understood Jeremy, but he knew enough of about both men to leave Jeremy alone...for now.

For now, was enough for Jeremy, he refused to think further ahead than the next twenty-four hours. Yukari was his only focus. Fortunately, Sam was available to smooth out many of the details of his work life. But Jeremy quickly realized that Yukari needed more of a structure to her existence and a roadmap into the modern world. She could not simply live in his apartment like a potted plant. That meant one of the most ambivalent of human experiences: high school.

A call to the Haras soon produced a transcript from a Japanese school. It was actually Yukari's original one, updated to make it appear as if she had been in high school in Japan last year. Her original high school had been destroyed by fire in WWII. A new one had risen in its place. Yukari had been an excellent student, though ironically not that good in English. Fortunately, her mastery of English had returned across the gulf of death with her.

To his surprise, Yukari immediately took to the idea of school. He'd forgotten that for a girl born in her time, an education was both prized and rare for a girl. So, he pulled strings to get her enrolled in Charlotte Classic, a high school with a reputation for good academics and low troubles. He wanted a safe environment for Yukari, and money was no issue. He'd made it clear that should that faucet ever start to close, the Hara family scandal would find its way into the news. In this he had the active support of Kei, and at least no active resistance from his father. Jeremy was taking no chances with Yukari's future. Powerful people owed him favors, and he ruthlessly called in every one he needed to get Yukari enrolled.

He found himself on a Monday, in the office of the admissions officer, a well-intentioned, if somewhat rabbity-looking, Ms. Weldon. He supplied her with one piece after another of notarized documentation and wondered how people who didn't have endless money and time accomplished any of this.

"We welcome students from all over the world," Ms. Weldon said, pushing her glasses back on her nose. "It is somewhat unusual to take one in mid-year. Fortunately, we are an all-year-round school."

"Very," Jeremy agreed. "Yukari's situation is very unusual."

"Yes," Weldon said, her lips pursed in sympathy. "How terrible about the loss of her family, a plane crash at sea..." She shook her head and sighed.

He nodded. "My family and hers go way back and we are, for private reasons, indebted to hers. My father promised that I would serve as a legal guardian for her."

"A lot of responsibility for one so young," Weldon observed.

He laughed. "Yukari is no trouble. I sometimes wonder who is looking out for whom. She is surprisingly mature and self-reliant for her age, perhaps less worldly than many of your other students, however. She's had a very traditional upbringing in a rural part of Japan, helping out a *ryokan*, an old-style inn that the family ran. So her acquaintance with modern conveniences is somewhat spotty."

"Good," Weldon said, "maybe she won't get scoliosis from bending over a cell phone like so many other children these days." Her professional mien reasserted itself. "Now as to these medical forms..."

Hours later, Jeremy met Samantha at Dilworth Coffee. The rebellious, self-proclaimed ex-hippy would not be caught dead in a Starbucks. He found her in the corner with a paperback. Sam had no use for Kindle either.

"Hey handsome," she said with a bright smile and a kiss as he tucked into the seat next to her.

"Hi yourself, beautiful," he replied. A waitress appeared at his elbow. It was still early enough for a European to order cappuccino and not feel silly. He could never get used to the American custom of ordering it "whenever."

"How is getting Yukari into school going?" she asked.

He grimaced, knowing there were two sides to that question at least. One was a genuine concern for Yukari; the other unspoken one was *when the hell are you getting back to work?*

Aloud he answered, "I wonder what would happen to this country if all the photocopiers and printers disappeared?"

She raised her eyebrows. "Isn't it all electronic?"

"Less than you think. There's no end to the bloody forms, and everything you complete then leads to another task. For example, I now have to get Yukari to a doctor."

"What for?"

"Well, she's a living person again, and there are a ton of shots that she needs."

Sam chuckled. "Yeah, I didn't think of that one. I should have. Has she seen a gynecologist?"

Jeremy stared at her. "Ah, well, she didn't say anything was wrong..."

"I didn't think anything was wrong. I was thinking more of birth control."

"Birth control," Jeremy said, "she's sixteen!"

Sam gave him a pitying glace. "You do have a TV set, right? You do turn it on occasionally? I seem to recall that you date women and, heavens to Betsy, have even slept with some."

"What are you saying? I mean she was born in 1918!"

"When a girl her age would often have been married and had a kid. Sex wasn't invented in the twenty-first century, Jeremy."

"Ah, so you really think this is necessary...."

Sam sighed. "Yes, and for two reasons. One, it would be a good idea if she was a normal sixteen-year-old."

"And the second?" Jeremy said, afraid of the answer.

"She's not a normal sixteen-year-old. She has, if not lived, been aware for over eighty-five years in that house. She's seen husbands and wives, lovers, people having affairs with the servants. Hell, she apparently saw you and the Queen of the D-cups at it in the wardrobe. She's not quite as innocent as she enjoys playing at, and she's more complicated than you think. She likes the fact that you're playing the big brother to her. It allows her to play the little sister, and she's happy to do so. To some degree, it's not quite play-ing; she didn't have a normal existence. No boyfriends, no husband, no children, so she's neither the sixteen-year-old, nor the centenarian."

"What do I do, Sam? How do I care for her? She's not like any of the women I've been involved with."

"With that big heart of yours, dum-dum, you won't go far wrong. But you can leave the birth control and doctor issues with me."

"Gladly."

Days after their conversation and up to her eyeballs in tax forms, Sam finally decided to enlist Yukari's aid with the business that was now shuddering to more of a halt. Jeremy had purchased Yukari a cell phone, and while most of its capabilities remained a mystery to the girl, she could manage the phone function.

"*Mooshi, mooshi*," Yukari said. "Ah, pardon, I mean hello, Samantha-chan."

"Hi, Yukari, did the phone tell you it was me?"

"Yes, Jeremy taught the phone to know you. Besides, only the two of you have this number, well, and now my school, I suppose. I am both excited and afraid at the idea of starting soon."

"It will be good for you to be in the swing of normal life."

"I hope so."

"I'd like to get your help with something."

"Of course, Samantha-chan."

"I know Jeremy is busy, but I kinda need him at the office. Perhaps if you expressed an interest in his work, said you wanted to see the studio..."

"Hai, Samantha-chan, we will be there without fail tomorrow. I cannot have Oniichan be remiss in his work for me. Others are depending on him. We will be there when the business opens. What time would that be?"

"Nine is fine. I will have coffee, tea, and snacks."

"Will there be cake?"

Samantha had to fight the desire to laugh. Japanese said cake as *cakee*, and it was too cute from Yukari. "There will be now."

"*Arigato*, Samantha-chan. We will see you tomorrow."

Jeremy found Yukari waiting for him when he finished with the computer for the evening, having arranged for still more false documents to be mailed to him. She had a determined look on her face.

"Something wrong?" he asked.

"No. Though there is something that concerns me. A little something, easily mended."

"What is that?"

"You have been spending uncounted hours working for my benefit—"

"It's my pleasure."

"Still, you have been neglecting yourself and your affairs."

"There is nothing in my life that cannot wait. Not for this."

"It is not fair to Sam-chan to have her do this all by herself. I would be ashamed if this was on my account."

Jeremy, recognizing when he'd been outmaneuvered and outgunned, surrendered gracefully. "I guess I should lean in more at the store, huh?"

Yukari smiled, gracious in victory. "I would like to see where you work and learn of what you do. Sam-chan also promised there would be cake."

"Well, if there is to be cake, then we should go by all means."

"I agree," she said gravely, before an impish smile broke out.

So, he resumed something like a regular schedule. The next morning saw them both at the studio. As a result of the collusion between Yukari and Sam, there was an abundant supply of cake on the desk. Since Sam was not overly fond of sweets, it was clear evidence of a female network.

He quickly realized that Sam had been right and was appalled at how far behind everything was, despite the pinch-hitting of the Templars. Clearly, he was going to have to rely more on the Haras and attend to his business. Samantha could do most things but was not a designer and her computer skills were marginal. Things needed to be different.

Already his old life seemed very far away. Templar work was of no interest to him, and he ignored any contacts that he could on it. He was between girlfriends at the time and decided that he was too busy right now to pursue a relationship with any of the women he'd met.

Gad, he thought, while signing tax forms, *I'm thinking like a modern single parent. This is probably God's revenge on me for some of the things I have done with women and creatures that looked like women.* There was no denying that now that he had a female in his care, he had begun to see crosshairs on males lingering near Yukari.

Days piled onto each other as Jeremy and Yukari settled into their new life together. Every day was a journey into a new world with Yukari, whose wide-eyed wonder charmed him. While he left some details of bringing the ghost girl up to speed on the twenty-first century to Samantha, he did all he could to acclimatize her to the world. Fortunately, she was a quick study.

"I'm surprised you didn't pick up some of this while you were haunting the legation," he'd asked.

"Such things rarely interested me," she replied, while frowning at her new iPhone. "To be a ghost is to be removed from the world, but aware of it. With no needs or wants, time had little meaning." She glanced at him slyly. "Jeremy-kun, it's not as if I was remiss in my studies."

He'd laughed at the time, but it was clear there would be large and odd gaps in her knowledge of the world for many months at least. He was confident the story of her having been raised in a small country town would cover such gaps. Still, from the way she took to her new iPhone, he thought she'd catch up with being a modern teen soon.

"Jeremy-kun," Yukari said. He put aside the school paperwork he was working on, thinking her puzzled by the phone, but Yukari was looking into the small curio-cabinet that stood in the corner. It held a few souvenirs: a knife from Languedoc, a glass pen from Venice, a small Florentine statue in gold and enamel. But the object that had her attention was a more cunningly and intricately wrought glass and gold wire amulet on a heavy gold chain.

"Yes," he said.

"I have been meaning to ask what this is." She pointed at the amulet. "It gives me a strange sensation when I look at it."

"Strange?" he asked, rising from the desk in concern.

"Not unpleasant," she hastened, "but..."

"I guess that I haven't told you much about my life prior to meeting you," he mused. "It's been kind-of a nonstop whirl since we met."

"*Suma*," she said with a slight bow.

By now he had learned to stop taking the apologies and bows as serious. They were the social oil of Japanese society, but he still did not like hearing her apologize so often. So, he merely smiled and walked over.

"Before I met you, I had help in my work. I was teamed with a guardian angel. Her name was Shadowheart."

"What!" Yukari said. "Angels are real?"

The incongruity of the ghost girl returned from the dead being surprised by the existence of an angel took him aback for a few seconds. "Ah, yes."

"But where is this marvelous person?" she asked, leaning forward as if she could see the angel in the clear crystal of the amulet.

And I am not telling her that story, he thought. "She was recalled to the celestial planes. I don't know for how long. Maybe forever, I have no way to know. But I hope to see her again someday. I think that she wanted to come back."

"She?" Yukari asked.

"Ah, yes she was female."

"What did she look like?"

"Well, she had different appearances. There were times she looked like a blond girl, a little younger than you. Other times she looked like a giant warrior-princess." He decided not to mention what she had looked like as a succubus, when they infiltrated the infernal regions and things had gotten totally out of control.

Yukari may have sensed that there was more to the story, but she also sensed that he did not want her to probe about why Shadowheart was gone. However, she could apparently not help asking the question that interested her most. "Do you miss her?"

"Yes," he said in complete honesty. "There were times we fought, and she drove me crazy, but I do miss her."

"Was she pretty?" Yukari asked.

"Ah, well, the older version of her was. The younger was more annoying."

"I see why the amulet called itself to my attention," she added. "It, too, is partly of another world."

"Do you want me to take it out?" he asked.

"No," she said after a moment's thought. "It is not something that should be trifled with, and should she return, this pretty angel of yours, I would not want to give her cause for offense."

He elected to change the subject. "The school has finally called with the go ahead for your transfer. If you don't object, I want to enroll you in school at a junior level. It will help her catch up on the world and acclimatize to modern life."

"As you wish," she said. "I think I will get started on dinner."

They spent a lot of time together. While he could and did work from home, Yukari insisted that he go to the small storefront that he used as part of his cover.

He bought her a Kawai baby grand piano, to her delight, and would enjoy evenings listening to her play. Music had served as their introduction and remained a special language for them both.

Sometimes, she would disappear with Sam on forays into Charlotte and modern life. He was grateful that Sam had taken to Yukari in such a matter-of-fact fashion. It was a lot to ask of even a close friend.

Today the two women had disappeared back into Southpark when Sam chastised him for Yukari's totally inadequate wardrobe with school almost upon them. He wondered how the pair was making out.

As for the Templars, he worked alone and unsupervised, as did most Templars, but they were beginning to express concerns about his lack of responsiveness. He could only plead injury and fatigue.

PTSD was as common among Templars as it was among other combatants, and after his experiences, the plea seemed convincing. Requests for aid locally, he just denied.

"I'm out of the game for now," he said to the local priest, who called to check on him. "Maybe out forever."

Yukari was standing by the window when Samantha pulled up in her Range Rover. The vehicle looked more like something the military would use, with its racks of lights and bush guards, and again she wondered just how wild the outskirts of Dallas, NC, were. She picked up her purse, opened the door and with a cheery wave to Sam, ran lightly down the stairs. Truth was she was excited by the idea of being out with a friend.

Jeremy had insisted that she treat herself to more clothes and necessities, especially with school in the near future. While she was reluctant to be any trouble or expense to him, she had to bow both to his insistence and the need to have more of the necessities of teen life. He'd handed her a plastic card with her name on it.

"Use this," he had said. "It's called a credit card. We use it in place of money, well some people use it instead of money. Get whatever you need."

So armed with this credit card, she opened the door on the vehicle, which gave a creak, and slid in.

"Hi, Yukari," Sam said. "You ready for a day of rampaging through Southpark Mall?"

"Yes," she replied, ignoring a tickle in her nose. Sam's car smelled of dogs. "I am very grateful for the time you are taking to help me. *Gomen nasai.*"

Sam grinned. "Happy to do it. Truth is that I need some girl clothes too. I spend too much time on my tractor and mucking about the homestead in field clothes. I need some nice things for work. Jeremy has been having me deal more with clients, and I realized my wardrobe is a bit small for it."

Sam drove over to the giant shopping complex, and they parked in a sunny spot. As they pulled up to a parking spot, Yukari stared at the massive collection of connected buildings in astonishment.

"All this is one place for shopping?" she murmured in astonishment. "It is bigger than the town I was born in!"

"Yeah," Sam said. "It's a temple to excess. It kinda functions as one immense building. Once you are inside, you can get to any of the stores."

Yukari found the pile of buildings intimidating, with the thousands of people wandering through it. As they walked into the mall, Yukari found herself overwhelmed by the sheer size and variety of the stores. Sam seemed to understand this, and Yukari knew that she was not overly fond of people either.

"Where do we start?" Yukari asked, looking about holding her hands together.

"Well," Samantha said. "Let's start from the inside out." She led Yukari to a nearby storefront.

"What is this place?" Yukari asked in astonishment. Women's underwear and more was everywhere. The walls were decorated with huge posters of the most beautiful women wearing nothing more, though some also had angel wings.

Sam gave her a curious glance then smiled. "It's called Victoria's Secret, a lingerie store. It's more aimed at younger women and girls. I usually buy at another store; I get kinda tired of this place's emphasis on size twos, but it's popular with your age group."

Yukari considered. "So, what was Victoria's secret?"

"I think that she was a slut," Sam said, "and it probably wasn't that much of a secret."

Yukari's face heated at the sight of such a wealth of lingerie and so much exposed skin. She suddenly grabbed Sam's arm. "There are men in here."

"Yes." Sam patted her hand. "Men are allowed here. Most are buying stuff for their wives or girlfriends."

Yukari was so disconcerted that she retained her grip on Sam's arm, who gave her a sympathetic look and led her to the back where a minute later they were examining bras and panties.

"It is hard to imagine," she whispered to Sam. "I have never seen such garments, the colors…the fineness of the fabric. One would have to have been very wealthy in my day to have such things."

"I can't believe that you've just been using the few pieces I bought you at Target for all this time. You must have had to do wash every other day."

"It was no trouble, Sam-chan."

"Well, while we are here, we should get you properly measured for a bra," Sam said. "I made a wild guess when I bought them."

Yukari nodded. She'd had to pull on the straps of the two she had to make them more comfortable. So, she followed Sam into a curtained room where an attendant was talking with a girl who wore a white bra studded with metal and panties that appeared to have no back. She gasped and tried to back up, but Sam reached back and pulled her in. The nearly naked woman gave her a curious side glance but returned to asking the attendant for a larger bra size.

Another woman in her late twenties, mercifully fully dressed, turned to them. "Hi, can I help you?"

"My friend here needs to be fitted for a bra," Sam said.

"Okay." She gave Yukari a professional smile. "I'm Jen."

"*Hajimemashte*," Yukari returned, figuring her use of Japanese would cover any slips she made. "My name is Yukari." It still felt bizarre to allow strangers to call her more than Kurita-san.

"Oh, where are you from?"

"Japan," she said, "though I have been here for quite a while."

Jen opened a curtain behind her and turned to Sam. "Do you want to come in?"

"I'll be next door," Sam said, trying hard not to laugh at Yukari's expression.

She followed the other woman in who took a measuring tape off her shoulders and gave Yukari an expectant look.

Yukari raised her eyebrows.

"Could you take your top off? It's optional, but I get a better measurement that way."

I am a grown Japanese woman, she thought, *I must stop looking like a fool in public and shaming my friend.* Schooling her face to impassivity, she took her knit top off, then turned to Jen, who nodded encouragingly.

"Well, you have a perfect shape for our bras," Jen said.

Yukari tried to control her breathing and nodded. *"Arigato."*

Jen moved in and began wrapping the tape around Yukari, her hands flitting about her body.

Where are you touching me? Yukari thought in momentary panic. *This is the second time I have been unclothed in front of others; I should be getting used to it. It's part of being a grownup.*

"So, an A cup," Jen remarked. "You're long in the body, so a pull on won't work well. It'll have to have adjustable straps. A racer-back would be useful. Since you aren't big, we can get you ones that snap in the front."

"While you're at it," Sam called from outside, "could you get an inseam and torso measurement? We need to get some regular dressy clothes for her too."

Yukari, who was wearing a skirt, nearly yipped as Jen knelt in front of her and ran the tape under her skirt and up her thigh. "Inseam 35."

Now I can never get married, Yukari thought. The prudishness of the old expression almost made her laugh aloud. A few more minutes of commercial intimacy had Yukari measured and ready for shopping. They made their way back into the store.

Sam picked up a couple for herself. They were an interesting mix of plain and daring. Sam caught her expression. "Have to have something for date night."

Yukari was again trying to control a furious blush.

She chose three of the plainer ones but with a little encouragement from Sam traded one in for a dark-pink bra with black trim and another in coral.

"Relax," Sam suggested, "and let's try some things on. You've got a couple you like for styles there, and if they don't fit, they can bring you the right ones."

Sam and she had selected all that was necessary. Yukari was

secretly embarrassed by some of what she had purchased, but also pleased by the daring of the garments. She didn't let herself think about who might see her in them next.

Once in the changing room, she was startled by how the garments looked on her and how they made her feel. They were different from all she'd worn before.

I am a woman, she thought, *and this is what a grown woman wears. Can it be that I look good in these?* The glimmers of a newfound confidence lit in her. She decided for the pink and black and some lacy coral underwear and picked a number of pieces Sam recommended, rounding it out with more practical everyday pieces.

With the trial of proper underwear behind them, they moved on to other clothes and shoes. Francesca's—with its trendy selection of studded clothes, gypsy, and boho—was rejected out of hand by Yukari, and they ended up at Express, where Yukari and Sam both selected blouses, sweaters, and other clothes. Sam got Yukari into pants and jeans but could not persuade her to be seen in public in them until Sam found a tunic length knit top to cover them.

At this point, both of them were at their limit for tolerating the masses of people around and retreated to the food court. Sam spotted a sushi place and motioned Yukari over.

Yukari spoke to the chef in Japanese until she realized that he didn't understand her. He turned out to be Malaysian. She watched him prepare sushi for some others for a minute then determinedly took Sam's hand and led her away.

They settled on a pizza place, which had intrigued Yukari with its smells. She found the idea of cheese, warm and covered with red sauce, much more palatable than ordinary cheese. Sam, whose love of pizza was second to none, readily agreed. After a few tentative nibbles, Yukari began to really enjoy the tangy flavor.

"You better watch that," Sam cautioned, "if you want to fit into those clothes we just bought you."

"How could anything that tastes so good be bad for you?" she returned. "Besides, I've never had any trouble with weight before."

"You weren't alive in twenty-first century America before," Sam said. "See a lot of thin people around here?"

"Well...no." She eyed her pizza slice. "Enemy of women," she said and bit into it as it were a live enemy.

"No need to panic just yet," Sam added with a laugh. "You're a teenager; you have years of misusing your body ahead of you before you have to pay the bill."

"I'm not used to the idea of aging," Yukari said ruefully.

"Don't rub it in," Sam replied.

CHAPTER TWELVE

A tremendous rupture in the Great Barrier Reef near Australia has occurred seemingly overnight. There have been no reports of an explosion, but an area several kilometers wide has vanished.

Dropping Yukari off at school proved to be a comical experience for them both. Since her resurrection, the two of them had been inseparable. Only with Sam had she departed his side. Now Jeremy had to leave her at a school and among strangers. They stood by his car in the parking lot of the complex, amidst the trees and multi-story buildings of the school, with waves of teens lapping around them. The sun was well up and the day promised, for once this strange year, to be seasonally warm. He walked her up to the broad stairs of a building with various flags fluttering around it.

"Oh, Jeremy-kun," she had finally laughed self-consciously. "Are we not ridiculous? I feel like a small child being sent to *hoikuen* for the first time. I am, after all, a hundred years old." She whispered the last to him, eyeing the crowds of young people around them.

Jeremy started to make a joke about his being a proud mother but opted not to. Reminders of her family were painful to her. So, he merely smiled. "You will be fine. I do wish the contact lenses had worked out."

Even the most sensitive lenses had irritated her eyes, so they'd settled on the excuse of the red-lensed eyes being a genetic trait of her family. At least she had learned to control the tendency of her eyes to glow. The eerie glow would not be visible in daylight anyway, but he reminded her to be careful inside buildings. Fortunately, there was a trend among teens to wear cosmetic lenses, sometimes yellow and cat-eyed, as a "thing."

Now they stood on the steps of the school, with Yukari dressed in the clothes Sam and she had picked. They faced each other as teens streamed by, some giving them curious looks. Jeremy was surprised by how reluctant he was to leave her and wasn't sure what to do with his hands. Yukari was far too Japanese to be hugged in public and a handshake seemed absurd.

She saved him by giving a small bow, a bright smile, and turning toward the school as if there was nothing unusual in the act. He stared at her graceful back as she went in and sighed. She was right; there should be nothing unusual about it. She was smart and resilient. Surely, she could handle high school without issues.

God, he thought, *I hope she has an easier time of it than I did. I think I would choose Hell over high school. Am I doing the right thing by sending her? Still, she wanted to go. It was a baby step into the world, and how else could he introduce her to the society she'll spend the rest of her life in?*

Even if he took her back to Japan, she would face a world changed out of recognition. It might even be easier here, where the strangeness of life in a *gajin* world would be expected. He shook his head ruefully. *Every female in my life*, he thought, *from Shadowheart, to Debbie, to the were-jaguar, Prosperine, would be laughing their ass off if they could see into my mind. Of course, Shadowheart could hear my thoughts and I was never sure she couldn't actually read them when she wanted to.*

The remembrance of his guardian angel brought a pang of sadness. He had not thought of her often in these busy past days. Now he felt the absence keenly. For all they had fought and driven each other to distraction, there had been no other relationship like it. Sometimes it had been like being friends with multiple women. Shadowheart had three manifestations: an annoying blond teen about Yukari's age; the giant, winged, raven-haired warrior-princess; and last, and most provocatively, the succubus he had infiltrated Hell itself with. Already, it was hard for him to bring up the memories of his final adventure with her across dimensions no other human had crossed and returned. The recollections warred with life in the human realm, but what he remembered most clearly was when her disguise as a succubus had buried them both in the part. They'd crossed a line that Heaven apparently had a problem with.

He shook his head as he got into his car. Shadowheart was beyond his help, and Yukari was not. He had to concentrate his efforts where they would have some effect.

Still, he thought, *dammit. I miss her. They shouldn't have separated us. Bastards.* The rage with which he sometimes faced Heaven reasserted itself, and a black mood wrapped him as he pulled away from the curb. He fought it down.

Besides, he thought, *Sam would kick my ass if I inflicted this mood on her.* Oddly, the thought cheered him up.

When he got to the studio, Sam was waiting for him. They did a video conference, and he finished one project, catching an error made by an overseas Templar. The interview in the afternoon with the new client was less successful. They turned out to be a religious conservative organization, and upon hearing the principals they wanted him to turn into a political campaign, he rose, frostily informed them that it had been a mistake for the Pepto-Bismol palace, as he thought of that particular church, to refer them to him and that he would not accept the commission. He rose and left the somewhat stunned audience without a further word. Sam trailed behind him.

"While I applaud the sentiment," Sam said as they got into the elevator, "should you be so cavalier about paying work?"

"I have come to despise most forms of organized religion," he replied. "But above all other things, I despise Hypo-Christians. I'd rather stick-up liquor stores."

"Well," she replied, "let's hope that it does not come to that."

"Tomorrow's client is a bagel shop," he assured her. "I can get behind Jewish donuts. No worries."

"I'm for home then if you don't need me any more today," she said. "I would like to get a jump on traffic."

He looked at his phone. "Yeah, I want to go pick up Yukari. I so hope her first day went well."

"She'll be okay," Sam said, rolling her eyes. "And if not, call me."

"I will."

CHAPTER THIRTEEN

On the island of Guam, a 13-year-old girl dying of terminal cancer has been found to be free of the disease. She claims to have been visited by an angel, which did not speak to her but only looked at her with "kind eyes."

Yukari held tightly to the brand-new Kate Spade bookbag containing the electronics now consuming so much of her attention. This was the aspect of her new life that she found most befuddling. It seemed the modern people lived as much in their machines as in the real world.

Maybe they won't notice me so much, she thought and then sighed. *That is probably too much to hope.*

She found her way to homeroom 12-A and, overcome by shyness, stopped just short of it.

"Are you Yukari Kurita?" a female voice said.

She gave a start, recovered herself, and turned to face a short, pretty Asian girl, wearing jeans and a knit top. She quickly made an apology and said hello in Japanese, when the girl raised a hand.

"Ah, sorry, I'm not Japanese. I'm Linh Pham, student council rep. Since I'm in the same homeroom, they asked me to help you get oriented.

"*Gomen…* Ah, sorry, I do not mean to be a trouble to you." She was surprised and somewhat dismayed. Japan had a terrible reputation in Vietnam and clearly the girl was Vietnamese with that name. Yet, she offered a pleasant smile.

Linh laughed. "Ah, I see you really are Japanese, aren't you? No, please don't apologize again, and the bowing will just confuse us Westerners. It's my pleasure to help you."

Westerners? Yukari thought. Well, the girl spoke English without an accent.

"Wow, you are the tallest Japanese person I've ever met," Linh said, eyeing Yukari, who stood 5'10" in wedge heels and was a head taller than her. She must have noticed Yukari's unusual eye color but was too polite to mention it.

Something about the girl's open-faced friendliness reassured her. "My father used to call me Beanpole."

"Well, that's better than what my dad calls me, which is Brat, which in Vietnamese is a lot longer."

She checked out Yukari's clothes and shoulder bag with strap. "Hmmm, fancy. That's a nice bag."

"Thank you."

"Well, you can call me, Linh," she continued. "I seem to recall that Japanese people use last names and san mostly."

"Yes," Yukari said, "but I know that is not the custom here. I must adopt the Western way."

Linh nodded, with a relieved look. "Yeah, if you insisted on being called Kurita-san, it will just put people off."

Yukari nodded. "May I turn to you for advice when I need it on how to fit in?" In her homeland a *senpai*, an upperclassman one could rely on for help, was a great advantage.

"Sure," Linh said, "but you're tall, pretty, and you have a lovely accent and an air of mystery. You will do fine."

"I hope so," Yukari said, fighting the desire to bow, which was nearly instinctive, so deeply bound was it in her culture.

To her surprise, Linh patted her on the shoulder. "Come on."

They walked into the classroom brightly lit by the sun bouncing off the trees outside. Large desks sat in the middle of the floor. That was a relief; the desks in Japan had always been too small for her. She was further relieved to find that the class was mostly girls.

Yukari was uncomfortable around boys. Memories of her death were still held at a distance, no longer utterly denied as before, which had twinned her soul, but she avoided them as much as she could. She did not like the close proximity of a male.

Unless it is Jeremy, she thought, remembering him carrying her through the woods. *That was nice...* With an effort, she pulled herself to the here and now. This was no time for daydreams.

"Hey everyone," Linh, said.

The class of about fifteen stopped looking at phones or each other. "Hey Linh," several chimed in. The class was nine girls and six boys and a mix of races she could never have imagined, either in Japan, or in the southern USA, back in 1932. Two boys wore glasses, and one of them simply stared at Linh in adoration.

"As Mr. Heins said last week, we have a new student joining us." She gestured at Yukari, who managed to nod deeply as opposed to bowing, though the effort hurt her back.

"This is Yukari Kurita, she's moved here from Kitashiobara, Japan." She stumbled over the rural town's name. Yukari controlled a wince. "While Japanese generally use last names, she would prefer that you call her by her first name, Yukari, just like you would talk to anyone else. She should be a senior, but she felt it would be better to start a junior year in our strange and wacky country."

A brief burst of laughter followed.

"Try and make her welcome and don't embarrass the USA too much."

She turned to Yukari. "Do you want to tell everyone about yourself?"

Yukari had prepared for this ordeal. This was a standard item for transfer students. *At least I don't have to explain about the kanji letters to my name.*

The tale that they had made, and Jeremy had drilled into her, rolled off her lips.

"I am from Kitashiobara, a village located in Fukushima Prefecture, Japan. It is about 300 kilometers north of Tokyo. There are about 2,500 people in the village. It is an area with heavy snow falls and bitter winters that I do not miss. You may notice my unusual eye color; it is a characteristic of my family, *gomen*.

"I lived well outside of the town itself in a small traditional inn run by my family. So, I am afraid my upbringing is very rural. We did not have TV or internet access when I was young. You will find that I am terribly ignorant of many things that are common knowledge to you."

She kept it brief. The boys then pushed to the front, which she found slightly disquieting, but Linh stood between them, heading off any inquiries she judged impertinent. Yukari quickly excused herself on pretext of finding a seat and began unpacking her stuff. Linh promised her that a seat by the window was untaken.

Before she had to deal with any further inquiries, the teacher, Mr. Heins, walked in. A middle-aged Black man, tall and angular with glasses and a kindly face, Heins wore khaki pants and a blue shirt with a matching blue and white tie. He squinted at Yukari. "Ah, yes, Miss Kurita-san, the new transfer student."

Having been addressed, Yukari stood up in a graceful move and nodded. "I thank you for using the proper form of address, but please, simply call me Yukari. I must adapt to the ways of my new home."

Heins did a small double-take on her, perhaps a bit surprised by her demeanor and adult manner. *Well, I am the daughter of a diplomat, more used to the conversations of adults than other children, even from my early days. I always wanted to make Father proud of how grown up I could be.* This brought a pang to her heart, but not her face. *I am a grown Japanese in public; no one may see below my face save at my invitation.*

"Well put," Heins said. "Have you been enjoying your time in our country?"

"It has been a most interesting experience. Every day is filled with the new and different," she replied in complete honesty. "My upbringing was far from the cities or even towns and many things people take for granted here are still novel to me. I sometimes feel like I have come here from another time."

"I'm sure." Heins gave a reassuring smile. "I am equally sure that Linh and the others will help you find your feet."

Yukari glanced down and wondered how feet might ever become lost.

"Do you have family in the U.S.?"

She was a little surprised by the direct question in public. Americans had a very different notion of privacy. "Not as such. My parents and grandparents have departed this earth." There was a brief murmur in the class, sympathy or dismay, she wasn't sure. It did give her a chance to deal with all awkward questions with one swing of the glove, as they used to say.

"I do not have siblings," she added. *Anymore,* she thought, containing the pain with her a Japanese stoicism.

"But," she allowed a small smile to touch her lips, "I do have a guardian, who is sworn to take care of me. He is very devoted, as much as any big brother could be."

"Was that the hot-looking, tall dude driving the red Min-Coop?" asked a blond girl with her hair in a twin-tail style.

"It was," Yukari said with a touch of pride.

A black-haired girl, whose skin looked like she never saw sunshine and who overdid her eye makeup, nodded. The skull earrings she wore jingled as she did so. "I saw him, too. Long, lean, and likeable."

"Sounds like the dangerous type," another girl with close-cropped hair over chocolate skin added, with a big grin.

"He is very strong," Yukari confirmed.

"Well, handsome young men aside," Heins said. "We should get to it, people."

Yukari slid back into her seat, sitting very straight and conscious of eyes on her as Heins rattled through various school topics. After thirty minutes, it was time to head out. Math class was next for Yukari. As she stood, she found herself surrounded by Linh, Skull-earring girl, and the blond Twin-tail.

"Yukari," Linh said. "This is Amy." She gestured at Twin-tail, who popped her bubblegum and winked. "And the Hun—"

"—Goth," said Skull Earring.

Linh gave a mischievous grin. "Sorry, wrong tribe, the Goth here, is Trice."

Trice extended her hand, and Yukari took it awkwardly. Handshakes were not a Japanese custom but occurred constantly among Americans. Still, it was unusual between girls. Her handshake was strong and firm, and Yukari noticed her black-painted nails.

"I go by Trice," she said, "since I hate the crappy name my parents gave me. Don't ask."

Yukari's brow furrowed. Trice was not a name she had heard before.

Amy came to the rescue. "She's called Trice because she rides a three-wheeler motorcycle. Plus, she's into threesomes."

Trice sighed. "Ignore her. The blond hair has penetrated what little brain she has."

Yukari gave a hesitant nod. She has seen some of this sort of dialogue between characters on TV during her interregnum in the Legation. Frenemy was not so hard a concept for a Japanese, and these two embodied it.

"We're all in the same math class," Linh said. "Why don't you come with us?"

As they left the class to head down the hallway, Yukari heard a commotion behind her. She turned to see one of the boys from her class, a smaller one, wearing glasses, picking up his books. Three taller, stronger boys stood by grinning. One kicked a book away.

Distaste tightened her sensitive mouth. The scene was a familiar one, even to her. Japanese boys were always competitive with each other and relentlessly conformist. Not conforming drew savage bullying. With the rise of the military in the Showa years and the brutal cult of Bushido, this became worse.

Pound flat the nail that stand up, she remembered the old Japanese saying. *Is it even true?* she wondered. *Or is it yet another cloak for brutality?*

The tallest of the boys caught her look and returned one that made her feel slightly soiled merely by encountering it. She controlled the shiver it gave her and turned away.

Another like Hara-san, she thought. *The world is full of them. Men are so vile.*

But not all boys are like that, she reminded herself. *Jeremy is gentle, but strong like a samurai should be.*

Her heart sped up a little at the memory of him. *I am foolish to think of him as a boy. He is a man and one who knows women, perhaps too many women.* The memory of him falling out of the wardrobe in an erotic tangle with the voluptuous Debbie came unbidden to her. At the time, she had thought it funny. Now she was unhappy with the memory. *She is not a fit or proper match for him. Sam is a respectable person. Of course, while they are close, she does not want him for herself. That is very convenient.*

She shook her head. *Enough about boys, back to the here and now. I must learn how the world works.*

After math class, she found herself in an English class, in which she struggled. She spoke it far better than she could write it, and unfortunately none of the three girls she had met was with her. There were two boys from her class, but they were as shy of her as she was of them. So, she was relieved after that to have a free study period in the library and still more relieved when she saw Linh enter. The friendly Vietnamese girl seemed to be looking for her and smiled when she spotted Yukari.

She came over and slid into the seat next to Yukari. "I didn't know if you had anyone to have lunch with, so I figured I would invite you to join me, Amy, and Trice," she whispered. "The cafeteria is not bad."

"I would be very grateful for the company," Yukari said, also in a whisper. "I did bring a *bento*, pardon, a boxed lunch with me."

"Sure. Are you ready?"

Yukari nodded and closed up her computer. The small and light machine slid into a padded pouch in her briefcase, which in truth she was beginning to wish she had packed with less. She had over prepared for the day.

They exited the library and headed down the crowded spiral staircase to the back of the building where the cafeteria sat, overlooking a small pond and the sports areas. It was green and pleasant, she thought as Linh and her joined the others.

Amy and Trice stood, obviously arguing about something. The two girls seemed very opposite, and Yukari suspected that either Linh was the glue that held them together, or that they so enjoyed their verbal sparring that it was an end in itself. They dropped whatever they were talking about when the two Asian girls joined them.

"Hi, Yukee," Amy chirped. "How's your first day going?"

"It was Yukari," Trice moaned. "Yuki is another name entirely and means snow."

"It does," Yukari said. "How did you know that?"

"I watch *Dragon-Ball Super*," Trice said, as if it explained everything.

"Ah," Yukari said, no wiser.

"Don't they use nicknames in Japan?" Amy asked.

"Not generally," Yukari said, "and never in public."

"What does Yukari mean?" Amy persisted. "Snowgirl?"

"There are various meanings depending on the Kanji, the Japanese letters used. The one my parents chose was, affinity, you could think of it was one who takes to things easily or is helpful."

"Americans always believe all foreign names mean something," Linh said.

Trice shrugged. "All names do, if you go far enough back."

"Okay, enough multiculturalism," Amy said. "I'm hungry."

"Why do you even go to school?" Trice said.

"I am hungry, too," Yukari said. "Though all I need is a drink."

"Come on," Amy said, hooking her arm through Yukari's, which made her control a gasp of discomfort at being touched so casually in public, even by another girl. But her discomfort was clearly not noticed as Linh and Trice immediately started talking about a double-date Linh wanted to arrange for a movie with a character called Deadpool. Trice didn't seem interested.

Amy pulled her along to the beverage area where she selected iced tea, which Yukari also choose, following the blonde to a line where she paid for her drink with a card. Amy was quite popular, with many people calling greetings. A couple of the boys made scandalous references that did not faze the girl, who shot back some sharp retorts. With her case containing her bento, she trailed Amy to a table by the windows. The girls sat by themselves, probably because they had Yukari with them. There certainly was seemed no shortage of boys noticing the trio. She seemed to have fallen among the school's power trio, a *gakubatsu,* or as Jeremy might say, the cool kids.

She unpacked her bento while the others settled.

"That looks good. Did tall and handsome make it for you?"

"No," Yukari said. "I do most of the cooking despite his attempts to help. He was raised in a place called Scotland where they are not very good with food."

"Yeah, I'm Scots-Irish too," Trice said. "Our people's food can be a punishment."

"Well, not today," Amy said. "The mac and cheese is good."

"Until it ends up on your ass," Linh said.

"My ass remains the pride and joy of this school," Amy replied with an airy smile.

"So many have seen it," Trice tossed at her, "it should be on the school flag."

A group of boys came in, and Yukari recognized them as the group that had bullied her classmate. Four boys hung behind their leader: a brown-haired boy as tall as Jeremy. Others moved away from them or watched them warily. He spotted Yukari again and gave her a slick grin, looking at her in a way that made her skin crawl before heading for the food line.

Linh noticed. "Yeah, him. Another transfer student, but not a happy addition like you. Name's Trent, he came in six months ago. The only good thing I can say about him is that he doesn't stay anywhere long. I have no idea how he got in here."

"Sure you, do," said Trice, the Goth girl, with a sneer. "Money, his family has it. With money you get what you want. The system is so fucking corrupt. He's a piece of filth. I'd advise steering clear of him."

"Oh, I don't know," said Amy, "I think he is kinda cool. He's tough."

"And you're a skank anyway," Trice said.

"What do you know, Lezzie."

"Knock it off," Linh said sharply, for all that neither of the girls, despite all their language were as worked up as Yukari expected, "before Yukari flees back to Japan."

Yukari looked at both of the other girls. Something in her gaze discomforted both. *My red eyes*, she thought, *it frightens them. Good, maybe it will scare some manners into them.*

"I am not so delicate," she replied. "I have already seen much, including things," she smiled, "that would scare the skin off both of you."

They exchanged glances. Amy shivered. Trice sat back.

Linh gave Yukari a speculative look.

"Sorry," Trice said, waving a hand at Amy.

"Forget it," Amy said, airily. "I'd still do you."

"You blond airhead," Trice growled. "I keep telling you I ain't gay."

Yukari sighed. The conversation of these young people tended to bore her after the initial novelty. What concerned them was of little interest to her. *I must make an effort*, she thought. *For better or worse, this is now my world.*

Yukari was waiting for Jeremy when he pulled to the curb. He saw her standing apart from the other high-schoolers. He sighed, there was so much that he wanted Yukari to have, but was it even possible? She had been sixteen going on seventeen when she died in 1932. What could she possible have in common with generation "who-gives-a-fuck?" The way she stood, silent and apart, it was as if she was still a ghost. Others were talking, goofing, and mostly staring at their phones. She was back, under a tree, her face in shadow, her bulging bag held rather primly in front of her, resting against her knees.

He pulled to the curb, parked the Mini Cooper, and stepped out. As Jeremy strode onto the sidewalk, he caught some resentful looks from the older boys. He was only seven years older than the seniors and probably could pass for one of them if, God forbid, he needed to.

He returned the looks with a cool stare. *I kill things,* he thought, *mostly things, but some people too. Mouthy teens I do not need.*

Yukari's face lit up when she spotted him, and she walked forward into the sun, which bounced highlights off her waist-length black hair. Any connection with her ghostly past seemed to vanish in the sunlight.

"Hello, Yukari," he said.

"*Konnichiwa,* Jeremy-san."

"So formal?"

She gave a slight smile. "We are in public. Jeremy-kun would be… too much."

"There is always just Jeremy."

"The habits of a lifetime are hard to break."

"Did you have a good day?"

"Oh, I did and even better just now."

"Oh?" he said, confused.

Now she laughed, a delicate, tinkling sound. "Yes. The other girls who have been studying me, because I am 'weird,' now see me being picked up in a fancy car, by a handsome young man who cannot be the brother that I have called him."

Yukari's eyes cut left, and Jeremy followed her gaze to see a gaggle of teen girls watching him. One was a cute blond with ponytails, the other was a Goth with hot eyes, and the final one was an elegantly dressed Asian girl. There was an outburst of giggling, and they vanished into the nearby doorway.

"Ah," he said, pleased. "I have added luster to your legend."

"Indeed," Yukari replied. "Perhaps I will have many new friends tomorrow. After all, I am the 'mysterious transfer student,' ne? I shall have to be the inscrutable Oriental and give nothing away."

"Ah, yeah," he said, a little uncomfortable with the old racial reference to the world of Charlie Chan.

"It will also serve to keep the boys at a greater distance," she added. "These young men are so crude. Dogs have better manners."

"Has anyone—" he began.

She raised a hand. "No one has done anything out of what is the ordinary these days. Though in my day, they would have been whipped through the village. I cannot have you menace a boy for acting as a modern boy."

"I'm sorry."

Again, came the laugh. "What, are you apologizing for the times? In my day, that I was just speaking of so fondly, I was little more than property. I could be sold by my family. So today the boys are rude, but I have rights. Overall, an improvement, ne?"

"When you put it that way," he said. "But this old-fashioned boy is going to carry your bag." He reached and relieved her of the case. "Shall we?" They walked back to the Mini and Jeremy made something of a show of opening and closing the car door for her, to her amusement and pleasure. He placed her bag in the trunk and, noticing that the gaggle was again watching, slid in and revved the Mini before pulling away.

CHAPTER FOURTEEN

Rogue waves have destroyed 15 ships in the Pacific in the last twenty-four hours.
Eternal Father, strong to save,
Whose arm has bound the restless wave,
Who bids the mighty ocean deep
Its own appointed limits keep;
O hear us when we cry to Thee
For those in Peril on the sea.

The next day was a repetition of the first. Less overwhelmed with the strangeness of the school, Yukari began to notice more of the many differences between her school in Japan and here. In her home country, both in her time and presently, the students governed themselves more. They cleaned their classroom, all the way down to mopping the floor. Student leaders controlled the classrooms when the teachers were not present, and certainly the lessons were far more rigorous than what she was experiencing now. Japanese schools had a dress code, and skirts were the norm for girls. She knew she probably appeared odd to her friends by not showing up in jeans. Yukari sometimes found herself longing for a dress code that would protect her from all the bewildering choices she had to make before school.

But there was an exhilarating freedom both of thought and action that came with it. She could say most things without fear of correction or intimidation. She had been used to having her thoughts as a girl dismissed or ridiculed. Compared to how she had grown up, the opinions of women and girls were now taken so much more seriously. The teachers were more interested in how she thought than necessarily what she thought, and she had to embrace the idea that there were multiple correct answers, or, even more, that there were issues that had no acknowledged correct idea.

For all that, she found her classmates were very quarrelsome with each other, willing to argue about everything and often with little knowledge of the subject. They were in many ways a disillusioned generation. They believed very little of what was told to them, least of all by their government, which had been wasteful of the truth. Seeing them, Yukari felt that she understood Jeremy and his doubts and fears better. He was only a little older than her fellow students and distrusted all forms of authority and dogma more than anyone she had ever met. These people might believe in each other, in their friendships, but the normal anchors for a Japanese were not there for them. Governments and employers were never to be trusted; even families took a backseat to peers. It seemed rootless to her.

What did blind obedience get my people, she thought, *militarism, disaster, decades of poverty? It is now a world of so many choices for a girl, for a person.*

The rush of clubs that were so much part of Japanese student life was less so here. She avoided the Japanese anime club for fear of the thousand little questions about life in Japan that she could either not answer at all or could only give responses that were decades out of date. She had seen such programs at the Embassy, but as was with so many things, they had not interested her as she drifted through her twilight world. Yukari joined two clubs, one for cooking, where she had both interest and skill, and the International Club where she could learn more about the state of the world, though there she did have to parry questions about her home country and its customs. So, ironically, she ended up using a lot of computer time to learn about Japan. There was no escape from being a novelty in her new school.

As much as she enjoyed her studies, she still felt very alien; sometimes, as if she was still a ghost. As Linh had said, she was tall, pretty, and exotic. Girls sought her out as a desirable friend. She did not mind this and especially with the younger girls who looked up to her, she enjoyed playing the part of a *senpai*.

As for the boys, she was startled to receive offers for dates and invitations to events on so little, indeed no, acquaintance. These she turned away with all the skill of a diplomat's daughter, though some of the boys did not take this well, and over the next few weeks she acquired a bit of reputation as either being stuck up, or a *yuri*, uninterested in boys. None of this bothered her. It was as if the boys, and to a lesser extent the girls, were shadows on her world, unreal, full of sound and excitement about nothing and meaning very little.

Yukari recognized this as part of her former ghostly detachment from the world, complicated by the fact that she had rejoined a world that moved on without her. *Perhaps I am the equivalent of the grumpy old woman telling the children under her window not to make so much noise.* The image of herself as an old woman both made her chuckle and think. Now that she was back, there was a chance that she would live to become that old lady. *If so,* she thought, *I must not become grumpy before my time. I wish to be the sort of old lady that everyone would praise.*

I must pay more attention to my new friends, she thought. *It would not do to lose my grip on a world that cost so much to obtain.*

One fly in the ointment of her new life was the school bully, Trent.

In her second month, she came across him and his pack of weaklings. They were blocking the way of some *shin'nusei*, some first years, a couple of girls who were looking up at them in fear. The boys were making rude comments to the girls. One put his hand on a girl's back, and she yipped and backed away.

"This is enough," she said aloud. She walked up, her heels clicking hard on the floor. Her determined stride carried her among them, and the followers unconsciously faded back.

"Excuse me," Yukari said. "Are you girls lost?"

"We were...were looking for the Student Council room."

"Don't worry about it," Trent said. "We'll take care of them."

"Please come with me," Yukari said. "I will take you there."

"Hey," Trent said, "didn't you hear me—"

Yukari ignored him and reached forward, taking the younger girl's hand. Trent made a move as if to stop her, and she turned her red-irised eyes on him. He froze for a second, and she used the moment to extricate the girls and push them ahead of her. She heard muttered obscenities behind her and ignored them.

"Thanks," whispered the smaller of the pair. "They were scary."

"Pay them no account," Yukari returned, big-sister like. "They are nothing."

As she did not see Trent or his gang that day or the next, she had put the incident from her mind. So, she was not looking for him two days later when Yukari turned onto the landing heading for the cooking club. He was lounging by the window and had clearly lay in wait for her.

She ignored him and made to continue when he came off the wall and stepped into her path.

"Hey, you," Trent said, "you made me look bad in front of my boys."

"You do not need anyone's help to make you look bad," she returned. "You are bad."

"Well not all bad, honey. I can be sweet to those sweet to me."

"What do you want?" she demanded. She glanced about, but there was no one in sight on the stairwell, though she could hear voices wafting up it. If she screamed, she would draw attention, but it might only make her appear foolish. She was not going to give him that much power over her.

"I like you," he said. "You've got some guts and you're not a skank like most of the whores here."

"What lovely compliments," Yukari returned, her lips pressed thin.

"Listen up, I don't need a bitch with attitude. So, start showing a little respect."

"For what?" she scorned.

His face darkened. "I can be very nice to you if you play along, or I can make every day at school a hell for you."

"*Baka*," Yukari shot back, a little amazed at herself for speaking so boldly to a boy. "I have more knowledge of hell than you can imagine."

"You know, I am getting tired of talking with you. I thought you might be fun to have, but you have too much to say about everything. So, one last time, don't get in my way around here, or—" His hand shot out and landed on her right breast and he squeezed hard. Yukari leapt back, almost tumbling down the stairs. She saved herself by grabbing the banister.

"Filth, Beast," she spat at him. "You will not touch me again."

"Or what?" he said with a leer. "You gonna tell the teachers; they're useless fucks, all of them."

Nothing has changed, she thought. *Those in charge still do not believe us when we complain of men.* She was shaking with rage, and something stirred within her. Her eyes heated and began to glow, her hair rippled as if there was a high wind.

Trent had started to follow-up his advantage, excited by her fear and anger, but the sight of her eyes stopped him. "What's wrong with you, freak?" he said. But he backed away watching her narrowly until he reached the door. "You've been warned, freak." He slipped through the door.

Yukari stumbled back onto the landing clutching herself with a small moan. Her eyes dimmed to normal, and her hair lay in its accustomed way. But in her mind, she was not on the staircase but in the legation with Shoji Hara, with him tearing at her clothes, forcing her down, the smell of him in her nostrils. Her breath tore in her throat as she fought the intrusive memories. Her dark self had held her safe from these memories. Now she had to face them as a living person. Yukari struggled for control, slowing her breathing, donning again the imperturbable face she had spent her living years building for herself. She reached into her pocket and found her phone. There was help there if she called for it.

No, she thought, *I must not trouble Oniichan more than I already have. First, I must see if I can deal with this myself. This is mere school bullying; it happens every day. It is no more than that.*

She would skip cooking club today; the library should be safe. She would wait out the rest of the day there.

CHAPTER FIFTEEN

Tsunami waves have struck the coast of Hokkaido...

When Jeremy pulled up to the curb, Yukari came away from the door, walking briskly. A tall boy, about eighteen or so, said something to her, but she ignored him. Something about his face said that his comment had not been friendly. Jeremy turned the car off and got out. The boy, who had moved as if he was going to follow Yukari, spotted him and stopped. He gave a sneer in response to Jeremy's flat stare, but turned away, heading toward a bunch of other male teens.

Jeremy searched Yukari's face. She looked tense, closed off.

"Yukari, is everything, all right?"

"Yes," she said, her voice clipped. Then. "*Sumimasen, Oniichan, konnichiwa and arigato* for coming to pick me up. May we go?"

"Did that clown say something to you?"

"It is nothing, Jeremy-kun," she replied. "May we go?"

Yukari being insistent and formal set off warning bells. He opened the door to the Mini for her, searching with his eyes for the tall, brown-haired boy. They drove to his house in silence, with his occasional forays into conversation meeting simple answers or none.

Later over dinner, Yukari's mood lightened as she served Katsu-don. He took advantage of the tension easing to raise the subject again. This time he was persistent.

She was hesitant. "The boys of this age, they are very forward. Their mouths need cleaning."

Crap, he thought. *I put her in CC because I thought the place would be safe.*

"But this boy, his name is Trent, he is, *ijimekko.* Ah, *gomen,* the English word is bully. He thinks he is handsome and that all girls should like him."

"Perhaps it is time he and I meet," Jeremy said.

"No," she said. "It is nothing. Mostly words."

His head came up. "Mostly?"

Yukari's hand had been resting on her right breast, and she gave an almost guilty start, then smoothly set it down. "Oniichan, it is nothing. Please enjoy your dinner."

Jeremy almost didn't hear her. The world had gone black to him, but with the discipline that he had used against the undead and unclean, he schooled his face to impassive. "As you wish, Yukari." He did not look directly at her, afraid of what she would see in his eyes.

Trent, he thought, calling up every detail of the other's face.

Later that night, he knew he heard crying from Yukari's room.

The next day, Jeremy arranged for an Uber to pick up Yukari, pleading some detail of his work. But he spent the day learning all he could about his target. Trent Udsell came from a wealthy family that had used that wealth to cover up the tracks of their vicious little offspring, but the tracks were there for those skilled with computers. Not to mention the fact that Udsell did a pretty good job of surveilling himself on social media.

Jeremy got to the school about closing, dressed inconspicuously. He watched Yukari get into the Uber and spotted Trent watching her, making an obscene gesture to two of his friends. The campus had good security, but Jeremy was not a Templar for nothing. His target lingered after school, not in any clubs but merely hanging around his group of imitation toughs, sharing a joint until they drifted off. He watched until Trent slipped away from campus, heading for a strip shopping plaza—the spot had recently turned into a location for hoods to sell drugs to suburban kids and the local police had not caught on to it. Jeremy had learned of it ghosting through the net. He followed Trent in. The area wasn't well lit. Perfect.

He walked up silently behind Trent, who'd taken up position near a dumpster. It was eight in the evening and the businesses in the strip had shut, save for a convenience store at the far end. None of the shops had windows out the back or in their rear doors. Better and better.

"You," Jeremy said, when he was a yard away from Trent. The teen, who'd been intent on watching the other end of the strip mall by the convenience store, jumped and spun to face Jeremy.

"What the fuck, man?" He glared back, all teen-tough and attitude.

"You," Jeremy repeated in a flat voice, devoid of emotion. "You're annoying Yukari."

"What. Oh, the Asian bitch. What, you fucking her or something, old man?"

Yes, perfect, Jeremy thought, *just what I wanted.* He stepped forward and slammed a snap-kick into Trent's balls and met his descending face with his knee as the teen doubled over. Trent went over backward with a choked scream and hit the pavement.

Jeremy quickly looked around then dropped on Trent, driving his knee into his sternum. He would have no air for screaming. It took some minutes for the gasping teen, eyes wide, face covered in blood from the broken nose, to get enough breath to speak. Jeremy waited patiently, calmly studying his work.

Finally, he said, "We were discussing Yukari. How you were bothering her. How you touched her when she did not want you to."

"I just grabbed her tit—"

Jeremy's fist knocked him flat again.

"Oh, God no. My parents will get you—"

Jeremy rose up and drove the knee back in. Trent gagged on blood. "No, please."

"What was that, Trent?" he asked, with a cold, distracted smile.

"What was that? No, please? Are those the words of a tough guy, Trent? You were pretty tough with Yukari, weren't you, Trent? Tough with others, too. Is that right, Trent? But I really only care about Yukari, you see." Slowly Jeremy drew the Walther from his back holster.

"Dude, what the fuck? Please."

Jeremy backhanded him across the face with the pistol, then pulled out the silencer. An ugly feeling, the like of which he had never felt, even against creatures of evil, welled up in him. He screwed in the silencer as Trent stared, paralyzed.

"You see, Trent," Jeremy whispered, "I'm going through some shit right now. Oh, shit like you don't even know exists, and I would really like to kill something. You see, I think it would really make me feel better. Not something important, not something that would be missed and, you see, you're that. You're a dime-a-dozen school bully. Your kind spawns on gym floors. We got lots of you. They can spare me one. No difference at all."

Trent's eyes were wide and the smile that sickled across Jeremy's face had nothing of humanity left in it. He jacked a round into the Walther.

"Man," Trent said, his voice high with fear and pain. "I'll never go near her again. I swear it."

Jeremy jammed the silenced pistol in Trent's mouth, chipping teeth. Some part of his mind was screaming at him that this was too much, that he had lost his mind, but it could barely be heard over the wave of pure pleasure lapping around him. *I'll kill him. It will make me feel so much better.*

Trent was sobbing now. Jeremy stared into his eyes, finger resting on the trigger.

"Why?" Trent wailed, the word barely recognizable with the gun in his mouth.

Jeremy froze. The word circled around him, buzzing like a wasp.

Why?

Doshte?

Sword handle in his hands. Horrible sensation of cutting. A girl facing him, turning, eyes wide in shock. Betrayal. Rags of substance in the wind. Gone.

Doshte?

Where am I, he wondered. *What am I doing? Right. I want to kill Trent. It will make me feel better. God, I want to kill him. But what happens to Yukari if I get caught? Why am I not thinking straight? He's a school bully in a suburban school. Can I kill him for that? God, he's just a kid, a rich man's fool child, but...*

Trent stared up at him, tears mixed in blood on his young face. A stink of urine bit at Jeremy's nose and the spell broke. It was like coming up from cold, deep, dark water.

Jeremy's hand began to shake with reaction. He took his finger off the trigger and pulled the silencer out of Trent's mouth. The boy was sobbing now.

"You listen to me," he managed, in a voice he didn't recognize as his own. "You'll never be closer to death than you were a second ago. Do you hear me? Blink twice for yes."

Trent blinked, gasping, hands up, beseeching.

"Bother Yukari, again, die. Mention me to the police, to anyone, die." There was no passion or anger in it, it was simply a statement.

"Never, never," Trent swore.

Jeremy stood. He felt as if he was wrapped in cotton; sounds were muffled, the light was strange. He couldn't feel much. Mechanically, he unscrewed the silencer and put the weapon away. He turned and walked out of the alley.

I was going to kill him, he thought. *I really believed shooting this piece of shit in the mouth and watching him bleed out would make me feel better. I was enjoying it.*

God, what's wrong with me. Murder? I'd never see Yukari again, or Sam. Who am I?

"Doshte."

"I've got to get hold of myself," he said, suddenly looked around. He'd traveled the better part of a mile from where he'd attacked Trent with no recollection of doing so. One second, he was in the alley behind the shops. Now he was at a Home Depot where he'd parked his car. He bleeped the car open and dropped into it.

Jeremy drove to a safe house well out of Charlotte that the Templars had set up for him as a drop for weapons, magical items, and other material that should never be seen. He pulled into the remote country house and unlocked it. Once there, he showered, cleaning himself and his weapons obsessively. There would be no DNA. Just for safety's sake, he switched Walthers and ditched the silencer. There were spare clothes there. He changed. His old ones went into an incinerator in the basement where the occasional hell-spawn had been consumed.

I will just have to hope I get away with it, he thought, still wrapped in that remoteness that had enveloped him in the alley. He got back into his car just as the phone buzzed.

He stared at it. It wasn't Yukari, thank God. He could not talk to her, not now, in this unclean state.

"Kai," he said, answering.

"Brother Jeremy. Dude, how are you doing?"

"I don't know anymore," he said, voice empty of tone.

"Doesn't sound good," Kai said.

"It isn't."

"Okay, this I can do something about. Meet me at the Kandy Bar near the Epicenter. I'm buying, bro. I owe you this much and more after all you've done."

"All I've done," Jeremy said and felt sick. "See you there."

CHAPTER SIXTEEN

The island of Midway was found to have been submerged in the Pacific, no explanation has been proffered by NOAH.

Samantha ran up the steps, two at a time, to Jeremy's townhouse at 2:30 a.m., but the door opened before she could ring the bell. Yukari stood there in a kimono, though this time it was of a simpler cut and pattern.

"Samantha-chan," she said in her light, breathy voice. "Thank you for coming. I am sure I am only being a foolish girl, but I am so worried."

"It's okay," Sam said, walking in as the tall girl held the door open. "This isn't like Jeremy at all. Our boy is nothing if not responsible." She pulled out her phone and hit recent to redial on Jeremy's number. It ran straight to voicemail again.

"And the car is not here," Yukari said, her hands knotting together.

"You know what his work life is like," Sam added. "He probably got a call for help."

"Yes," she said, "but Oniichan always promised he would call me if that happened and a promise," she hesitated, "a promise is very important to him."

ONIICHAN

"Yeah," Samantha said, knowing that there was more behind the comment than she was getting just then.

As Yukari went to close the door, a yellow cab turned the corner and pulled up.

"Wait," Sam said, peering at the cab. A young Asian man got out of the cab and made his unsteady way to the other side of the cab. As he opened the door, Jeremy practically fell out, only saved from hitting the ground by the other man's grab.

"Oniichan," Yukari whispered, obviously distressed.

"Who's that with him?" Sam demanded.

"Kei Hara," she replied, "a recent acquaintance." There was no mistaking an icy edge to her voice.

Kei got Jeremy's arm up over his shoulder, and they started to weave toward the door. The smell of alcohol preceded them.

"They're hammered!" Sam said astonished. She didn't know Kei, but in all the time she'd spent with Jeremy, she'd never seen him drunk.

"Yo, yo, yo," Kei said, breezily. "Look at the hot chicks waiting on us, bro."

Sam studied Kei and did not like the hip-hop imitation street that she saw. The clothes were expensive, new and street right down to the Bulls cap. A wannabe.

Jeremy raised his head and tried to focus on them. His eye met Sam's, and a furious blush covered his face. He tried to speak, but it was unintelligible.

"Get him on the couch," Samantha ordered. She moved forward to get Jeremy's other arm, but Yukari slipped ahead of her.

Oh well, Sam thought, *she is taller.*

With Kei's dubious help, they got Jeremy onto the couch. As soon as his head rested on a pillow, his eyes fluttered closed.

"Hara-san," Yukari said, her voice cold. "What is the meaning of this?"

Kei shrugged. "Now don't be like that. Man's got troubles, baby."

"Troubles?" Samantha growled.

Kei staggered slightly and gave her a goofy grin. "Who you be?"

"I'm Samantha Pelton," she replied with a cool correctness others would have recognized for the warning it was. "I understand you're Kei Hara."

"You got it, baby. Kei's the name. Don't wear it out. I know my boy was hurting, so I decided to take him out. Wooo, we did party. Jeremy wanted to pick up some girls, but I reminded him bros before hos, and I just kept buying the drinks."

"Too many," Yukari said.

"Hey, when a man has trouble, he needs a belt," Kei said, waving a hand.

"I'm glad you feel that way," Sam said and threw a hard straight right catching Kei on the jaw and dropping him.

"Samantha-chan!" Yukari said in shock.

Sam hauled Kei up by his shirt.

"Hey," he managed. "What did ya do that for?" His hip-hop persona slipped, and he suddenly just looked like a drunken college kid, not a gangsta.

Sam put her face near his. "I'm going to put this down to being young and stupid and not ill-intentioned, but if you ever do something like this with Jeremy again, I will hunt you down and beat you to death with a rock."

Kei felt his jaw and seem to have sobered up some. "Damn girl, I mean, miss. You didn't have to slug me."

"Hara-san," Yukari interrupted. "Your cab is still waiting for you. It must be time for you to go home. Doubtless your family will be concerned about you."

He focused in on her. "Hey, are your eyes glowing red again? You didn't bring back any spooky powers, did you?"

"I do not know, Hara-san, but we may find out shortly."

"All right, all right," Kei said with a grieved air. "I'm just trying to get my boy past his pain."

"Yeah, yeah, leave the rest to us. Go home and sleep it off," Sam said.

Grumbling and feeling his jaw, Kei weaved his way out the door.

"I'll get him to bed," Sam said, wondering if she could. Jeremy was almost a foot taller.

"I will help," Yukari stated.

"It will make him even more unhappy tomorrow if he knows you had to deal with this."

Yukari have a small sad smile. "Samantha-chan, I have already done as much for my father. In our culture and my time, it was not unusual for men to behave this way."

Sam nodded and turned to her prone friend. "Jeremy, honey, it's time to go to bed."

Jeremy opened his eyes. "Oh. Room spinning. Sam, Sam I am sorry. Yukari, sumimasen."

"Oniichan," Yukari said softly, as she pulled him upright with Sam's help. "No talking for now. Time for bed."

"Sorry," he repeated thickly. "Sorry. Shouldn't have done this."

Yukari put a finger across his lips, and he subsided.

It took both of them and all their strength to get Jeremy up to his bedroom. Sam let Yukari hold him while she turned down the sheets. The tall, slender girl was evidently stronger than she appeared. She lowered Jeremy into the bed.

"Okay," Sam said. "I'll get him undressed and be down to talk with you in a few minutes."

"Samantha-chan," Yukari said with a note of reproof in her voice. "I will take care of Oniichan."

"That's nice, dear, but I think I had better do it. You're only sixteen, and he's not actually your brother."

"My body may be sixteen, but I am far older."

"Jeremy said you were sixteen, so you are going to be sixteen, young lady. Downstairs you go."

Yukari gave her a mutinous look but bowed and swept out of the room.

Sam gazed down at Jeremy. There was only ten years difference between them, but it struck her how young and vulnerable his face looked. There were shadows on it now, that had not been there before. He'd had to fight things most people couldn't even imagine,

123

and like many other soldiers, carried scars that could not be seen. She wondered if he woke up screaming at night and then wondered why she didn't know the answer to that.

She slipped him out of shoes first, then carefully secured his holster with its Walther pistol, putting it in its lock box before removing the rest of his clothes and pulling the duvet over him. Experience made her leave a large glass of water at his bedside. She decided a bucket would be also good idea. When she opened the bedroom door, she found Yukari just on the other side, already holding a bucket.

"Right," Sam said, "you have done this before."

Yukari marched in, surveyed Sam's arrangements, and placed the bucket by the bed before scooping up Jeremy's clothes.

"I have made tea, Samantha-chan. Will you please come with me?" Yukari left the door slightly ajar, doubtless so she could hear if Jeremy stirred or, more likely, puked his guts up.

Yukari maintained her delicate, flowing gait even as she descended the stairs. As a concession to her upbringing, Jeremy had added a *kotatsu* to the dining room. The low Japanese table was surrounded by cushions. A tea service sat on it now, next to a slender vase with a single chrysanthemum in it.

Yukari plumped a cushion for Samantha and settled on her knees on the opposite side. Sam dropped on the cushion with less delicacy, on her butt. They sat quietly while Yukari poured tea in the exquisite little cups. The small ceremony and tea settled both their nerves. Yukari decorously refilled the cups, then, in a nod to more recent customs put a small plate of cookies on the table.

Good Lord, Sam thought, *even the cookies are arranged, with the yellow center cookies surrounded by white cookies for petals over some with pistachio, making a stem.* It seemed a shame to break the pattern by eating one.

"Yukari," Sam began, "things have not been right with Jeremy since I've returned. I've been waiting for him to tell me why. I can't wait any longer given tonight. Your arrival and Shadowheart's departure are the two big events. I can't ask her, so I am going to ask you."

Yukari looked down at her teacup, clearly unhappy.

"I know it's not you, yourself. When he sees you, he looks a kid who got a Christmas puppy." Samantha gave a small laugh.

"I am glad," Yukari said, her voice controlled, but shaky, "that my presence makes him happy. Truly, I feel as if he is the big brother that I wanted in life. You see, I was the eldest and so much fell on me and I was only a girl..."

Have to work on that, Sam thought, *but hell she was from 1932 in a country where girls could still be sold in her day.*

Yukari sighed. "But you are not correct, Samantha-chan. I apologize, but I am the source of the pain that has brought him to this."

"Tell me," Sam said, putting her cup down.

She looked down at the table. "I am sure Oniichan will be able to tell you in the morning."

Japanese people rarely say no directly, Sam thought, but shook her head. "I'm sorry Yukari, but I'm going to be a pushy Westerner and demand you tell me what you know. You can tell Jeremy I gave you no other choice. He knows me and will believe it."

Yukari met her eyes. "You will take responsibility?"

"I will."

"Very well. You know I was a ghost, even divided into two parts. One part was very angry, powerful and intent on wreaking vengeance on the Hara family."

"Having met Kei Hara I can understand that."

"Samantha-chan," Yukari reproved. "Hara-san's ancestor, Shoji Hara, murdered me after taking my innocence. He then destroyed my family."

"Oh, my god," Sam said, reaching across to touch the girl's hand. "I am so sorry."

Yukari's face was cold, remote, like carved ivory. "Jeremy became friendly with the other, lesser ghost. The gentle part of me you might say. We felt a..." now, she blushed, "a resonance with each other immediately. There was something more than chance in that meeting, for Jeremy, alone of all people, could touch me when I was a ghost."

After a moment's silence, she continued. "Jeremy hurt me with an exorcism spell meant for my darker self when he first came to the mansion. He didn't even know I was there at first. After we spoke, and he realized I was not the threat, I extracted a promise from him that he would not hurt me again. He swore it as a Templar oath.

"My angry self, with its mission of vengeance was the far stronger side. It was about to burn Kei's family to death in a fire that would shrivel soul and flesh alike. How terrible a fate." She shook her head and her voice quivered. Now it was Sam who looked down at her cup.

"My gentle side could not stop my dark ghost. The vampire Debbie could not. Jeremy could not reach the Dark Yukari in time. He could only reach me."

Sam froze reaching for her teacup.

"The sword was very cold as it cut through me, severing the threads of fate that bound me to this world. I felt myself dissolving. I had a moment to turn to him and ask, why? Oh, oh, his poor face..."

Sam put her hand to her mouth and fought sickness. "I can't...I can't imagine anything worse."

"It was the only choice," Yukari said flatly, "a great crime was unfolding and had to be stopped."

"How did... the..." She gestured at Yukari. "How did this happen?"

"As I began to fade, I became one person again, whole and in charge of myself. I thought, ah, well, so now I will know peace. But as I began to fade from the world, I saw Jeremy and realized that he was about to throw himself on the same sword he had struck me with. I wanted to reach out to him, to tell him it was all right, but he could no longer hear me. The vampire seized his arms, but I knew she could only stop him for the moment. With all my strength, I willed myself to his side. The forces drawing me from the world relented.

"I do not know why I am flesh and blood now. Perhaps it was the only way that I could remain in the world. A ghost is the most unnatural of the unnatural.

"Jeremy-kun cannot rid himself of the pain of striking me down against his sworn word. I do not understand it. There was no choice then, and it has proved to be the gate for a new life for me."

"He didn't know you would come back?"

"No, even I had no idea of that."

"Then to him, he struck to kill a sixteen-year-old girl."

"I was already dead."

"Not really, Yukari. You had a different existence. Jeremy told me a little about you: how you would play music, talk, how you would show him your favorite things and spots in your little world. It may not have been a human life, but it was not death as we know it.

"To Jeremy, you were always alive in some sense. He cut you down after promising the good Yukari she would be safe. He's ashamed, sickened, and guilty."

"I have told him again and again," Yukari insisted, her fingers pressed against the table top, "that he should not feel so. Even had I been destroyed, it would have been a blessing to me. There must be a special Hell for those who destroy families. I was saved from that."

"Jeremy has been at war," Sam said slowly, "all of his life. A war with no end, as neither evil nor good can triumph while humanity is what it is. I think that it has added up on him. Then this last was too much."

"Can you help, Samantha-chan?"

"I can try. I owe Jeremy my life. He's my people, and I don't ever give up on my people."

"I am very glad."

"I am going to stay here tonight if that's okay."

"Of course, Samantha-chan."

"If you have a pillow and a blanket, the couch will be fine."

"My bed is quite large. Please sleep with me."

Samantha opened her mouth then shut it. There seemed too much to easily explain.

Yukari smiled as if divining her thought. "It will be fine, Samantha-chan. It's a large bed."

CHAPTER SEVENTEEN

Reports of giant ants three meters long are being denounced as a hoax.

When the sun woke Sam, she was alone in the bed. She sat up vaguely remembering that Yukari had risen much earlier. She blinked. At the foot of the bed were her clothes, neatly folded, and she realized after picking up her shirt, freshly laundered. Next to her clothes laid a robe and towels. She wrapped the robe around her and peeked out into the hallway. The scent of coffee wafted up to her.

Sam padded down the hallway to Jeremy's room. The door was open. He lay face down on the bed and a faint smell told her that he had been sick during the night. She checked the bucket, which was empty, and noticed the bathroom smelled of cleaning products. Yukari had been busy.

A groan came from the bed as Jeremy rolled onto his side. A bloodshot eye opened. "I always thought that if I saw you in my bedroom, in a robe, it would have been more fun than this."

She fought the grin off her face. "Well, if you can flirt with me, I guess you aren't as close to death as you look."

"No," he said, struggling to sitting. "Death was last night. God, I forgot what hangovers were like."

"Fortunately," Sam said, "you have had a recent experience with returning from death."

"Oh, God," he said paling. "How am I going to apologize to Yukari for this? I've been a complete ass. She must have been so worried."

"Yukari," Sam said, "is a very strong and understanding girl, and I think she would forgive her Oniichan anything."

Jeremy, the sheet in his lap, met her eyes and they looked at each other for a long moment before he half-turned away. "You know."

"Yes, sweet-boy, I know. I'd have waited for you to tell me but for last night."

He nodded. "Maybe it was easier this way." Then with a start, he turned back to her. "Wait a minute; did you slug Kei last night?"

"Dropped him in his tracks," Sam replied, "and promised to beat him to death with a rock if there was any repeat of this."

"Oh, Sam. He was just trying to cheer me up."

"Do I have to send for my rock?"

His response was cut off by a gentle knock. The door swung open. Yukari walked in with a tray in her arms.

"Oniichan," she said with a bright smile. "Good morning. I have brought you weak tea and rice porridge for your stomach. Samantha-chan, there is coffee for you, cream, two sugars, as you like it."

How does she know that? Sam wondered bemused. There seemed no limit to Yukari's domestic ability.

"Yukari," Jeremy said, pulling his sheet higher, "thank you, but I am not dressed."

She raised an eyebrow. "You were wearing less when you fell out of the wardrobe with Miss Melons."

Jeremy blushed.

"Miss Melons?" Sam asked archly.

"Uh, Debbie, long story…later."

"Hah, I can imagine."

Yukari put the tray on Jeremy's lap. He looked a bit green as he studied it. "I'm not sure I could eat—"

"Oniichan," Yukari said with an unmistakable sternness. "You have nothing left in you and you need warm, soothing food and drink."

"Oh Christ," he said, putting a hand over his face. "It was you last night when I was sick. You got me to the bathroom."

"It is nothing, Oniichan. I did as much for my father when he would drink too much, as my mother would not see, or speak to him, at such times."

"This is a disgrace," Jeremy whispered, "absolute disgrace."

"This is not common for you, Oniichan. Please do not think of it again." She sat on the bed with such delicacy that it didn't disturb the tray.

Sam reached for her coffee in the silence that followed, and Jeremy picked up his tea and had few mouthfuls of porridge to Yukari's evident pleasure.

He put the spoon down. "*Gomen*, Yukari-chan, *gomen nasai*. This is my most grievous fault."

"You are troubled, Oniichan; I would have you be untroubled. Take comfort in all you have done for me. And so that you know, I told Samantha-chan everything last night. *Gomen*."

He shook his head. "I was too much of a coward to do it myself."

"Why?" Sam demanded. "Did you think I would turn my back on you?"

Jeremy studied his porridge.

"My friendship is stronger than that," Sam said softly.

"I know," he replied. "It was just too hard to say the words."

"I understand the pain," Sam said, "but not the shame."

"Samantha-chan," Yukari said, standing. "Will you join me downstairs? I have made a breakfast more suited to Western tastes for you. Perhaps after Jeremy-kun has showered, he will feel like something more substantial."

"Thank you, Yukari," Jeremy said. "That sounds good."

Yukari gave a small willowy bow and looked at Sam, who took the cue and followed her from the room.

It's going to be difficult to talk about things, Sam thought, *with Yukari running interference.* She protected Jeremy on an instinctive level. It suddenly struck her that Yukari and Jeremy were very similar in this aspect. The more, she thought about it, the more they seemed emotionally twinned.

Yukari gestured to the Western style table in the kitchen, where several covered dishes sat on a warming plate. "I have learned to make French toast and sausage. Do you like such a thing?"

"I love French toast but will pass on the sausage. I'm a vegetarian."

"Ah, there is fruit then."

"Yukari," Sam said, as she sat, "you are going to spoil the hell out of people with this kind of behavior, particularly a single male like Jeremy."

She smiled, looking slightly puzzled. "It is my pleasure to keep our house. It makes me feel useful."

"I was just thinking how alike you and Jeremy are."

Yukari paused in picking up the coffee pot. "Ne? How so, Samantha-chan?"

"You both have overly developed senses of duty, honor, and obligation. I think that things most people would either laugh off, or consciously try to forget about, stay with both of you. I can also see that you are as protective of him as he is of you."

"Perhaps so," Yukari said with a hint of color to her cheeks.

"And maybe," Sam said, taking a piece of French toast, "you both enjoy having someone to take care of."

"That is certainly true for me," Yukari replied, sipping her tea. "When I was reincarnated into this world, I had no one. Jeremy took me in. He has acted the part of my older brother in every way. So yes, I enjoy taking care of him. But surely, he has other people in his life. There is you, of course."

Sam nodded. "We've been friends since soon after we met, and we work together, but that is quite different from keeping house together."

"Debbie Middleton?" Yukari asked, evidently eager to take the chance for some girl talk. "He is reluctant to speak of her."

"The vampire," Sam snorted. "She hardly needs any looking after. More like looking out for."

131

"It seems, ahem, a rather intimate relationship?"

"Honey," Sam replied, "that one you will have to talk over with him. Short version, it's more about lust than liking."

"Are there others?"

"Well, he isn't a monk... Well actually, he's supposed to be... It's kind-of complicated." Sam hesitated, thinking of Prosperine the were-human. *Note to self*, she thought, *possessive. Perhaps jealous, streak confirmed. Maybe my being gay will be handy here.*

"He had a close male friend," Sam added, "but he moved away, and not many people know the truth of what he is. It makes for a compartmented existence."

The door to the bedroom upstairs opened, saving Sam from further explanations. A freshly showered Jeremy, in jeans and a loose t-shirt came down the stairs slowly, holding on to the rail. His face was drawn, but he smiled readily enough at them.

"Do you feel better?" Yukari asked,

He slipped into the chair between them. "I owe you both a huge—"

"Would you like more tea, or are you ready to face that foul Western coffee?" Yukari interrupted.

"The French toast is good," Sam added. "No, actually it's excellent, and there's sausage for you devourers of small animals."

Jeremy paled at the mention of sausage.

"Or I could make something else," Yukari said, looking anxiously at him.

"The coffee and a little French toast will be fine." He started to rise, but Yukari was up instantly and pressing him back in his seat before heading for the kitchen.

"She shouldn't have to work so hard," he said.

"Let her wait on you," Sam whispered. "It's her way of restoring normalcy, and it makes her happy when she is taking care of you." After a moment, she added, "It makes me happy sometimes too."

Jeremy placed his large hand over hers and gently squeezed it. She noticed that he let go of it before Yukari returned with more breakfast.

They talked of inconsequential things over the food, both of them interrupting Jeremy's attempts at further apologies. After a while, he stopped.

"Ah," Sam said, after they finished the last of the French toast. "I have a bunch of things to do at my house, and I don't have a beautiful young girl to do my laundry at the moment."

"Thank you for coming, Samantha-chan," Yukari said, rising to give a graceful bow. "I am in your debt."

"Anytime you need me," Sam said.

"She will not need you for anything like last night again," Jeremy said. "There will be no repeat of this sorry episode. And I, too, am in your debt."

Sam walked around the table and kissed Jeremy on the lips, catching Yukari's surprised look out of the corner of her eye. *Whoops,* she thought.

"I will see you tomorrow at the office for our catch-up Saturday," she said. "And we will talk."

Later that morning and after only a little sleep, Yukari sat quietly in the front seat of the Mini, while Jeremy drove with unusual care toward the school. He was playing the radio very low, instrumental music from an album called *Porcelain* that they were both fond of. Jeremy did not seem inclined to talk. As she did not want to embarrass him, she did not press. She wondered what had triggered last night's misadventure. She did not like Kei Hara, and not merely because of his ancestry. He struck her as a proper fool who had no idea who he was, or how to act. The fact that he had any influence over Jeremy made her unhappy. Still, she could not pick his friends for him, well, perhaps not yet.

With all of the excitement and the early morning, she fell asleep in the car. He woke her after pulling up as close to the school entrance as he could since the day was rainy.

"I'm going to spend some time at the office. I may not get that much done tomorrow when Sam is in. I think she will be bending my ear most of the morning."

"Please do not overdo it," she cautioned. "You have had a rough night."

For some reason she did not understand, this made him chuckle.

"Yes, dear," he said. "You have a good day at school. You call me if you need anything, or if there is in any trouble."

"Hai," she said, reaching for her umbrella. To her surprise, he gently rested a hand on her wrist. She looked at him.

"Call me for any trouble, large or small. Right?"

"*Wakarimashita*," she said, brightly.

"Okay. I sent a text to your home room teacher so everything should be all right. I will see you later."

Yukari opened her umbrella against the light rain and ran into the school. She turned back to wave at him. As usual, he waited until she actually entered the building to drive off.

While even he could not have told it, she was deeply troubled and reluctant to part. If she could find any fault with Oniichan, it was that he felt everything too deeply and thought about matters with great seriousness. Something had happened, she was sure of it. From everything Samantha-chan said, the drunken behavior was unknown, and he certainly appeared ashamed of himself. Even the *baka*, Hara, if she could make herself put aside her dislike of the young man, had seemed motivated, if stupidly, to comfort Jeremy. If the event was related to her, or to the other stresses in his life, most notably his separation from his guardian angel, was unclear. She would have stayed with him, but she sensed that he needed to be alone to have time to think and adjust.

It is so often the nature of men, she mused, *that when wounded, rather than turn to those who care about them, they seek isolation in which to nurse their wounds, like hurt animals.* To her mind, it was foolish behavior, but then, men were often fools. Still, it was unlooked for in Jeremy.

Not now, she decided. *But I cannot allow this to go on if there is a reoccurrence. He almost gave up his life for me once. I will not have it so again. I will press for answers if this happens again.*

With a deep sigh, she put her worries aside for the day. *I am the Queen of compartmentalization*, she thought, *even among Japanese. It is my duty to learn here.* She walked in, still finding it peculiar that she did not have to change her shoes. In a Japanese school, there would have been shoe closets, but then that was the least of the differences between Japanese and American schools.

At least, she thought, as she made her way to her homeroom, *I don't have to clean the classroom or bathrooms here as we would in Japan. Still, I think it might not be a bad thing if these American youngsters had to clean up after themselves sometime.*

Many students were standing in little clusters, and there was more than the usual share of excited talking going on. Many were looking down at their phones, though that was not unusual. She caught some glances directed at her and was surprised by the mix of curiosity, even a little fear she detected in them.

She opened the door to her free period class and slipped in. The usual class was present, and their buzz of conversation dropped as she entered. She looked up in surprise.

"Konnichiwa." Her classmates liked the smattering of Japanese she dropped in conversation; it made her interesting and sophisticated to them. Truth be told, when she was surprised, she sometimes slipped back into it.

A chorus of hellos and good mornings came back. She quickly made her way to her desk and to the safety of her surround of Linh, Trice, and Amy.

"Hey, I thought you were going to be out?" Trice said. "That's what Mr. Heins said."

"There was a minor issue that needed to be resolved," Yukari replied.

"You need to learn to drive, sister," Amy said.

"Ah, but I enjoy having Oniichan drive me and pick me up," she said with a teasing smile. "How could I give that up?"

"Man," Trice said, shaking her head. "Sometimes I wonder what century you come from."

"I wonder about this 'older brother,'" Amy said. "I'm not sure all this affection is so familial."

"Wow," Trice said, "did you learn that big word in class today?"

"Please, no fighting," Yukari said.

"Pay no attention," Linh said, "it's just background noise with them."

"So, did you hear?" Amy began, her eyes shining, as was the case whenever she had gotten hold of a juicy rumor.

"Hear what?" Yukari said, placing her bag under the desk.

"You're kidding?" Amy said. "Have you looked at your phone?"

"No," she said. "Why? Did you call me?"

"Call? By voice?" Amy said. "Is this the 1950s?"

Yukari laughed. *1950s,* she thought, *if you only knew...*

Meanwhile, she'd fished out her phone to the amusement of Trice and Linh and slight annoyance of Amy. When it lit, she was startled. There were over a hundred text messages going back and forth among her schoolmates, not all of whom she knew.

"What has happened?" she asked.

"I wondered if you might know," Trice said with an enigmatic expression. Linh gave her a curious glance, but Amy could no longer restrain herself.

"The school's number one bad boy got turned into hamburger yesterday," she whispered. "Word has it that Trent was in a drug deal gone wrong."

"How did you learn this?" Yukari asked, last night had driven thoughts of Trent from her mind.

The others gave her a pitying look.

Trice waved her phone at her. "It's a net, sweets. Trent's buddies got word from him, and once it's out, it's out. I think everyone but you knew last night."

"He has admitted to this buying of drugs?" she asked.

"No," Amy said, "but knowing Trent, it was something gangsta like that. Only he wasn't as tough as he thought and ended up in the hospital."

"Too bad it wasn't a pine box," Trice said.

"Well," Yukari said, "at least we will be spared his company until he recovers."

Linh shook her head. "Oh, it's better than that. He's not coming back; he's moving to California to be with his mother."

Yukari shook her head. "You should be with the *Kempeitai*...the secret police."

"Like Trice said," Linh replied. "Networks and networks. I'm on the student council, and we just got that word just before I came down here. Trent is out and the goon squad is without a leader."

"For now," Trice said. "There's always a Trent around, but perhaps the next one will be more careful of whose grill he gets up in."

Yukari shook her head; slang sometimes still eluded her.

"Meaning," Trice said, "it got around that Trent and his bully boys were hitting on two underclass girls recently when they were saved by a tall, mysterious Japanese girl with the reddish eyes. Apparently, she walked right into the middle of them and rescued them. Trust me, the story was all over the school in an hour. You have quite the fan club among the freshman year."

"It was a minor matter," she replied.

"With Trent," Linh, said, raising her eyebrows, "I doubt that; you made him look bad—"

"He is bad."

"—and weak," she finished.

"He is that as well," Yukari said tartly.

"So, we wonder if maybe there was a Round Two," Amy said.

Trice sat up, a serious look sliding over her usually indifferent expression. "No, we don't. Don't answer that."

Amy seemed as if might argue, then seemed to realize something. "Oh, yeah, question withdrawn."

The pieces slid into place for Yukari at the same moment. She had told Jeremy enough for him to put together that Trent has harassed her. He had seen more deeply than what she had admitted to, as was his wont.

"I see," she said slowly, upset that trouble had come to him again through her. *Of course*, she thought, *he would be furious with me for believing I have any responsibility in this. He is so unlike the men I knew, and the times are so different.*

Trice looked at her narrowly. "According to a guy I know, who knows one of the hoodlums, Trent said he was jumped from behind and there were a bunch of them, and he didn't get a good look. So, he claims he can't identify his attackers."

"And you believe that?" Amy scorned.

"No," Trice said. "Another source has all Trent's injuries on the front, meaning he was facing whatever he'd stirred up. But the cops won't care. He's leaving town, it didn't happen on school grounds, and it didn't make the news. That may be why they are hustling him out of town. His family has money, and the story wouldn't look good for them, no matter how it turned out."

"So," Linh said, giving her a knowing look. "We are rid of one menace and maybe the school returns to what it was before Trent organized his little jock squad."

"One can have such hopes," Yukari concluded.

The start of class interrupted further discussions. But the remainder of the day was abuzz with the downfall of the school bully. Yukari felt eyes on her often. She was surprised when the two girls she rescued ran up to her trailed by a couple of their friends. They were delighted to hear that the scary boy was gone. Yukari wondered if, as he had done with her, Trent had harassed them further, or had his thugs do it. In any event, she found that she was very nearly a hero to the younger girls.

Good, she thought, *even here, I can be a proper senpai.* She agreed to the girls request to have lunch with them but begged off to another day. There was too much on her mind for today.

As she moved from class to class, she spotted two of Trent's minions. One gave her a frightened look and changed course, taking a stairway he had not been going toward before. The other gave a stiff jerk of his neck, acknowledging her, as if he dared not to. She wondered what had happened, now surer that Jeremy had dealt with Trent in some way. Also, she wondered what Trent might have told his followers. Americans were terrible at keeping secrets and teen Americans were even worse. Still, it seemed best to downplay everything and pretend nothing that had happened has any connection to her. There was a Japanese saying, *Iwanu ga hana*, the unspoken are flowers.

After lunch, Yukari had study hall while Linh and Amy had classes. Trice was free and came with Yukari. They found a quiet spot in a corner of the commons. They had fallen into this habit over the past months. The Goth girl and Yukari might have seen an odd combination to others, but an affinity had built between them. Amy was always dashing off to be with one of her many boyfriends, and Linh was busy with her duties as an honor student on student counsel and with her huge family. She spent what time she could with Trice and Yukari, but the pair were often left alone. This was, in part, because of a bad breakup Trice had gone through with her boyfriend.

"No more boys, or particularly fixer-uppers, for me," Trice had said. "I am over my bad-boy thing."

Yukari agreed that this was wisdom.

"So," Trice said, as they settled into their quiet corner. "You seem to have lucked out. This Jeremy seems quite the catch. Does he have any brothers?"

"No," she said. "He doesn't speak much about his family. I know his parents are overseas and that they are estranged from each other. He does not seem to be in contact with either of them."

"Does he have a girlfriend?" Trice probed.

Yukari considered her answer carefully. "He is...popular with women from what I have learned, but there is no one serious in his life. His career causes him to travel, sometimes for long periods on short notice. He was recently off to a very hot climate for several months and has not yet gotten his life back in order from that. Then, of course, there is me. My moving here has caused him no end of trouble."

"How long have you known him?"

"In a way, I feel like I have known him all my life. But we have not been together that long, really. Yet the time has been intense and filled with excitement. I hope that we are together for a very long time."

"That sounded kinda romantic," Trice said with a smile.

"Perhaps it is," Yukari admitted.

"Well, he's a few years older," Trice said. "That could be kinda cool. Maybe more mature and less selfish. As long as you know what you are getting into."

"Well, I cannot claim to know that," Yukari said ruefully

"You don't seem too sure of what you want," Trice added.

"My experience of boys," Yukari managed, "has not been good. I find it difficult to trust them."

"Yeah, sometimes it seems sex is all they want from us."

Yukari shivered trying to suppress a memory. "But Jeremy is not like that."

Trice gave her a skeptical look.

Yukari laughed lightly. "Hey, we are here to study you know."

CHAPTER EIGHTEEN

An Avenger torpedo bomber from WWII was found sitting in the Tampa airport, its engine still warm but there was no crew found...

After dropping off Yukari, Jeremy drove off, his mind still dulled by fatigue and reaction. The only thing that made him feel better was his certainty that Trent would not bother Yukari again.

All I can hope, he thought, *is that the little rat-bastard is too yellow to call the police. I've disposed of the evidence as best I can. At worst, it's my word against his. Maybe he'll tell his parents a story about getting rolled by some toughs from another school or getting mugged by some kids from the hood.*

He headed for the studio where he knew he would be alone. After last night's late sojourn, he wouldn't see Sam until tomorrow. So, he parked and looked up at the sign over the storefront that he rented. On it was a symbol he'd created, angel wings wrapping a sword over the words, graphic designer. *A fake*, he thought, *like the rest of my life.*

He rested his head against the steering wheel. *Unburdened of one shameful secret*, he thought, *and burdened with a new one. I almost murdered a teenage boy. How long will I have to live under that sword, wondering if and when it might fall? God, I wish Shadowheart was here. I never imagined how much I would miss her. Will we ever see each other again? Is she as lost as I am? Is she thinking of me?*

No answer came to him.

He got out of the car, grateful for the sunny, but cool day. It dried the sweat that had broken out on him worrying about the future. He swayed a little and leaned back on his car, struck by an exhaustion more of the soul than the body, for all of hangover and lack of sleep. He turned, and with a mute apology to Sam, headed into a nearby Starbucks. There was one every thirty-feet in Charlotte. Having to control his desire to throttle the barista after the fifteenth question about how he wanted his coffee took his mind off his problems. The drink was welcome when he finally got it. He returned to the office, punched in the code, and slipped in.

It took the better part of three hours to make progress on the calls, emails, and dead-tree mail. It had piled up, despite Sam's best efforts, and those of the Templars overseas, and was threatening to turn into a real mess. There were also projects that required his last burnishing and professional touches. Given his secret backing, he had more leisure to throw money at problems than a real entrepreneur.

At least for now, he thought. *I better make use of it while I can. I just don't know that I can, or want, to keep doing this. If it ends up being just me and Yukari, I'll have to buckle down like a real adult, make money, get health insurance and the rest.*

Before he knew it, the afternoon sun was slanting through the window. While he still felt like he had been run over by a truck, work had been a tonic for his soul. He checked his phone for the tenth time and there were no calls from Yukari or, worse, the police. Sam sent him a text, checking on him, but being wise enough to realize that he would not want to talk save in person. He shot her back a few lines, assuring her that he was well and would see her tomorrow.

Once he finished with that, he opened the small bag that Yukari had pressed on him as they left for school that morning. Inside was a small lacquer box with a pair of chopsticks. He opened it to find rice and fruit, and some bland chicken, arranged in the shape of a bird. He couldn't stop the laugh that burst out of him. There was also a small thermos of tea decorated with an intricate pattern. Jeremy slowly and carefully ate only a little of the lunch, though he finished the tea, appreciating all of it.

I could get used to being looked after like this, he thought. *How is she so good-natured after all she's been through?* He shook his head in silent amazement. It was already hard to remember what life was like before Yukari. It had certainly led to some changes in the household. Meals were now regular, good, and spent in company. He had fallen too much into the American habit of eating any premade garbage at random intervals. His diet had become distinctly Asian, but he had no complaints, save for an aversion to sushi. That aversion had matched Yukari's reaction to his efforts to introduce her to French cheese. Even a diplomat's daughter had been unable to conceal her horrified expression. He'd taken to eating cheese only when she was not in the house.

Ah well, he thought, *of such compromises is life made. It will be good practice for me if I ever have the chance to get married.*

Hah, he thought, *not much chance of that.* Right now, there was no woman in his life but Debbie and there was no possibility of anything there but friendship with benefits. In his heart, he knew it wasn't a good idea, but Debbie provided a number of advantages. She wasn't fragile of heart or body. Involving a normal woman in his life exposed them to insane dangers or involved him in a fatiguing web of deceit that Batman might have balked at.

Damn, he thought ruefully, *I'm part French. I should be better at lying to women than this.* But he wasn't, so only the most casual of liaisons had worked for him. That left him very alone in the world.

Except for Yukari, he thought. *Now is it she that needs me, or that I need her?* He shook his head. Too much thinking in his state was not a good idea. If he thought too much about her...

A sword whispering through the air.

"No," he said aloud as his gut clenched. "Can't think that way. It's enough that I have the chance to take care of her."

He finished a little more of the lunch, dug back into the design project, and spent a few more surprisingly effective hours before it was time to go get Yukari.

I guess I will have to get her into Driver's Ed too, he thought as he closed and locked up. Surprisingly, Yukari had not been enthusiastic about that idea. In life, she'd never given any thought to driving, rarely apparently ever being in a car and never in the front. She also pointed out that Americans drove on the wrong side of the road.

Traffic was not too bad as he made his way to her school, arriving a few minutes early. He debated whether to hide and then decided to brazen it out. There was no point to trying to duck such trouble as he may have spread if it was waiting for him. He got out and leaned back against the car. There was never enough parking spaces, and he had to stay with the Mini.

The campus was shimmering in the bright sunlight; the trees rustled with a breeze that didn't penetrate to ground level. Young people, well, younger than him, wandered around, most involved with their phones. Some yelled and ran, a few walked side by side or held hands. He did not see any sign of Trent. One boy who looked like one of Trent's crew came down some stairs, but his eyes slid off Jeremy's without recognition. Jeremy let go the breath he hadn't been aware he was holding.

Yukari came out a side door, wearing a blazer and skirt. She was with a small troop of other girls as they paused on the colonnaded steps of the main building. Her face was light and carefree, which was the best news he could have had just then. As he was early, he did not wave, content to watch her with her classmates. Yukari was developing friends. He had seen this particular trio around her before. One was blonde with a figure that belonged on an older girl. The next was the small Asian girl. The last wore leather, short black hair, and eye makeup like Avril Lavigne and was almost as tall as Yukari, in her boots at least.

It occurred to him that there would soon be others in their bubble world, friends, and though he grimaced at the thought, probably boyfriends at some point. He sighed, problem for another day.

She spotted him after a few minutes, smiled, and waved. He waved back, which fueled a fresh burst of discussion among her friends. Yukari excused herself with a small bow that her classmates returned with laughter added. She headed toward him. As she did, a curious change came over her, almost as if she was putting aside her teen personality, donning her more adult face. He shook his head to clear it of the curious notion.

"*Konnichiwa*, Oniichan," she said

"*Konnichiwa*, Yukari-chan. How was your day?"

"Good," she replied. "Class was interesting. Some of the girls wanted me to go with them to Imaginon. They have a karaoke machine there and we can make a video."

"You should go," he said. "Call me later. You have money and a card—"

She gave him an amused look and shook her head. "No, Jeremy-kun. I am enjoying the company of these young people, but only so much. They are like fresh flowers, bright and full of energy, but knowing nothing of life. Their conversation is pleasant and diverting, but also shallow and full of nonsense. We both know more of the light and dark than they do, ne?"

"Yes," he said, a little concerned about her serious tone, "maybe too much so."

"But we cannot hide from what we know, from what we have been or, at least in my case, from what I have been." Unexpectedly, she giggled. "The other girls believe that I am very adult and very, very serious. Amy even suspects that I may be a 'kept woman.'"

He wasn't sure how to respond and merely nodded, though he expected his ears were burning. *How is it she makes me feel like I'm sixteen and she's twenty-five?* he wondered.

She walked forward and took his arm, a surprising act for a Japanese, who would rarely, if ever, be affectionate in public.

"Perhaps," she added, with a mischievous air, "it is that I prefer the conversation of older and generous gentlemen."

"Hey," he said, "I'm only eight years older than you. Hardly ancient."

"Why just so," she replied. "You are certainly suitable." Again, came the giggle.

Yukari's high spirits had lifted his. The cloud of uncertainty that had hovered nearby retreated further. He took her bag with its burden of laptop and books then opened the car door for her.

"Ah," she said, "and manners too. Another virtue of the older male."

He closed the door, hopped in his side, and started the engine. They pulled into Charlotte traffic and ended up in a valley formed by SUVs fore and aft.

Jeremy glanced over at Yukari, who looked totally relaxed and was fiddling with the radio; mercifully, her taste ran toward classics and jazz. Finally, he decided to probe a little more on her day.

"I didn't see any of those jerks from earlier in the week," he mentioned with an off-hand air.

"Yes," she said, giving him a sidelong look. Her cheerful expression did not fade, but she turned alert. "Trent is no longer my classmate."

"Oh?"

"Yes, the teacher said that he had gone to live with his mother in California. I will not see him again."

"Small loss," Jeremy managed.

"No loss at all," she added. "He was unpleasant and the instigator of much that was mean in the school. Without him, the others are even less of account."

"Good."

Again, the sidelong look. "Let us forget about that one. He is not worth more words. Tell me of your day, Oniichan."

"Blessedly boring," he said. "I am just about out of the hole of overdue projects."

"Good," she said with a decisive nod. "We must not allow your business and Sam-chan to suffer on my account."

"It's not," he protested.

She raised eyebrows at him.

"Much."

"Well, you do look like you are feeling better too. Perhaps I can make something more flavorful for our dinner."

He realized that he was hungry and had made little dent in the lunch she had made him. "That sounds wonderful. You know you don't have to do all the cooking. I can manage some dishes."

She smiled. "It pleases me to make them and to run our home." Then she blushed.

"Everything okay?"

"Oh, yes. *Gomen*, I was merely listing what is needed for dinner and the weekend in my head."

He raised his eyebrows at her and she, caught, burst out laughing.

"We can stop at the Trader Joe's in the Metropolitan and get some things," he added.

"Ah, a quiet evening at home," she said. "I will play the piano for you if you like."

"You know, that does sound just great," he responded.

CHAPTER NINETEEN

Earthquakes in Mexico City have tumbled a dozen buildings into dust.

The next day, Jeremy felt he needed to be as good as his word to Sam and headed to the office after a call to Kei Hara. The younger man was still nursing a sore jaw from where Sam had popped him and seemed unusually subdued. He'd evidently caught hell from his fiancée and family after he stumbled into the house that night.

"I appreciate your coming out for me," Jeremy said, "even if I don't even want to look at a bottle of liquor for the rest of the year."

"Kinda the point," Kei said in a surprising flash of insight. "You've been locked in your head since...well since you know when. You aren't the only one with a debt to work off. Call me anytime you need anything."

"Thanks, amici," Jeremy said.

"Just don't tell your killer vixen. Peace out."

Jeremy put away his phone and pulled up to the studio. With a deep sigh, he walked in. Samantha the killer vixen was there. She smiled, ruffled his hair, and slid a coffee in front of him along with a stack of paperwork.

"Okay," she said. "The whole story, once and done, from the beginning, hold back nothing. I think I know the worst of it already."

And so he began, telling her the whole of the tale and sparing nothing. Being Saturday, the phones were off and there were no interruptions. Sam watched him and when he came to the point where he struck down Yukari and could not stop tears rolling down his face, she held one of his hands in both of hers.

"So now you know how my life is bound to hers," he finished, "and the size of the debt that is owed."

"Yes," she replied. "I can see that. But I can also tell you that the last thing Yukari wants is to see you suffer. You're nailing yourself to this cross."

"Her face..." he managed.

"It was necessary. She said so herself. No, the problem here is you. You sometimes feel too much and too deeply, especially for the things you have to do and to face."

"I am who I am," he replied.

"And I don't think she would have you change, and I know I wouldn't. But it comes with its burdens."

"I've never done anything that stopped me looking in a mirror before," he said. "Don't care for it, not one damned bit."

"I don't think you have now, but it doesn't matter what I think. It doesn't matter what Yukari thinks. It matters what is going on in there," she tapped his chest, "and I see more confusion and pain than there should be."

"It gets better as I take care of her," he said.

"A lucky girl then."

"But I am not quite myself yet."

"I know, and now I understand what part Hara has in this and why. I almost regret belting him one."

A laugh escaped him to his own surprise.

"Now enough of this," she said. "You need life to return a little bit more to normal."

He smiled at her understanding and turned on his computer. Three hours of controlled chaos followed, and he was grateful for it.

Ordinary work allowed him to stop seeing the terrified face of a teen and the rags of black twisting on the wind. He didn't hear the whispered, *"Doshte."*

They worked through the day with a tacit understanding to let things lie. Perhaps she realized that there was not much more he could, or would, say. He was mutely grateful.

"I'm going to drop off the graphic portfolio with Manny's Bagels," he said. "Manny likes the personal touch."

"Manny likes the fact that you buy the drinks at lunch so his wife can't complain," Sam returned, eyebrow raised.

"It will be one drink for me," he said, "if that."

"I wasn't concerned," Sam said, giving him a direct look.

He nodded. "This will get better."

She nodded. "Again, I wasn't concerned."

"See ya, Sam."

Hours later, Jeremy's mind was on other things as he walked into the lower level of the parking deck. Manny had, as usual, chewed up a good bit of his time along with lunch. The day had warmed with a tropical mugginess that had come up the coast with the morning rain. He wore only a shirt and jeans. The shade of the garage was welcome, though he felt a chill as the reduced temperature bite through his damp shirt. Sometimes, Charlotte required two or three changes of clothes in the spring months.

He had a to-do list that emptied slowly and refilled quickly. As he was contemplating the latest difficulties in working with the Haras on Yukari's documents and financing, he didn't see the man standing in the shadows until he spoke.

"Well, well," he said, "if it isn't Jeremy Leclerc."

Jeremy spun to face Bob Diablesse. The banker was leaning against a column and, as always, was dressed impeccably in a suit and tie. He appeared to be a handsome, slender man in his thirties, manicured, pedicured, his hair looking freshly cut and set. But he wasn't a human, for all his apparent love of human luxuries. Bob ran the Bank of Stone in Charlotte. The demon preferred his evil on the financial side, not that he was above a bit of slashing and cutting if the chance came for it.

Jeremy glanced around. They were alone. This wasn't good. While he and the demon had a de facto truce, there was no reason to trust the demon's word on it.

Bob came off the column and walked to within a few steps of Jeremy. He was conscious that he had only his Walther riding in an ankle holster. Not a good location for a quick draw, if the weapon would even work on the demon.

"Bob," he said, coolly.

"So, how's it hanging, Templar?"

"What? Are you curious about whether it leans left, or right?"

Bob shot out a wicked grin. "Never interested in boy parts. Well, not without seasoning and sauce."

"Yuck."

"Not carrying around your sword?" the demon asked innocently.

Jeremy snorted. "Little hard to wear a duster in these temperatures. All these cosplayers and Renfesters make it look easy, but swords are a pain in the ass to carry. They keep getting in the way, especially when you sit."

"People don't appreciate how you suffer for them. Oh, by the way, where is tall, dark, and beautiful as heaven? Normally she'd have signaled her presence by now, you know, with a demon being around her baby."

"Bob, I don't have time for your shit today," Jeremy said, starting for his car.

The blow caught him by surprise before he could block, and he was thrown to the concrete, partly stunned. He snatched for his pistol only to find Bob's foot on his ankle, pinning the Walther.

"You know, kid," Bob said, "you're kind-of mouthy for a guy without his magic letter opener and Mama-angel."

"How much you want to bet on that angel not being around, Bob?" Jeremy demanded, knowing his only choice was to brazen it out.

The pressure on his ankle increased as Bob smiled wider. "I hear you were bending Shadowbitch over on a table on the Hell Express during your last escapade. Yep, you are regular booty-bandit, Leclerc. Ambitious too, I mean it never occurred to me to bang an angel. How was it?"

Jeremy twisted and kicked with his free leg, knocking Bob's foot off his. He continued to roll and grabbed his Walther.

Bob hadn't followed up and just laughed at the Walther pointed at him. "Pathetic. You better adjust to the new reality. When you had that angel and were carrying that sword, you were somebody. You could walk and talk big. What are you now? You gonna shoot me with that popgun? I may get pissed off. You wouldn't want that, boy. You better learn to walk small and keep a civil mouth, or you won't walk at all."

Jeremy kept the pistol leveled at Bob as he stood.

"What dickwad, you still pointing that toy at me?"

"So, what have you heard, Bob?"

"That's Mr. Diablesse to you, asshole. You used to be on people's radar back when you were important, before you and Shadowheart traipsed off on an adventure in Hell itself. Oh, what a story. And you know what the other Realms have in common with this one? Three of any being can keep a secret if two of them are dead.

"So, word gets out that there's no angel with you and why. Word gets out that you rescued some little ghost-girl and then you hacked her with the magic throat-slitter and got all bummed."

Jeremy was shaking, not only with rage. Each of Bob's words put him back at the scene: smelling the flowers of the garden, hearing the screams of the Hara family and worst of all, hearing Yukari's anguished cry of *"Doshte?"* the terrified, betrayed look on her face. The pistol almost fell from his nerveless hands.

"Now, Bob," came a soft Southern voice. "I think you've had enough fun for today."

Both men started and turned to face Debbie Middleton as the blond vampire moved out from behind a nearby van. She was dressed as inconspicuously as her figure allowed, in jeans and a blouse under a light jacket. Her eyes glimmered with a vampiric shimmer.

Bob snorted in irritation. "What the hell are you doing out and about? The forecast was sunny."

"Amazing how much you can travel underground in this town. I love the skybridges too. Sun can't get me that easy through even regular glass."

"Hit the road, Vamp. I'm having a serious talk with numb nuts, the weak sister here."

Debbie smiled as broadly as if someone had handed her a julep. "No, you ain't. You're all through now and ready to go on about your evil little day. Ain't you, honey?"

"You're lining up with the wrong team, Middleton. Pretty boy here doesn't have the throw weight he used to. Bang him one more time and drink him dry. I'll make it worth your time."

"Do I gee or haw at your voice?" she asked.

"Ah, hell, don't go all country on me," he growled.

Debbie sidled over to Jeremy's side.

"You're punching over your weight, Vamp."

"I'm a pretty good scrapper, honey. Plus, a bellyful of nines is going to slow you up."

Bob looked at Jeremy. "This is what it's going to be like from now on, Leclerc. No sword, no angel makes you nobody. Vampy here won't always be around to help."

Jeremy said nothing. Provoking Bob gained them nothing but a fight that even with Debbie's help, he might not win. Bob walked off, and Jeremy returned the pistol to its ankle holster in case some civilian came by.

"He's done for today," Debbie assured, but her mouth was a tight line. "You get in your ride."

"What about you?" he said. "I don't like leaving you alone with a pissed off demon in the area. We're too near the Bank of Stone; he may have an army of creatures below it. I know he's been using all those old gold mines to hide things and critters in."

She studied him. "Okay," she said finally. "You got something to cover me so I can lie in the back?"

"Always," he said. "I try to plan ahead. But maybe not as much as you."

"How do you mean?"

"Were you watching out for me? What are you doing in this part of town?"

"Actually, I was watching him. Without you holding him down, Bob's been exerting himself some and running into more problems with the FOE. I wanted to see what he was up to and figured he wouldn't be watching for me in daylight."

He gave a brief bitter laugh. FOE was an old joke between them: Forces of Evil.

"Let's go." He clicked the key for his Mini. Debbie slipped in the back while he got a blanket out of the boot.

"Next time we get in the back seat of something," Debbie grumbled, "make sure it's big enough for us to have fun in. I couldn't even get my legs apart in this thing."

"I am going to have to reconsider the Mini's allure as a studmobile," he said ruefully.

"Get a big black Cadillac," she said.

"I'm not with the Sopranos."

He started the car and headed for his condo.

"Don't get pulled over," she called from the back.

"No worries. I'm driving like a sixty-year-old."

"Watch the cracks about age, boy."

Ten minutes later, they were at his condo. He slid the Mini into the one-car garage and barred the sun by dropping the door. Debbie unwound herself from the back seat. He opened the house door and leaned in. "Yukari, we have company."

"Sam-chan?" she called.

"Not quite," Debbie called.

They found Yukari in the living room, staring at a computer. She rose gracefully as they came in.

"Middleton-san," she said, bowing slightly. "How nice to see you again."

"Oh, honey, you can call me, Debbie."

Yukari blushed a little. Calling someone by their first name without an honorific in her culture was an intimate act. Jeremy knew that Debbie was far more educated and cultured than she let on, and he suspected that she knew this and was playing with the ghost girl for some reason.

"Debbie-san, then," Yukari said, but she was staring at Jeremy. "Oniichan, what happened to your face? Were you in a fight?"

"Nothing to worry about," he replied. "Just an old acquaintance with a sense of humor."

Yukari looked from him to Debbie then back, and then her face settled into its most reserved Japanese expression. "There is tea for our guest. Please, Debbie-san, sit."

Jeremy and Debbie sat at the table, Jeremy wincing as his ankle twinged. In moments, Yukari returned and, in a series of delicate gestures, poured tea for them both and set out a small plate of cookies.

"I don't suppose you have some O+ on tap," Debbie asked.

Jeremy scratched his chin. "I have a few pints of plasma—"

"Huh," she said. "I was kidding, but thanks. The tea will be fine, and I think a cookie would be quite welcome. Of course, the two of you are both appetizing, but I don't suppose..."

"Nope," Jeremy answered for them both.

They chatted about inconsequential things with Yukari present, who did not press him further about his injuries. After cookies and tea, Debbie called for a rather particular Uber, which showed up in a black van with smoked glass. It pulled up to the back. Jeremy raised the garage door and with a careful check of the bright outside, the vampire sprinted into the van and slammed the doors.

After Debbie left, Jeremy took an icepack from the refrigerator along with a cool beer and walked out onto the back deck over the garage of his townhome. Yukari followed him out. The deck over-looked a small alley that ran down to the parking lot nearby. He was surprised to notice that the deck now sported an array of planters and flowers. A small glass windchime emitted an occasional high sweet note.

When did all this happen? he wondered, as he took a sip from the beer. He eased into a rattan chair by their small table. Overhead a jet rumbled by. This close to downtown, it was rarely silent. Still, the back deck was insulated from South Boulevard traffic and only cars owned by residents used the alley. Many of the owners were young professionals like what he was supposed to be, and it was rare for them to use their decks, even on the weekends. The financial world was dog-eat-dog, even when there were no demons involved. No one else was out on theirs.

"Jeremy-kun," Yukari began as soon as she sat opposite him, "I must know the truth."

He looked into her red eyes, and the lie he had planned died on his lips.

"There is a local demon," he said after taking a sip of his beer and placing the icepack on his cheek. "He runs the Bank of Stone—"

"A *yokai*, here?" she said. "Running a bank?"

"You could argue that all bankers are essentially demonic," he said with a smile that she did not return.

"Jeremy this is serious, a *yokai*, actually living among humans... Wait, don't we do our banking with the Bank of Stone?"

"Well, they have the best money-market rates...but anyway not the point—his evil is chiefly financial, at least since I got here."

"Why is this?"

"We made a deal. He has substantial assets in the area, so tangling with him would be dangerous, maybe impossible. Apparently, he felt the same about me, then. We agreed to leave each other alone and concentrate on the blood and guts evil that threatens people's lives. For me, it was an opportunity to neutralize the most powerful evil in this region—"

"But he continues his, how would you say it, financial evil?"

"So do the Republicans, and for the most part he does less harm than they do."

"And he gets?"

"Immunity from me, so long as he does not harm humans directly, plus it's a chance for him to clean up any competitors that might be considering unseating him. Bob has sophisticated tastes; blood and guts interest him less than fine wine and Cuban cigars. Our arrangement makes life and profits more certain."

"So," she said, "sensible so far."

"Until now," he said, sipping his beer and wincing some. "He's found out somehow that I am not carrying that damn sword anymore. My angel...my angel, Shadowheart, is gone and there is no one to back me up now.

"I guess it hadn't registered on me that while I have benched myself—sorry, while I have taken a leave of absence from being a Templar, that not everyone necessarily sees it as a timeout. Some people and creatures may see it as a time to make their move in Charlotte and the area around it. Things have become unsettled, and it's all seeking a new balance. Others may feel they have a score to settle with me, and in my line of work there's usually no second round and no rematches.

"But Bob is another matter. The truce between us was based on mutually assured destruction. Now that's changed. He knows way too much about me for my safety. I'm not sure what would have happened if Debbie hadn't showed up."

"I must be grateful to Miss Melons for that," Yukari said. When he didn't laugh or smile in response, her expression became serious again. "*Gomen nasai,* Jeremy-kun, this trouble has come to you on my account."

"No," he stated. "Bob and I have been an issue since I landed here. This is not your fault. As for Shadowheart, well that, too, predated my knowing you."

"But the sword—"

"Is also not your fault," he said, fighting to keep anger from his tone. Ever since he had fought...ever since he had nearly murdered Trent, he feared his temper like a recovering alcoholic feared Scotch. "They gave me a weapon, a thing I could not trust, again, not your fault."

"Perhaps not my active doing, but we both know why you will not touch—"

"Please," he managed, hand clenched on the bottle.

She stopped, her lips pursed. They sat silent for a while.

"If Shadowheart would only come back, things would be different, but I have no way of reaching her."

"You have not mentioned much about being connected to this celestial being. Tell me of her."

"Well, it was something of a one-way relationship," he replied. "She knew all of me, but I only knew her in a narrow range. She often appeared as a teenager, blond hair, what you would call a twin-tail hairstyle, shorter than you and overly fond of chewing gum—"

Yukari gave a surprised laugh then covered her mouth as if in apology.

"I suppose it doesn't sound that much like an angel," he added.

"Hard to say," she responded, "Susano, who is a mystical being in Shinto, was often a rude and childish character."

"She had another form. Shadowheart could rarely act directly in the Realm of Earth, but when she did, she was a warrior angel, black-haired, green-eyes and over seven feet tall with great black wings."

"Oh," Yukari said, her eyes wide.

"I don't think I realized quite how dependent I was on her."

"Why…" she hesitated.

"Isn't she here?" he finished.

She nodded.

"It's difficult to explain," he replied. "Almost as if there has been an inhibition placed on me. I can only say that we left the Realm of Earth for a mission to correct a mistake in the Underworld. While we were there, well things got a little complicated, and Shadowheart was recalled to her origin. I don't know if there is any chance she'll return."

Yukari did an almost visible battle with her curiosity and then simply nodded, discretion, to his relief, winning out. "Perhaps something will turn up."

He started to say, *that's what I'm afraid of*, and then thought better of it.

CHAPTER TWENTY

Mysterious lights were seen on Alcatraz Island.

J eremy had no choice but to go about business as usual on Monday, but he was better armed and wary now. He doubted the efficacy of the crosses and sutras he carried but knew that the silver-tipped bullets in his Walther worked on most of the forces of evil. He'd parked his car in an open surface lot and attended his meeting with an accountant, finishing off a major project and getting substantial payment for it. He should have been feeling good. Instead, he was moodily surveying the cityscape below him as he stood on the top outdoor level of the Epicenter, Charlotte's hangout for the young looking to do something after work in the downtown area. Though he always experienced a flash of irritation at the squabble over the use of the terms downtown or uptown among the influencers of Charlotte, civic boosterism insisted that uptown sounded classier.

Right now, he was wondering what was going on below the levels of the city and in the shadows that would lengthen with sunset.

"So, you're what passes for a Knight Templar in this crapfest of a world?"

Jeremy started. He was sure he was alone atop the Epicenter, but when he turned, a woman about thirty, dressed in a sharp business suit, and with a short, yellow helmet of hair was staring at him in disdain. His senses tingled, and he knew that whatever she was, human wasn't in the cards. His hand twitched, but he kept his hand away from his weapon.

"Who are you? How did you know who I am?" he demanded.

"Always with the questions. God, you're just as much as pain in the ass as I was warned of."

Jeremy simply stared. The wind riffled his hair; his arms hung loose, ready for a quick draw.

"What? You thinking of shooting me, motherfucker?" she rasped.

"Language, please," Jeremy said. "I have delicate ears."

"Shit," she said, crossing her arms. "Well get this straight. I'm your new guardian angel, Abathar Muzania. That's Muzania to you."

"What happened to Shadowheart?"

"None of your business. You've done enough corrupting of her. They realized you need a firmer hand."

Jeremy sighed. "I'll miss her."

"You'll get over it."

Then he turned his back on her and headed for the stairs. "And I won't work with you."

Shock must have silenced her for ten steps. "Hey, wait a minute, you bastard."

Jeremy stopped then looked back at her. "A foul-mouthed excuse for an angel? It must be time to be done with this Templar nonsense. How dare you think that you can sunder me from Shadowheart as if she didn't exist? How dare you think that all she and I suffered, and fought together, would mean so little? She wasn't just my friend; she was part of my soul. She knew me, faults and all, better than anyone else. And I am to accept you as a replacement? You and your God can handle it all from here without me."

She glared daggers at him as he padded down the stairs.

Jeremy was looking forward to a quiet night at home, with none of the alarms of his old life when he pulled out of the Epicenter parking lot. He'd dismissed the harridan angel from his mind and paused only at a custom jeweler in NoDa to arrange for a present for Yukari. Her seventeenth birthday was coming up soon, and he had his eye on a jeweled comb for her hair.

So, it was late when he pulled up in his car in front of the townhouse. He hopped out, anticipating dinner. The weather was fine, and Yukari had told him they would eat on the back deck under the stars, so he went around back to greet her. He froze when he saw Yukari dressed in a modest dress and light cardigan facing the angel of the afternoon, in the kitchen. Her stance was tense for all that her face was calm, almost serene.

Jeremy raced up the stairs two by two and this time; useless though it might be—the pistol was in his hand. He shoved open the sliding doors. "You, what are you doing here?"

"Trying to find you, you insubordinate bastard."

"I told you I wasn't interested in working for you."

"Oniichan," Yukari asked, "who is this person?"

"She says she is a guardian angel," Jeremy gritted, slowly replacing his pistol. "I find that hard to believe."

"Since Clueless here," Muzania said, "isn't going to introduce us, my name is Muzania."

Yukari merely nodded, eyes narrowed.

"Not big on hospitality," Muzania said.

"Were you invited?" Yukari said. "*Sumimasen.* I must have forgotten."

"She was not invited," Jeremy said, moving to stand between Yukari and the angel. "Nor is she welcome."

"This is not Shadowheart then," Yukari said in obvious relief.

"No, Shadowheart has manners."

"Well, while we are still in introductions," Muzania said, walking over and dropping herself onto the sofa. "Who is this? My senses are confused. They say dead human and live human at the same time."

"What did you miss the Facebook updates in Heaven?"

"I do not have the link with you Shadowheart did, that was part of her undoing."

"Yukari is a reincarnated human. Short version is I'm her legal guardian, and she lives here."

"You've got to be fucking kidding me."

"Hey," Jeremy snapped. "Language!"

"I have heard curse words before, Jeremy-kun," Yukari said, her usual composure back in place. "But never from the mouth of one who claimed to be a heavenly creature."

The two females locked eyes, red ones versus blue ones.

"As I said before," Muzania said, "we need to talk, Leclerc."

Muzania wasn't going to be easily dissuaded, and with Yukari at hand, he was more worried about conflict with the angel. "Let's take this outside. I did not invite you into my home."

Yukari put a hand on his arm. "Jeremy-kun, I will stand by your side."

Despite the glowering angel, Jeremy smiled. "No, Yukari. I will be fine. Please respect my wishes and remain here."

Yukari bit her lip but nodded.

"You, follow me," Jeremy snapped at Muzania. He slipped out the sliding glass doors to his deck and found Muzania had appeared there waiting for him. They stood, leaning against the railing, hearing the busy traffic of Charlotte's South End. Lights glittered in storefronts and streetlights.

"So, this is the new look for angels?" he said, eyeing her severe business suit.

"Doubtless you'd prefer garter belts and red panties, you miserable excuse for a monk."

"You don't like my work. Good, you don't have to be part of it."

"You're a Templar. You need guidance. Frankly, I think you need a kick in the ass."

"So much of my sense of self-worth depends on your good opinion of me."

"You're supposed to be fighting evil—"

"I have found lately that good and evil are harder to distinguish than I expected," he replied, "and I have found that in the course of doing what is called good, that I have had to use evil means. The sword of justice I was given seems a cruel as any other blade."

"God, you are the weak sister," she sneered. "What a pussy."

"Again, language, you foul-mouthed harridan."

"Look, the battle between good and evil is not a cartoon. There are complexities. Sometimes you have to break a few eggs to make an omelet."

"Then you break the eggs. I can't get the eyes of the last one I broke out of my mind. I have a chance to make good on that. Nothing will stop me from that."

"If you want to play house with a little Japanese girl in your off time, it will just get added to your list of sins. She looks underage to me—"

"Can it, Wingless. I look after Yukari as if she was my sister." He swung to face her. People passing in the distance looked at them but hurried on.

"I have wings, I just didn't bring them," she snapped, folding her arms.

"Sure," he returned, sensing a sensitive spot.

"Look," she said, pointing a finger at him. "You're a warrior of God—"

"Never met the guy."

"—and you're special at that. Only a handful have ever paired with an angel. You're a resource that cannot be casually forgotten. Or have you forgotten the evil that you faced here?"

"How could I?" he said. "Sometimes I see them in my dreams. We call it PTSD."

Muzania rolled her eyes.

The light rail rolled by, pausing their vocal battle for a few moments. Passersby ignored them as a couple of some sort having a spat. A street musician up the block began playing something on horn.

"I have no interest in battling evil at the moment," Jeremy said, as the rumble died away. "I'm battling my own demons just now and expending myself in a never-ending conflict doesn't appeal."

"And what of those who need aid?" she snapped.

"Talk to your all-seeing, all-powerful God. He made the place; let Him fix the leaks."

"He sent you."

"I must have missed orientation that day."

"You've been entrusted with an angel and one of the most sacred of relics, Joseph of Arimathea's bloodsword."

"You want it back," he said. "I think Yukari keeps it under her bed. I'll go get it."

"No fucking wonder I had no idea what was going on here. You haven't touched the sacred sword in weeks."

"I thought it was a sin to play with your sword by yourself."

"Oh, shut up," she growled, hands on her hips now. "Look, you may want to forget about supernatural evil, but do you think it wants to forget about you? Much as it pains me to admit it, you've done horrific damage to Evil Inc—"

"And look what I got for a reward...you."

"You fucked your last guardian angel on top of a table in Hell!"

"Who sent us into Hell?" He returned folding his arms and leaning on a lamppost for the light rail. "She didn't choose to pose as a succubus." The setting sun on his back was a comfort, and he realized he was sweating.

"Whether you like it or not," Muzania grated, "you're a player on a big board and not a pawn." She reached into her pocket and took out a gold and gemmed locket on a thick chain. "You're going to need me and, God help me, I'm ordered to aid you."

"Jeremy-kun," Yukari called softly from the window. "Will you be coming in soon?"

"How fortunate for you," Jeremy began, "that Yukari is within earshot. I was going to tell you where you could put your angelic housing in your own idiom. Allow me to rephrase it for more lady-like ears. You may place your pendant in a location where it will be safe from exposure to daylight."

A spasm of rage passed over Muzania's face and she was gone.

Wearily, he turned toward his own door. *This crap I do not need.*

How could they send me this disgusting excuse for a guardian? The whole universe seems to have gone mad.

Once inside, he slumped in his chair at the kitchen table, aware of Yukari's nearness.

She leaned forward. "This new angel, she has upset you?"

"When the angels are less pleasant than the demons, it's a sad state of affairs. I have no intention of being paired with that…thing."

Yukari merely stared at him.

He sighed. "My joining with Shadowheart was a matter of choice, and it was very…intimate. It was an opening of a soul, closer than some marriages, I guess. There is no possibility of such with this Muzania."

"There is more, Jeremy-kun," Yukari stated and suddenly her cute teen personality was submerged in something older and more experienced. "You are angry; terribly, terribly angry. I believe you are enraged at God himself."

"Why shouldn't I be? I've done things in the service of this so-called God that have gouged out pieces of my soul. I've met things that no human should. They call themselves demons and angels. I don't know what they actually are, perhaps players in some vast pretense? Even you, who were dead, know nothing of what comes after as you never left this world. I never reach the main player, the lead actor. He is always hidden in the wings, and I never get a glimpse of him, never get a chance to ask my questions of this God."

"And that question is?" she prompted.

"Why?" he said. "I want to know the why."

"And there is no room for faith in this?"

"I have no faith. I have never found anything I could believe in beyond myself." Fatigue struck him, and he yawned. "Let's have a little dinner, then I think I'm gonna turn in. I'm ragged."

She rose and returned with a glass and wine bottle. "Sit here and enjoy a glass. I will make dinner."

CHAPTER TWENTY-ONE

The Mississippi Side-wheeler Mark Twain is reported missing.

Despite the appearance of Muzania and a general increase in supernatural events, the next weeks proved uneventful. Jeremy was more careful in his movements, wary of both Bob and Muzania. But as nothing threatened, he returned his focus to the only things that now mattered to him, Yukari and his job, which was likely to be the staff for their future if he quit the Templars entirely.

Spring was almost over, and it had been an atypical spring, with sudden chills and cold rain, even an occasional sleet. It seemed as if all the world shared Jeremy's unease. School progressed for Yukari, who continued to adjust to the world. But either her Japanese reserve, or the sheer difference in her experiences, prevented her from developing a very close friend. It was perhaps too much to expect, but he was glad for the small group of girls who invited her places. Between Trent and her past though, she evinced no interest in boys, for which he was more grateful than he probably should be. But there was something that he was looking forward to...

June 17,1918, Jeremy said to himself. It was hard to believe that

Yukari's birth was so early in the last century. It was the conundrum of the girl's existence; time had stopped for her after her death in a way. She hadn't changed for all that she had existed in the interregnum of her ghosthood. She hadn't aged through the rituals of a human existence, but neither had she remained totally static, experience and knowledge had accumulated, albeit in a narrow band.

None of this musing, he thought, *is helping me figure out what to do about Yukari's seventeenth, or one hundredth and a bit, birthday.*

Having her friends from school over seemed risky, away from the restrained environment of the school. He decided that as long as he was out and about, he would drop in on Debbie, who as a member of Club Undead had the most similar existence to Yukari. He pulled out his phone at the next light and called the vampire.

"Hey, sweetie," she twanged in his ear. "Is this a midday booty call?"

"Actually, I was in your neck of the woods, and I wanted to get your advice on something. Feel like a little company?"

"Sure. Daylight is passing slower than usual, so any distraction is welcome."

"Yeah, daytime TV is pretty bad."

"Oh bother, I'm taking the Great Courses online, working my way through international economics. Daytime TV would make me take up sunbathing."

"See you in a bit." He put the phone down before the car behind him could beep and moved on. He sighed. When he had first arrived in Charlotte, no one used their horn. It was usually the last thing heard before a crash, a kind of admission that all steps to avoid the accident having failed. *So sorry and we hate to be a bother, but we got to let y'all know we're gonna crash.*

Now, with the influx of northerners, the tenor of the town was changing. With more progressive politics came more impatient drivers.

Well, some of us retain our manners, he thought, as he pulled into a Fresh Market, emerging minutes later with a tribute of flowers and chocolates for the vampire. A short drive took him to the rundown Northside apartments she made her lair. Debbie had enough portfolio to afford a rooftop apartment downtown, but she found life among the downtrodden and undocumented, with its inherent lack of visibility, far safer. The poor in any society were easier to move among and less inclined to deal with the authorities, particularly the police, and particularly these last few years in Charlotte due to some dubious police shootings.

He parked his now too conspicuous Mini next to an old Accord with two different color doors. As he got out, he eyed some men sitting on a staircase, who gave him enough of a cold regard that he switched the flowers to the arm with the chocolates and reached under his jacket to unsnap the thumb strap on his Walther. They recognized the move and might assume he was a cop. They continued to eye him and make comments among themselves until he reached the door that led to Debbie's apartment. Then the oldest slapped one of the others on the arm, and they all disappeared into an interior hallway. Deb's apartment faced the back of the complex and had no exposure to the sun at all. He entered the short hallway, dimly lit by one fixture, and walked up to her door.

Debbie opened the door at his knock. To his relief, she wore a sweater and jeans. He'd resolved to keep this visit platonic, but he'd resolved that other times and found Debbie in lingerie impossible to resist.

Her eyes lit up when she saw the bouquet of mixed spring flowers and chocolates. "Well, ain't you sweet. Thank you, honey. I'll have to get these into a vase. Come on in and set yourself down. I'll get you some sweet tea."

The apartment inside was the antithesis of the complex: filled with beautiful furniture, fine original artwork, mostly of sun-drenched landscapes and fixtures. He'd rarely been in Debbie's lair since his first disastrous attempt to kill the vampire after he landed in Charlotte. He'd ended up tied to her four-poster being ridden into submission by Debbie, who'd fortunately fed earlier. Only later did he realize that it had all been part of Debbie's plan to obtain a White Pass, a mark of safety from the powers of light, for those of the dark who pledged to do no harm.

Debbie hummed as she pulled out a Mikasa vase and set about arranging her flowers. Satisfied, she disappeared into the kitchen to return with the chocolates in a crystal bowl and a pitcher of iced tea on a salver with two glasses. They sat on the same couch, but as he sat second, he gave enough space so as to put temptation at arm's length at least. Debbie's look at him was affectionate, but not sensual, as if she was aware of his mood.

Of course, she knows, he thought ruefully. *After more than a century and a half, what doesn't she know about men? God, she does do good things for sweaters though.* He forcibly pulled himself back to the reason for his visit. But Southern-like he knew better than to bring it up immediately. He sipped the tea and bit into a proffered chocolate, as she did so as well.

"I'm always amazed that you have all these riches here and no security system, no bars on the windows."

Debbie chuckled. "Hah, I'm more worried about your fancy Matchbox car outside. Well, not much worried. People don't mess with anything, or anyone that parks in the spaces near my apartment. Officially, no one here knows what I am. Unofficially, of course, the accumulation of weirdness lets them know something is amiss. I occasionally have to make an example of some asshole who's just moved in.

"The men whistle at me from a distance, and the women make the sign of the cross, but they're glad I am here. Anyone who steals from me, or messes about in a way I don't like, I hunt down by scent. I don't want the police coming here, so I tend to take care of trouble myself, quiet-like and no fatalities, as we agreed. No one dares me twice. Your matchbox is safe."

"Good to know."

"So, what was it you wanted to talk about?"

"Ahem. Well, about Yukari."

"What a surprise," Debbie said dryly.

"Saturday is her seventeenth birthday. I'd like to do something for it. You know, like a birthday party."

Debbie stared at him.

"I mean, she never got this—"

"Oh my god, you're serious. Tomorrow." Debbie pinched her nose before dropping her had back to her cup. "You realize that she's not... not really a teenager."

"But not really not a teenager either," he returned.

She sipped her tea and looked at him with raised eyebrows.

"She got cheated out of a lot of things the first time. This time will be different." It came out with perhaps more force than he intended. Perhaps.

"You're the person," he continued, "with an existence most like hers. I understand that it is different in detail—"

"I get it. How does someone with a greater lifespan deal with birthdays and holidays?"

He nodded.

"It's probably the hardest part of it," she admitted, after a long silence. Her Southern accent had moderated, as it often did when she was being serious. "I'm not human anymore, not physically or psychologically. I live the solitary life of a predator. But I was human once and I remember. Never had family, but I was luckier with friends. I miss that.

"But my prey and I look alike. It's almost literally like befriending someone you might eat, least before I mended my ways some. Think of it as if your favorite pet could beg for its life in your own language. What other predator has to put up with that?

"So, I know I have to do without any real friends, have to do without Thanksgiving dinner and Christmas morning and birthday parties. If I still had a human soul, I would have long since gone mad and walked into the sun. But I'm not that human anymore. I'm more like a tiger in a sense. I live alone and I don't really need anyone. Not even you, boy, though I do enjoy your company."

"That seems a contradiction," he said carefully.

She shrugged, "Maybe just a bad habit. After all, I was the one and am now the other. A tiger would always have been a tiger.

"Anyway, Yukari may have been like me when she was a ghost. Now she's alive again. She really is, 'Girl Interrupted' but she's not seventeen except biologically." Debbie played with the chocolates for a moment. "I think she's much more on your side of the line. She's going to need friends, lovers, and holidays."

He sighed. "I feel so too. But I don't know that she can hold up on close scrutiny so soon. She doesn't know the kids at school well. I think she's having trouble relating to them. She finds them—"

"Young, dumb, and shallow," Debbie said. "I do too. Least I can bite 'em."

"So... well, I thought we might have a little party of us in the know. You, me, Sam, unfortunately the only other person is Kei Hara, that won't—"

"Ah, Jeremy, aren't you being just a little dense just now. You really think Yukari wants me at a birthday party with you?"

"Huh?"

"After the closet caper?"

"I don't know how much she really saw. Anyway, it was a wardrobe."

"Doesn't matter and don't change the subject. It's less a matter of her watching than of her being aware of it. But she knows we did it furiously and not for the first time. When she was little Miss Ghostly, she might have been amused by it, but she's not now."

"Debbie, I don't think jealousy is—"

"God, how is it men got to run the planet when they are so dumb? You better wise up; she is playing at being little sister because it keeps her close to you."

He could only give her a confused downcast look.

"Oh, Hells Bells," Debbie finally said. "If it will get that look off your face, I'll come to your little party, bring a proper present and all."

A smile shot across his face.

"I worry about you," she grumbled.

"You're a very understanding predator," he assured her.

With Debbie sorted, he stopped on the way home to attend to his grocery list, spending more time than he wanted to filling the cart and dissuading an overly chatty clerk from signing him up for a loyalty card. He paid and rolled the cart into the parking lot.

"Having fun, Templar?" Muzania's voice sounded next to him.

He controlled the desire to jump and tug at his pistol. After composing his face, he turned to face Muzania, whose pinched face glared at him from across the small shopping cart.

"Is it senior day at Whole Foods?" he replied.

"Still with the wisecracks?"

"What do you want?" he said, giving her neither name nor title of angel. He assumed people around them could see her from the curious stares they were getting. She looked like a corporate lawyer, and their demeanor to each other was not friendly. Not waiting for an answer, he started to load groceries in the back of the Mini.

"To get your head out of your ass, and your sword back on the line."

He emptied the cart and gave her a cool glance. "I have not changed my mind about you or anything else. If Shadowheart were to return—"

"Dream on." She gave a malicious grin.

"Then you can go fu—"

Muzania growled, and Jeremy found that he couldn't breathe. But it was only for a moment, and the angel jumped and cursed as if stung.

Now he returned her unpleasant smile. "Violate a rule, Wingless? You weren't sent here to run the world, were you? Humans aren't your playthings."

"I was sent to get you back to your duty," she hissed. Now they were definitely attracting attention. *Probably they think it's a fight between a cougar and her boytoy,* he thought weary of the tableau and so-called angel's presence.

"I have no use for you," he added, "nor do you have power over humans."

"Don't be quite so sure of yourself," she replied, fury dancing in her eyes. "Not everyone you are connected to is fully human. Your little ghost girl—"

He slammed down the boot of the Mini, turned, and stalked up to

Muzania. A mother nearby grabbed her young daughter and hurried to her Mercedes SUV.

"Do any harm to Yukari," he said, in a flat, iron-tinged voice, "and I will take up the sword again, long enough to plant it in your chest. Do you understand me, witch?"

Muzania stepped back, uncertainty on her face for the first time. She spun on her heel and stalked off.

A pleasant faced, heavyset man with an armful of groceries gave Jeremy a sympathetic look. "Love can be a bitch, right?"

"Too true," Jeremy returned and turned back to the car. He slipped in behind the wheel and started the engine but knew he was too upset to drive.

Breathe, he thought. *Let the anger and the terror pass. Muzania can't do much against humans and harming Yukari would bring me to war against her and anything she values. She wouldn't have to worry about Bob then.* But even he couldn't face the prospect of active angelic enemy with equanimity.

After a minute he felt calm enough to put the Mini in gear and head out. *Maybe she'll head back to whatever snooty suburb of Heaven she hung out in when she wasn't serving as a recruiting poster for the forces of evil.* But he knew in his heart that there would be another round with her.

He put the angel out of his mind, somewhat, and started thinking about Yukari's party. He wouldn't share the news about Muzania with anyone, particularly Yukari. He had preparations to make, and he would let nothing mar her birthday.

Yukari's birthday was to be a small affair at a café in the fashionable South Park area. Debbie and Samantha met them at his condo. Debbie appeared dressed modestly, at least for Debbie, with a bouquet of yellow roses for Yukari, who set about arranging them in a blue vase. Sam showed up in a thigh-length sweater over leggings, the weather had continued its odd jags and tonight had turned unexpectedly cool.

"I'm surprised you picked a French restaurant," Sam said, hugging the tall girl.

"I'd assured her that a Japanese restaurant would be fine," Jeremy added, "but to my surprise, she'd opted for Monte."

"I wish to learn more of the land of your birth," Yukari said, finishing with the flowers, then she paled slightly, "but I will pass on the cheese, if you do not mind."

"I'll save you from any stray brie."

"It could be worse," Debbie said. "He was born in France, but educated in Rosslyn Scotland, and no one can face the thought of Scottish cuisine with equanimity."

"Shall we go?" Jeremy said. "The limo is waiting."

Yukari donned a wrap over the long dress she wore; she seemed to feel the cold less than most teen girls.

The trip to the café was quick. Once there, they were shown, amidst some curious glances by the staff and customers, to a quiet section in the back. A piano player was tinkling away, and the place was full, but not too noisy.

Despite his fears, there was no tension at the table. Perhaps it was the champagne that he had opened. He was annoyed by the fact that Yukari, who was underage, had to make do with some feeble nonalcoholic champagne. He'd had his first wine at ten but now lived in a country where you could buy a gun before you could have a glass of wine. Absurd. He switched his glass with hers after the waiter left.

"A toast," Jeremy said. "To Yukari, long life, good health, and much happiness."

"Well said," Sam added.

"Happy birthday, baby," Debbie said.

"Thank you all so much for sharing this time with me," Yukari said with a demure smile. She sipped the champagne and wrinkled her nose. "Oh, it tickles."

"If you're lucky," Debbie said.

"Almost everything sounds naughty when *you* say it." Sam gestured with her champagne flute.

"I am the Queen of Misbehavior," Debbie acknowledged, with a defiant toss of her blond hair.

The return of the waiter saved anyone from having to come up with a response to that. Yukari asked Jeremy to pick for her as she did not know much about French food. The meal was a variety of French classics. Jeremy opted for a cassolette and a savory crepe for Yukari. Sam, as usual, went for Lobster Thermidor. Debbie, who never had to worry about gaining weight, chose blanquette de veau despite a dirty look from Sam the Vegetarian.

Afterward, beautiful strawberry shortcake was served with coffee; then it was time for presents.

Debbie's gift was a garnet pendant that matched Yukari's eyes. He wondered if there might be a double meaning in that gift. Still, since Yukari was so delighted with it, he dismissed the concern. For her part, Yukari protested the expense, but Debbie waved it off.

Sam gave Yukari a Himalayan salt block candle holder. The salt block would glow as if lit from within when the candle was lit.

Jeremy's gift was twofold. The first he presented with a flourish, a cloisonné hair comb in the shape of an orchid. The second, he handed her with a more subdued air. She opened the package ornately wrapped in the Japanese fashion, to reveal a small gold and jeweled woman's compact.

"Ah," Yukari said, pleased. "This is very beautiful and quite old."

"Yes," he said. "It was my grandmother's. Her mother's before her."

Everyone sat still.

"Jeremy," Yukari said into the silence. "This is very precious, surely a memento of your grandmother—"

"Is indeed precious," he said softly, "and it is to you I give it."

She looked down at the beautiful small compact as if to hide her eyes, started to speak, then could not and covered it with a delicate sip of champagne. "This then will be a treasure to me."

"I'm glad," he replied, smiling broadly. "Happy birthday."

"Yes, a happy birthday. I, who never thought to reach seventeen. This is indeed a happy birthday. Thank you all. I am so grateful." She very carefully refolded the paper around the compact and placed it within her purse. The comb ornament she picked up and with a few deft motions placed in her glossy black hair.

Jeremy settled the bill, after which they stepped into the unseasonal chill, and he waved for the limo. The short drive was interrupted by some unexpected singing. Debbie and Sam belted out "Rock Me Mama" and "Amazing Grace." Sam was staying over, and everyone had hit the champagne significantly including, to Jeremy's surprise, himself. Yukari, who had sipped real champagne from his glass was slightly tipsy but covered it by being extra correct. Debbie, as usual, showed no sign, just being herself, perhaps more so.

They decided to brave the chill on his back deck. Jeremy felt stuffed from dinner and his body was busy turning the sturdy cassoulet into heat. He did have a heater outside and plugged it in, to Sam's relief.

"Coffee, tea anyone?" he offered.

"Decaf," Sam said.

"Cognac, for me," Debbie said, smiling.

"I would like some warm tea," Yukari asked.

"I'll give you a hand," Sam said, from where she sat practically on top of the heater. She scampered in behind him, sliding the door close.

Ghost girl and vampire found themselves alone and eyeing each other under the stars. Music was sounding from a party at another condo down the block. The rumble of a jet vied with the light traffic from South Boulevard.

"A special evening," Debbie said.

Yukari sighed. "Perhaps only you, Debbie-san, would begin to understand how special."

"Perhaps," she returned. "We are, or rather were, different versions of the same thing. I'm rare, despite what humans show in the movies. You, however, are singular. If a ghost was almost unknown, how much less so a returned-to-life human? It's not like you're a reanimated corpse. I could tell."

"Yes," Yukari said tartly, "and so you did, even mentioning my virginity."

Debbie chucked. "Sorry. Well, have you done anything about that?"

"Debbie-san!"

"Oh, please," Debbie said. "Can we drop all the smoke and mirrors and level with each other, undead to undead?"

"Debbie-san, I do not understand what you mean."

"Yukari, honey, you're no more seventeen than I'm twenty-eight. We've both logged decades of moving about after we were croaked. Shall we both agree that we're over the age of consent?"

Yukari shifted and a trace of annoyance flickered over her face. "Hai, Debbie-san, though I have not consented as frequently as you have."

Debbie showed teeth, but not in a smile. "That's right, and I have consented with Jeremy on a number of spectacular occasions."

"I have not been so lucky," Yukari said, looking away. "My one experience didn't involve my consent and my death followed soon after."

Debbie studied the pensive girl for a few seconds, then sighed and put a hand on her shoulder. "Hey, listen, I'm sorry about that. Really, I am, and I am even sorrier if I was rough on you a moment ago."

Yukari gently patted Debbie's hand. "Thank you, but I was the first to play the cat, so it is my own fault. *Sumimasen.* But we were discussing Jeremy."

"We were," Debbie agreed, dropping her hand back to her side.

"I am a living human again. Jeremy is only eight years older than I. More, I will not be seventeen forever, as you will remain at twenty-eight. If I decide that my...relationship with him is to be...different, well then, I will travel through time with him until one, or both of us, pass through the gate of death to what is after. That is something I can do—"

"And I can't," Debbie finished. "But you said, if..."

Yukari gave her an atypically direct look. "Debbie-san, you enjoy sex. I have not."

"Baby doll," Debbie said gently, "you were raped. You've never had sex."

She nodded. "Nor do I know if I want to try."

"It's a big piece of life to leave untested."

"Perhaps, but it is not all of life, or love. Yet, I do not want to close that door. I...I... This is difficult to say aloud but I...do love Jeremy. For right now I am content for that love to be as it is. For him to be my oniichan. As for the future, well perhaps he is my Mr. Knightly."

Debbie considered. "Okay, Emma, I understand, but you shouldn't expect me to hang around waiting on you to make up your mind."

"Nor do I ask you to. What will be, will be."

"I don't believe in karma, girl."

"*So deska?* Fortunately, it believes in you."

The two eyed each other and laughed.

At that moment Jeremy and Sam appeared, sliding the doors back. "Drinks are up. So, what are you too laughing about?"

"Women's secrets, Oniichan," Yukari said quickly.

"Ah," he replied, realizing he would get no better answer. Sam just rolled her eyes.

ACT III

CHAPTER TWENTY-TWO

"It's the pause before the plunge."

Another month passed in relative peace; nothing immediately threatened the little world Jeremy and Yukari inhabited. But both the human world and the supernatural world roiled with war and rumors of war. The overseas Templar network buzzed with engagements, and casualties were not light. Yet Jeremy was able to refuse travel or involvement. His spiritual loss had crippled him, he claimed, as had his recent bout of PTSD. He could no longer wield his sword. While he would provide no details of what had happened between him and Shadowheart in the Realms beyond Earth, he advised them that the angel was no longer with him. About Muzania, he said nothing. Shock had answered him, but the sword would only resonate for him. While he lived, no other could use it. He refused any visitation or support. The Grandmaster, an ancient and wise man, decided to leave Jeremy alone to heal and turned to the global campaign against evil and chaos.

This was what Jeremy wanted most. He lived only a day at a time, working on his business and, more importantly to him, taking care of Yukari. This was the medicine that he craved.

As for Yukari, she too enjoyed the relative peace. Her friendship deepened with the other girls, and they became inseparable at school. Trent's old crew avoided Yukari at all times. With the newfound confidence in her ability to navigate the human world, she decided to take a bolder step...

Yukari waved as Amy's magenta Civic pulled up to the garage entrance below the deck to Jeremy's townhouse. The sun was fading, but there was still light in the sky.

"Ah," Yukari said, "they are here." She could not quite contain a flutter of nerves. It was the first time her friends would visit her house, and she'd had to overcome Jeremy's reservations about having them here.

"Well," he'd said finally, "it's not like they have guessed anything about you from school and you will only get closer with them over time."

Tonight, he only smiled. "Go let them in."

She nodded, noting with approval that he had put on a fresh white shirt and stood muscular and handsome in his jeans. There was a clean, lean look to him, and she detected a bare hint of cologne.

She slipped down to the garage and hit the opener, just as the three were getting out of the car. Trice wore her usual leather pants with a retro-t-shirt that said *Ramones*. Amy wore heels, tight red pants, and a top that showed her shoulders. Linh was more sensibly dressed in a blouse and jeans. A chorus of greetings met her.

"Please come in," Yukari said. "Oniichan...Jeremy is looking forward to meeting you." She turned and led them up to the living room. As they entered, they were greeted by the smell of gourmet cupcakes. To her surprise, Jeremy had a plateful on the center of the table surrounded by glasses and a pitcher of lemonade and sweet tea. He stood by the table, smiling and once again, she was conscious of how handsome he was.

"So, you're Yukari's friends," he said. "Welcome. This is a great pleasure."

"Jeremy," Yukari began. "This is Trice."

"Ah," he said, walking over, "she whose real name must never be said."

"Yep," she said, surprising Jeremy with her trademark strong handshake. "You have hard hands for a graphic designer," she said, hanging on to his hand for a few more seconds than Yukari approved of.

Jeremy raised an eyebrow. "Martial arts. My parents started me when I was small."

"Yeah," she said. "I saw the heavy bag hanging in the garage. And I get the feeling that is not just a decoration." She gestured to a stand in the corner of the room in which a katana stood. "Sweat stains on the handle wrappings."

"Well," Jeremy returned easily, "I spend entirely too much time sitting in front of a computer. It's train or soften to death."

The girls chuckled appreciatively.

"And this is Amy." Yukari gestured.

Jeremy took Amy's hand in an old-fashioned way that charmed her, judging by the brightness of her smile.

"I love your European accent," Amy said, "but I can't quite place it."

"It's a bit of several places," he replied easily but with instinctive evasion. "I had thought it had faded out under y'alls and bless their hearts."

"And this is Linh," Yukari added.

"Yukari has told me so much about how you helped her get settled in during her first days at school. I'm very grateful."

Linh responded with a shy smile and struggled with finding something to say, settling for just, "Thank you."

"Actually, I am quire grateful to all of you. Yukari knew no one here when she arrived, so it is both a relief and pleasure to see that she has found some good friends, and all so pretty too."

Amy giggled. Linh blushed. But Trice grinned. "Oh, you are a smooth-talking devil, aren't you?"

"Mostly on the side of the angels," he replied, enjoying the word play, "even though some have expressed doubts.

"Please." He waved a hand at the table and in a minute had all four girls seated and had poured drinks.

"Don't suppose there's a shot at a beer?" Trice asked.

"Trice," Linh scolded.

"None whatever," Jeremy said, smile intact.

She looked up at him. "That was the right answer."

"Oniichan is a very serious person," Yukari said with pride.

"Yes," Trice continued. "You seem to have lucked out for a guardian. So how did a handsome twenty-something end up with a Japanese teen?"

"Sorry," Amy said, putting a hand to her head. "Trice is the blunt trauma of conversation."

Jeremy showed no sign of discomfort. "Mostly by good luck is my answer. But to your question, my family owes hers a debt of honor the like of which you cannot imagine and that, sorry, is not open for discussion. You will have to work it out of her and good luck to you on that."

Yukari gave them all her most mysterious smile.

Trice only laughed. "We've already given up on that. She has more ways to evade questions than a CIA agent."

"All this," Jeremy said, "is cutting into your gourmet cupcake eating time."

"Good point," Amy said, reaching for one with an avaricious gleam in her eye.

"Better watch those calories piling up on the hips," Trice said.

"An argument that might have more weight," Linh interjected, "if you didn't have two on your own plate."

"What are you, a fanatic?" Trice cracked.

Jeremy laughed outright, and the girls joined in.

"Wow," Trice said, looking at the Kawai. "Nice piano."

"Yukari plays wonderfully," he said.

"It does take up a lot of space," Yukari said, running her hands over the dark wood instrument. "And you should not have spent so much."

"I was happy to part with the space and money to hear you play. As far as I am concerned, I came out ahead."

The conversation continued in a light tone with Yukari a little bemused by how much her friends were vying for Jeremy's attention. He, for his part, seemed to enjoy it, listening intently to what they said. He surprised Linh by knowing a few words of Vietnamese.

"You have a very nice home here," Linh said, looking around at the antique furniture and decorations. "I thought all single guys lived off bean bags, crates, and IKEA."

"The old stuff is mainly the product of coming from an old family. However, I cannot deny that there has been a marked improvement in décor and cleanliness since Yukari arrived."

"It is my pleasure to keep our house," she said. "It seems the only thing I can do for you."

"You do vastly more than that," he said, suddenly serious. "The flowers, your beautiful rice paper paintings, all these things are merely icing on the cake. It's your presence here that is the treasure."

"Oniichan," she said, startled, and blushing, delighted and embarrassed in equal measures.

Realizing this, he opted for lightness. "So, karaoke, huh? Sounds like fun."

"Depends on who is singing," Linh added, with a pointed look at Amy, who wiggled the middle finger holding her lemonade glass.

"We haven't heard Yukari sing yet," Linh added.

"She sings beautifully," Jeremy replied.

Trice shook her head ruefully. "Is there anything she doesn't do well?"

"Instagram," Yukari replied, provoking laughter.

"Not the best with technology," Jeremy admitted.

"My village was very primitive," she said.

"Primitive," Amy said. "You might as well have been a Flintstone. Honestly, just landlines and not many of those!"

Yukari's mind drifted back to the family country home, remembering the first time a car had driven through it, the first light bulb, and the first phone. Aloud, she said, "And what is this, Flintstone?"

This provoked still more laughter and rolled eyes.

With the cupcakes devoured, Yuri invited the girls up to her room, but only after Jeremy several times shooed away her attempts to help him clear the table. "Go be with your friends."

Yukari sat on the bed with Linh, as the others sprawled on chairs.

"Nice room," Trice whistled, "ensuite bathroom and all." She picked up a Totoro plush toy from its shelf and gave Yukari an amused look. Amy, meanwhile, had seized on an expensive teddy bear.

"Jeremy is generous in all things, but honestly, sometimes I wonder if he thinks I am twelve years old, not seventeen."

"Oh, I'm not so sure about that. The way he looks and talks about you. I think he has it bad. How much older than you is he?" Amy asked.

"Only seven years now."

"Only," Amy said with a knowing glance at Trice.

"Only," she repeated in the same tone, "and handsome, strong, and owns his own business…"

"So," Amy purred, "has he made any moves yet?"

Yukari's eyes flashed, literally. "Oniichan would never do anything dishonorable." The heat of her response took the other girls back a bit.

"Okay, okay," Amy said, raising a hand. "My bad. I just mean that he's a great guy. Maybe I'm even a little jealous."

"Yeah," Trice added. "Sorry. Color me a little green too. Especially after the last asshole I dated."

"Yes, of course," Yukari said quickly. *I must remember that these Westerners will think anything and say most of it.* "I did not mean to snap. It's just that, well, I am of two minds, which is not unusual with me." Then motivated by an impulse she couldn't control and feeling greatly daring. "I have had a very bad experience with a boy before. I…do not feel comfortable with most, which is why I have turned down invitations even from the boys in our homeroom. With Jeremy though… I think I could spend forever with him."

"Ah," Amy said softly, "but as the little sister, or as an adult?"

The room was silent for a few seconds. Finally, Yukari said. "I don't know. For now, I am happy with how things are. But this role and this place will not always be available to me." She sighed. "In any event, I have time. I do not think that he sees me as I am now, hence all the plushies. And I know he would not consider anything until I am eighteen, if he realizes it then. So, I have time."

"Hey," Trice said. "If you ever need to talk about…about what happened before. We are all here for you."

"Thank you, but I would not darken your days with such a tale."

Trice nodded. "Offer remains open."

She gave the Goth girl a wan smile. She'd now mentioned this twice in her presence, but Trice, for all her bluntness, was sensitive enough to conceal the earlier admission from the other girls. Though they seemed polar opposites, she felt closest to the rough girl.

"But enough of all this serious talk," Yukari exclaimed. "Are we not going out to karaoke?"

"We are," Amy said, seeming to sense and agree with Yukari's need to back out of the intimacy of the last few minutes.

"Yes," Linh added, "unlike the rest of you. I have a curfew to deal with."

"Yes," Yukari said. "Or Oniichan will be up here with another plate of cupcakes."

"Oh no," Amy said, patting her pert butt. "He bought more?"

"He is never less than generous."

"Does she ever answer a question directly?" Trice asked of Linh.

"You know how inscrutable we Orientals are," Linh said, "Yankee."

The girls trooped downstairs to find Jeremy watching Trevor Noah. He stopped the show and stood just as the front doorbell rang. He gave Yukari a puzzled look. "Were you expecting another friend?"

She shook her head.

He walked down the short hall to open the door. When it swung open, Debbie Middleton stood on the front step. The vampire's hair reflected the streetlight and glow of the full moon. She wore sandals and capri pants under a light sweater that hugged every curve of her. The effect was riveting.

"Hello, sweetie," she said. She caught sight of the foursome of girls. "Oh, did I catch you at a bad time?"

"Ah, no," he said. "Yukari and her friends were just going out. I just wasn't expecting you."

"I was just in the neighborhood, hadn't seen you since Yukari's party, thought I might drop in."

"Come in," he said.

With a broad smile of red lips over perfectly even teeth, she followed him back. "Hi, girls."

"This is a business associate of mine," Jeremy said, "Debbie Middleton." Jeremy quickly introduced the girls as the vampire, who in her instinctive way of ingratiating herself with prospective meals, chatted easily with the three.

Jeremy went to get the drinks from the kitchen, more adult ones in this case. Yukari used the chance to slip up to his elbow. "Oniichan, is there trouble?"

"No," he whispered back. "Not immediately anyway. She looks too relaxed for that. Don't worry about it. Go and have fun."

She glanced at the voluptuous vampire, so different from her own slender figure. "I think I should stay. She may bear important news."

Jeremy took her by the elbow while balancing two wine glasses in the other hand. "No, what you should do is go out and have a blast with your pals."

"So," Debbie said, as they rejoined them and she lifted a ringed and braceleted hand to take her glass of white, "girls' night out?"

"Yep," Amy said. "Karaoke."

"Well, ain't that sweet."

Yukari abruptly felt both childish and uncertain in the vampire's presence. *I am over a hundred years old,* she thought furiously. *No woman should be able to make me feel like a child, even if the kappa is twice my age!*

"You kids have a good time, watch out for pimply boys and hickeys." Debbie turned back to Jeremy as if they had already left.

"Yeah," Linh said. "Let's get a move on or I'll be late."

"But," Yukari began

"Enjoy," Jeremy called over his shoulder, moving to take a seat on the sofa.

"Come on," Amy said, giving Yukari's sleeve a tug.

"But…" Before she could protest further, she was swept out the door and down the stairs by her friends.

With Yukari and her friends gone, Jeremy turned to Debbie, who had draped herself over the sofa with a practiced and sensual ease. He sat opposite her with a sigh.

"Must be rough," Debbie smiled. "Being surrounded by teeny-boppers all the time."

He chuckled and raised his glass for a sip. "Actually, this is the first time I've met her friends. It seemed a safe time to have them over."

"Hope you can get used to the scent of Clearasil and Pink's perfume line."

"They do seem so young," he replied, "even if it is only seven or eight years."

"A lot happens in those. Especially for you."

He shrugged. "Can I get you a cookie or something?"

"No, honey I'm fine. Girl's gotta watch her figure."

"Which in your case, never changes, no matter what you eat."

"Or who."

"Behave," he said wagging a finger at her.

"Even too much virtue can be a vice, you know."

"Who said that?"

"I may be paraphrasing Thomas Aquinas. Or maybe Paulo Coelho, I forget."

"So, what does bring you to my door?" he asked.

She gave him a speculative look. "Maybe I thought you could use some more adult company…"

The desire for the vampire stirred in him, and he was aware that it was his desire—she wasn't glamouring or casting for him. But two things held him back: one was the fact that Debbie was never the safest of interests, and second, he was not so thick as to be unaware that Yukari had been distinctly unhappy about leaving the two of them alone. He did not put it past her to double-back on some pretext. While who he did what with was not really hers to say, he nonetheless felt a strange desire to avoid her disapproval and disappointment.

"Hmmm," she said, "even cautious, you don't usually keep me waiting."

"I'm a little reluctant to complicate things just now. Still finding my feet in my new life."

"Oh, boring, boring," she said.

"Aren't you the same one who said you were evil with a capital E? Always urging caution on me."

"Usually," she grumbled, "you don't listen worth a damn."

"Women," he replied, "you can't win. But I don't believe a booty call is what brought you here."

"Partly right," she said, sipping her own wine. "There's so much going on in the human world right now, wars, rumors of wars, and more than the usual share of unexplained happenings."

"I haven't been following the news much lately, when I do, all it does is depress the hell out of me. Still as you say, things have been odd. Wouldn't be surprised to find a Sasquatch running around Sharon Road."

"This has been mirrored in the supernatural world," Debbie added. "There is strange shit going on."

"What have you heard?" he asked, sitting forward.

She rested slightly fanged teeth on her lower lip. "Well, that is the problem, it's bits and bobs, as my granny used to say. Human-derived supernaturals don't have the network that the un-damn-naturals have. Even they don't share info the way the Forces of Light do."

"We used to have a Templar joke that Forces of Evil were their own worst foe for that."

She groaned. "Don't book yourself on Bill Maher; you have no future in standup. You're better at lay down."

"Anyway," he pressed.

"The rumor mill is that all across the world FOE have run into trouble, large casualties, or unexplained disasters. Knowing my side, it may be that they are attacking something they shouldn't, but what that is, I ain't got a clue. What I do know is that Bob is pulling in his forces. He's filling the tunnels under Charlotte, the old mines and such, with as many of his critters as he can. It's like he's getting ready for a war. Now, that don't make no sense given what we both know of Bob."

"Could he be clearing out any competition?" he asked with a guilty feeling. Without an operating Templar and angel, Charlotte was suddenly more welcoming to the Godless.

"I think some of that is going on too, but there's not that much around this part of the world that Bob couldn't handle with what he already had here, or if it came to it, deal with himself. I'm not sure you ever quite understood how powerful he is, an actual demon from the hellish regions. Frankly, I'm not sure how we got out of that garage with our skins intact."

"I've wondered that too."

"So, Bob is in duck and cover mode, but I don't think even he knows from what. Have you picked up anything on your side?"

"No," he returned, again with a guilty feeling. "I have been leaving the Templar network alone, other than some business support they were giving me, which I have largely discontinued, and they, at my insistence, have been leaving me alone. It's not that unusual for Templars to disappear or go inactive when they can take no more. Many return to the monastery."

"The walls would fall in if you did that."

"Jeez, was I that much of a horn dog?"

"You were banging a vampire, a were-jaguar, assorted airline personnel—"

"Hey, how did you know—"

"Oh, for crying out loud, honey, you're a Templar. Toss in a magic sword and angel, you were probably the most dangerous member of the FOL running around the planet. You get noticed. Anyway, you ain't known for celibacy."

"Anyway, back to the point," he said. "I have no information and I can't reach out to the Temple, not unless I don't have any other choice."

She gazed at him. "You'd take Yukari's part, even against the Temple?"

He was quiet for a few seconds. "Debbie, I will kill anyone and anything that threatens Yukari."

She was quiet in turn for little. "I believe you."

"It's what I have left," he added.

Debbie drained her glass. "On another night, let's bend a bedpost or two."

Jeremy grinned. "Yeah, let's do that. You going to stay in touch?"

"Oh, your Freudian slip is showing," she replied with a smile that weakened his resolve almost to the breaking point.

"You're welcome here," he added.

"Good to know," she said, rising. He rose with her and accompanied her to the door. They paused and she slid into his arms. The kiss was slow and sensual and made him regret his scruples even more. But she winked and slipped out the door, which was probably for the best.

CHAPTER TWENTY-THREE

"The administration insisted that absolutely nothing occurred today at grid coordinates 7.4256° N, 150.5508° E."

The girls settled in with sodas and snacks in their private room, but the microphone for the karaoke machine remained untouched. The subject of the conversation was the intruder, Debbie Middleton.

"So, this Debbie?" Amy asked. "A friend?"

Yukari had been thinking so hard about leaving the vampire alone with Jeremy that she almost didn't hear her. "It is as Oniichan said, Middleton-San is a person he has done business with in the past. I would not say friend, rather acquaintance."

The look all three gave her was eloquent of what they thought of that statement.

"What business is she in?" Linh followed up.

"Lingerie model for Victoria's Secret?" Trice suggested.

"Nah," Amy said waving a hand. "I don't think they make em that big. For Crissakes, what were those E's?"

"Nah, G's" Trice said.

"G's!" Linh yipped.

"Yeah. Gee those are too big," Trice said.

"And they cannot be real. I mean, she must be in her late twenties, right? Those things were high and tight," Amy added.

"She's only 5'5" too; her back must hurt," Linh said. She looked down at her own chest and sighed. "Guess I will never have that problem."

"I am," Yukari added, again overcome by her desire to confide, "not happy about this connection, for all that she has been helpful to Jeremy in the past. I cannot say that Middleton-san has not been kind to me, or that I have not...owed her better behavior in the past. Still, I don't think that she is a suitable friend for Jeremy."

"A skank?" Trice said.

Yukari hesitated. "She enjoys her life fully, and perhaps frequently."

Amy raised her eyebrows. "Isn't that a bit prissy? I mean she's an adult, and you said she was single. I mean if she was a guy getting lucky, no one would say anything."

"A skank is a skank," Trice insisted. "I wonder if she is a porn actress or something like that."

"What would he be doing with a porn actress?" Linh said in exasperation.

Trice sighed. "So innocent."

"She is not a porn actress," Yukari said, unwilling to allow a falsehood to attach.

"Well, anyway, there's no way those things were real," Trice said.

"How can breasts be unreal?" Yukari said, puzzled and annoyed at the turns of the conversation.

They looked at her.

"Ah," Amy said. "Cosmetic surgery."

"Boob job," added Trice.

Linh finally took pity on Yukari's ignorance. "Surgical enhancement to make a woman's breasts bigger."

Yukari placed a protective hand over her own chest. "How ridiculous!"

"The Patriarchy loves big un's," Trice said darkly.

"So anyway, we come to the big question," Amy said. "Is she his girlfriend?"

"No!" Yukari stated.

"You sure?" Amy said.

"Well," Yukari sniffed, color and temper rising. "There may have been some involvement in the past."

"Oh," the three said.

"That sucks," Trice added.

"Come on," Amy said. "He's a hot guy. Did you expect him to be a virgin, or never to date? Expecting him to ignore her is like expecting a dog to ignore steak."

"Um, could we not compare her Jeremy to a dog, please?" Linh said, raising a soda.

"No offense," Amy added hastily.

"All men are dogs," Trice said.

"I can't believe she referred to us as kids," Linh added, "how dismissive."

The free-flowing conversation and the ease which with the girls volunteered such thoughts was intoxicating to Yukari, while at the same time being annoying beyond words. No Japanese in her day would have spoken so. It almost took her breath away.

I am not going to cry in front of these children, she thought. *While I may have the body of a teen, I am one hundred years old!*

Or am I? Or have I just had the one year over and over since my death? I am of both the light and the dark. I have been so happy since I came back to life, with even the smallest matters of being alive, that this reckoning has been postponed. I have not faced my past, not faced what I really am. Sometimes, it is like a veil has been drawn over my time as a yurei. It seems so distant from my existence now. I have been reborn. The world I came from is gone, and no one knows me from then. Should I not live just as a girl of this time?

"Hey, Yukari," Trice called. "If we've been insensitive bitches, please just tell us to fuck off. This is your life we are talking about."

"I would never," Yukari said, shocked.

Trice smiled. "No, I don't suppose you would. Honestly, you have the most beautiful manners. Sometimes makes me wish I wasn't—"

"A Satan-worshiping, foul-mouthed, Goth, chopper-chick," Amy finished.

"Exactly," Trice said. The round of laughter broke the tension.

"Hey, aren't we supposed to be singing our troubles away?" Linh said, reaching for the mic.

"What troubles do you have?" Trice demanded.

"Spend two weeks in a conservative Lutheran Vietnamese family," Linh said, "then talk to me. At least you get to go out on dates with guys."

"And look how that worked out for me," Trice said.

"Wrong guy," Amy said,

"And how do you find the right one?" Trice asked

"Sample 'em all," Amy said. "Hey, what a great line for a song."

The next two hours were taken up with singing, mostly badly, bad jokes in an effort to take Yukari's mind off of Debbie, and school gossip.

Yukari realized a few things while the others tried to cheer her and divert themselves. First, that she greatly valued her night out. Never had she dreamed of being able to express herself so freely, without fear of punishment or censure. But it also occurred to her that she might have been wrong about her earlier assessment of how much time she had to make decisions about her life with Jeremy. After all, Debbie Middleton had fairly warned her that she would not wait on Yukari's decisions.

Finally, all sung out and with Linh's curfew nearing, they decided to wrap up for the night. Amy drove Linh home first, then dropped Trice off near the school, where she'd left her Trike. She pulled up in front of Yukari's home. Amy wasn't even going home. She had a date with her current boyfriend. The girl's energy amazed Yukari.

"Good luck," Amy said, and then to her astonishment, she leaned in and kissed Yukari on the cheek.

A slightly dazed Yukari got out of the car and fumbled for her keys as Amy sped off. As she approached her own door, Yukari was wracked with questions.

Is she still here?

Why did she come?

What will I do with if she is still here but behind the door to his room?

What do I want?

She opened the door, and to her immense relief Jeremy was sitting as before in front of the TV, though that was not a common activity for him. She realized he had been waiting on her return. He was wearing the same clothes and his hair was not wet from a shower. Likely nothing had happened. Good.

"How did it go?" he asked. "Did you have fun?"

"I did," she replied, "but I am still glad to be home."

He smiled. "I saved two cupcakes."

A wave of something washed over her. She decided she would not ask what had brought Debbie to their door. Oniichan was not able to dissemble with her. Had it been urgent or pertained to her, he would have spoken of it first. She smiled, put down her jacket and sat down to tea and a cupcake and told him an edited version of her night. And she wished, while knowing it futile, that nothing would ever change.

After she left Jeremy, Debbie spent the early morning hours on her couch with a Blood-lite, which is what she thought of stored human blood as. She was out of sorts and listless and didn't feel like going through the seduction necessary to get a human to part with some blood and life energy. The sun would be up soon. She raided her emergency supply and sat on her couch and watched Oprah. She normally avoided daytime TV the same way she avoided sunburn, but today she could not focus on her portfolio or the Great Courses. Debbie had four masters degrees already and knew more about economics than the Fed did. None of this vast supply of knowledge or experience was helping her just now.

She had felt this way since the birthday party with Yukari weeks before. It had been fun, despite her misgivings, but when Jeremy gave the ex-ghost that damn compact, it had created a tremor in that long-gone heart of hers. Last night's visit had only reinforced that. She knew his attraction to her and knew that he wanted her. But he was holding back, unwilling to further complicate his life. She knew that was about Yukari. The girl had become his focus. As yet, she suspected that he didn't realize he was in love with Yukari, well a form of love. He had chipped out a very nice pedestal to put her up on and admire.

I wonder what he will do if she decides to climb down off of it? At some point he better wake up and realize she's a woman.

What do I care? she thought irritably. *They can play house all they want. It's not like I want him or anybody full time on my pillow. Am I really competing for this human boy? Am I in this horse race? Why do I feel this way?*

She actually growled as she thought about it. While she had earned her White Pass from Jeremy and the Knights Templar and no longer hunted any human that did not hunt her, she hadn't fully considered what it would mean for her future, beyond not having to fear the Church and other anti-vampire organizations. She now had more time than she could fill with sex, drugs, and rock and roll. Or was it that she just didn't find it quite as fulfilling?

Unlike Yukari, she thought, *I can't turn back into a human. I'm a hunting animal, and I can't afford the emotions of a human. I don't love people; I have sex with them. Even if I liked that boy and decided to make him mine, how long could I possibly have with him? Vamps live a long time; most are killed by humans because they only think with their fangs. Stay in one area and the bodies pile up. Only really during a major war could a vamp subsist on humans without drawing enough notice and enemies to overcome them.*

I don't have any living enemies, and I have immunity from the forces of light. If I don't screwup, I could live for a thousand years or more. I don't know of any of my kind that has ever succumbed to age, though a lot of the older ones have walked into the sunlight.

So again, why do I feel this way? And can I afford any of this?

After more hours than she cared to count, the sun finally went down again. Debbie packed her curvaceous body into club threads and headed into the Friday prime hunting night. Somebody was going to get lucky tonight and then they were going to get bitten.

She satisfied her needs with a UNCC student who was curious and healthy. A nip and a sip from her, after a tussle in the back of her car relieved the edge of her hunger, but to be on the safe side, she bounced a bouncer at the White Horse.

Relieved, and in a much better frame of mind, she decided for a long walk on the Greenway. No one else would be on the isolated paths except for a police patrol, and she would sense them coming long before they could spot her. She could simply stand in woods while they passed. Insects and animals would not bother her. Not even southern mosquitoes were tempted by her undead body. Poison ivy was no threat either. So, she wandered, once again pleased by her own company and the stars.

"I am not going to call Jeremy for a while," she said to herself. "That boy is too close to me. I like him. I like his little pals, but I'm not sure this is going to work out. I wonder if it might be time to move on. Goddamn it though, I like it where I am. Maybe a vacation in Alaska where the nights are months long...."

The miles disappeared under her shoes, though she never really lost track of time. A vampire had an internal clock that always ticked down toward sunrise. But she was as much lost in her own thoughts as she could be, heading back to where she had parked her pink VW bug when the chill struck her. That brought her head up. She couldn't remember the last time that temperature had bothered her. Now she felt a cold like she had never experienced before, not even when she'd had the more delicate body of a living human.

She turned slowly and saw him, or her, or it. The unearthly beauty of the being at the top of the stairs to the parking lot seemed to balance between the genders. It was tall, with slender, graceful limbs that projected from the robe-like garment it wore. Long, golden hair tumbled over the shoulders and framed a face with features more than delicate and less than strong. It gazed down at her with eyes that held a distant beneficence.

They stood still as no living beings could, regarding each other.

Debbie dared not break the silence. She could normally tell gender with her sense of smell, but though the being opposite her was real and not an apparition, it had no scent. Supernatural being that she was, she sensed that it was not entirely present. What she was seeing was only part of something larger and more powerful. She concentrated with vampiric senses and while the image of the being did not change, she could swear that she saw the traces of huge wings behind it, as if someone had sketched them with a single pass of a pencil.

The being smiled at her. Something in that smile both warmed her with its beauty and chilled her with its complete self-assurance.

"Greetings, Nightwalker," it said, in a voice of beautiful music.

The sassy response natural to her died on her lips as she stood under those timeless eyes.

"Hello," she managed, hating how small her voice sounded.

The figure stepped forward, seeming to glide down the stairs, barely touching them. Debbie wasn't sure about its clothes, if it wore any at all; the details of the body were behind something that could be a mist or a light fabric. Debbie backed as it came within arm's reach. The figure stopped its advance.

"Do not fear me," it said. "Had I meant you harm, you would never have known I was here."

"Who...or what are you?" Debbie asked.

A gentle smile wreathed the beautiful face. "Were you here when the first light came?"

"I don't...I don't understand."

"I was not young when the command to light the universe came," it said.

And fear struck Debbie. The thing before her was an angel. She had feared Shadowheart, Jeremy's guardian angel, but this was not that gentle-hearted messenger, however inimical Shadowheart could be to Debbie's kind when provoked. This was a fallen angel, an original being that had defied all creation in its pride and power and ignorance. It was entropy, the opposite of life, evil in a way that no mere demon or werewolf could be. It ran counter to the principle that organized space-time. By all the laws by which the universe worked on, this could not be standing in front of her.

"Who are you? How are you here?" she demanded before wisdom could silence her.

It regarded her quizzically. "But I am not here. At least not fully, else you would simply shrivel in my presence. As for my name, it cannot be rendered in the tongues of this world being a sound of the chord of music that started all. Few now exist that know that music, most came long after.

"My true name would be too hard for you to sing and take longer than even a nightwalker exists for it is the tale of all I have done."

"What do you want?" she whispered.

"I want nothing," it said, as if the question was very strange. "I am merely here. You happened to enter my sphere."

She backed away. "Forgive me for disturbing you. I intended no disrespect. Let me leave you to...well...whatever you were doing."

It looked away as if Debbie had suddenly ceased to exist.

I am going to get out of here before that turns out to be the case, she thought. She slipped away, heading for another staircase a hundred yards away. She didn't want to trigger a hunting instinct by fleeing, but when she couldn't see the angel, she ran at a speed no human could match, car keys in hand.

CHAPTER TWENTY-FOUR

A missing teen was discovered on an island in the delta; she claims to have met a divine messenger.

Jeremy opened the small boot of his Mini and dropped in the packages he had, weary from a very long Friday. Much against his will, he'd been sent on a shopping trip by both Sam and Yukari, who had pronounced his wardrobe of casual clothes as terminal.

"How long since you were last on a date?" Sam had asked, holding up a worn-out shirt in one hand and a sweater with a hole under the collar in the other.

Yukari had given her an enigmatic look but agreed about his clothes. "You have nice business clothes," she said, "possibly because you wear them so seldom, but Samantha is right."

He managed to abort the shopping expedition that was gathering steam by promising to stop by South Park and pick up some new clothes. Both females expressed considerable misgivings about his ability to properly dress himself, but he held firm, pointing out that he had been wearing clothes when he met both of them. Seeming more puzzled then persuaded, they relented, and he went on his own.

Business had kept him running about until well after normal hours. Then Barbara, an airline pilot he had dated once, called and asked to meet for a drink. She'd been surprised when he suggested they make it coffee. It was pleasant to see her, but she quickly picked up that something was different. She asked if he was seeing someone, and he gave her the carefully edited version of his life with his new ward. Barbara, who had no lack of admirers and no desire to be involved in anything complicated or committed, gracefully let it all go with a promise to get in touch in the future. He watched her leave with a mixture of regret and relief at having one less complication to face.

Given that he was now stuck with a useless increment of time, he decided to grab a slice of pizza at the food court and get the shopping done. He'd parked in the deck by the Belk's, figuring that it should be safe enough even at this hour. As he hated shopping, he found a staffer who looked good and asked for advice. Nine hundred and fifty dollars poorer, and only an hour later, he was headed out.

The hair on Jeremy's neck stirred as an updraft from the open landing in the parking deck brought up an animal scent with a familiar tang of a were-creature to him. For a moment he wondered if it was Prosperine, sometime friend, lover and were-panther. But she would not have returned without warning, and this scent was deeper, rank, and unpleasant. He reached for the sword in his duster unconsciously, his hand encountering nothing and slid on to the butt of his Walther. He pulled the pistol and jacked a round in. He'd been holding the duster in his hands the weather being so bizarre lately, the night was still a bit warm, but it was such a habit to carry it. He was glad for the coat now, as he could swathe his gun arm in it as he moved over to the open stairwell.

Something was stalking him, one of Bob's henchies? Somehow, he doubted it. The demon had clearly relished the chance for some payback, but his escape from the banker had been too easy. If the attempt had been serious, he wouldn't have lasted long enough for Debbie to interfere despite Bob's professed a dislike of "wet-work." He was full demon to Debbie's half. Not to mention that the abandoned gold mines below the city itself were full of Bob's minions. No, there was something in that encounter that he had not yet figured out.

One thing he knew was that Bob did not use werefolk, sharing the demonic prejudice against human-originated menaces such as vamps and weres. Prosperine had been an exception; she was panther first and a human second.

Jeremy stalked forward and peered into the stairwell. He saw nothing. Rising air brushed him, bringing up the scent from below. The lower levels were partly underground as the building was banked into a hill.

No more garages for me, he thought. *I'm taking the Blue Line from now on.*

It struck him that whatever was going on below might not be aimed at him. *What if it's not? I'm no longer a Templar. But if there's a were down there, whatever its hunting wouldn't have a chance. What the hell is it doing in this part of town? It must have come up the greenway by the sewage treatment plant.*

I don't have to do this. I'm on the sidelines now. It's not my problem. What if I get killed? Who will look after Yukari?

It wasn't enough. Soft-footed, he made his way down the stairs, keeping his pistol under the coat. It wouldn't do to wander into the CMPD coming up the stairs.

A shriek drove all caution out of his mind, and he jumped the rest of the way to the next landing, spinning about and almost losing his balance.

An elderly man lay against a sedan, his face mask of blood. Pressed against the car next to him was a young woman, her eyes wide with horror as she looked up at the were-creature standing over her—one paw upraised to strike. The creature was a mix of its human and animal natures, hairy, bestial in its distorted face, yet towering on two man-like legs.

Werebear, he thought even as he aimed. The werebear, distracted by the sound of his landing, turned, a snarl on its malformed face. Jeremy fired and it gave an unearthly howl. He was alternating squash-head dum-dums with crosses cut in with silver-tipped bullets. The silver was the more lethal with this beast.

The werebear turned and with a speed astonishing in its bulky body, raced away, dropping to all fours. He knew he'd hit it but wasn't sure how many silvers had struck. It vanished in seconds, toward the band shell for the symphony that backed the South Park Mall. He heard the crash of cars and distant shouts. A closer vehicle peeled out, and he saw a car racing out of the parking deck. They had clearly seen the werebear but hopefully not him.

He turned back to the girl, but to his shock, Bob Diablesse was standing there. The girl stared at him with a vacant expression. Bob looked down at the man and shook his head. "Gramps has breathed his last."

"What did you do to her?"

"Take it easy, Whitehat, it's just a trance spell. She won't remember a thing." The girl slid down the car to the ground, apparently deeply asleep. "We need time."

"Time for what?"

"For you to recover your brass, asshat—you slapped out five rounds—and for us to get out of here before the cops show up. I'm interfering with CMPD communications, but it will only buy us so much. Everyone has an effing phone and now a goddamn camera. I'm casting glamour over us that should frustrate even an Android. Come on."

"The werebear—"

"It headed for the woods by the sewage plant. My people run it. It won't get far, now you got a silver in. I'd dispose of the girl if it was up to me—"

"It isn't, you leave her be."

"Still talking tough, kid?"

"You're still not killing me, Bob?"

"As I said, no time for chats." He gestured with his hand, which emitted a sour green glow. From where they'd been ejected, the brass cylinders of his expended ammo leapt to Bob's hand. He wrapped them in a silk handkerchief and threw it to him. "Walk and talk, Templar, walk and talk."

Sirens began to sound in the distance as they went up the stairs. A security guard appeared and raced past them, evidently not seeing them at all. He glanced at Bob's, whose face showed strain. Even for a demon, distorting reality this much was a drain. They reached the level with his Mini.

"Get in the car," Bob managed.

Jeremy opened the Mini, and they jumped in. He started the car and raced for the exit. "Someone will see us."

Bob grunted. "Not so much, with the car all I have to do is change the appearance. You're driving a Honda sedan right now. Shut up till we get to Tyvola."

He drove out. Blue lights were coming from all directions, but the collisions caused by the werebear created enough confusion, that in the darkness of late evening, they were able to drive away.

Once out of sight of the mall, Bob sighed and sat back. "Okay, you're a Mini again. Pull over at Park Road Shopping Center."

Jeremy turned in and parked in the back near the Indian restaurant. The back of the old center was filled with small buildings and shops.

He got out and faced Bob across the hood of the Mini. They stared at each other.

"You weren't there by chance were you, Bob? You could have stopped it."

"Could have," Bob said with a shrug. "But since when is protecting humans my job? I was watching tall, smelly, and hairy because he's been poaching on my turf lately. You're showing up was fortuity, but I wanted to see what you would do."

"You let a man die for that?"

"Actually, you let him die, Templar. Low order trash like that avoided Charlotte when we had an angel and a magic chopper here. Now what is there?"

Jeremy stared at him, unable to speak.

"Beat it," Bob said wearily. "It will just be another mugging gone wrong, and they'll blame it on some Black guy. Or maybe they'll think it was a real bear; nice of him to run away on all fours for the witnesses. Now I'm tired, not the least because it was hard to disguise your hipster ride. Buy a fucking grownup car some time."

Bob shoved the door closed. He walked away, heading toward the old folks home that backed the shopping plaza. Then Bob paused, glancing at his phone, which lit with a text. "You didn't do too badly," he called. "Dead werebear in the greenway; we'll dispose of it. The girl will live. That's not too shabby for you on your own."

"What?" Jeremy managed faintly, his mind in turmoil.

Bob looked back at him. "Do you even know who you are anymore? Any idea what you want to do beyond playing with your ghost girl? I think you need to start asking yourself, why?"

Why?

Doshte?

Blade cutting through something was not air.

When he snapped out of the flashback, Bob was gone. He rubbed his face with his hands. "Home," he said thickly. "Got to go home. Figure it out tomorrow. Home."

CHAPTER TWENTY-FIVE

Dust storms have cut off the city of Austin, Texas, from road and air traffic.

Yukari opened the door; the smile froze on her face as she looked at Jeremy. His face was pallid, sweated, his eyes haunted.

"Oniichan! What has happened?"

He almost stumbled in. She looked out at the street a few people were walking by. A couple glanced at them curiously but with no malice. There was no threat in the street that she could see.

Then she spotted Muzania leaning against the lamppost. The angel was not easy to see, and Yukari knew that only her connection with the supernatural had let her spot it. Even for her, the angel was unclear, she saw it as they had earlier, but as she stared, it assumed an animal aspect that she recognized.

Later, she thought, as she pulled Jeremy inside and closed the door.

"I'm alright," he said in a voice not much above a whisper.

She checked him over. He was not physically injured. She took hold of his arm and led him to the table. He collapsed into the chair. She sat next to him. After a moment's hesitation, she took his hand in hers and placed an arm across his shoulders. Westerners were so much more touch-oriented than her people and drew so much comfort from it.

He raised his head and gave her a wan smile.

"Jeremy-kun," she said softly. "Share the truth with me, *onegai*. What has happened? Was it the angel? Did this Bob attack again?"

"No," he said, "though he is involved in my troubles."

"You may tell me anything," she coaxed.

"I don't know who I am anymore, Yukari. I don't know what to do with myself. I know what I want to be…"

"And what is that?"

He faced her for the first time. "I want to be the man who cares for you. I want to be free of the darkness and all that moves in it, so I can be that person."

She stroked his hair. "Oniichan, you are that man already."

"But the darkness keeps reaching back for me. Tonight, a man was killed by a werebeast, a shape-changer."

"You speak as if this was somehow your fault?"

"When I was a Templar, and now I must admit that I have not been since…since the night you returned to life, things such as that avoided this town. They feared me. They feared the informal alliance that I had with Bob, knowing that there was no protection for them there.

"Bob said…he said, it was my fault. He had no duty to defend humans."

"Manipulation," she stated. "Emotional manipulation, Jeremy. You cannot be everywhere, nor do everything. The beast existed; it did what it did wherever it was before. This time it struck here. That is all."

"But if I had been what I was, it might not have been here."

"Then it would have been somewhere else, and another, or more, could have died. The world is the world, Jeremy. You Westerners always think that you can manage karma; it is not so. Even when you had your angel and…were at your greatest power, you could only protect the place you stood in.

"Do not fall for such talk. Indeed, be angry that this Bob thinks you are such a child to be troubled by such nonsense."

209

The problem, she thought, *is that he is innocent in such a fashion, almost a child in this. Why is that?* she suddenly wondered. *He was raised in a cloistered way but was always disobedient and willful. Yet, still there is this streak of naiveté...*

A rueful smile flitted across his face, almost too quick to be seen. "Yes, *senpai.*"

She pinched his cheek as if he was being a naughty boy.

But the face he turned to her was open and troubled. "All I want is for us to live our lives together. Why won't they leave me alone?"

"The darkness is troubling, but not all evil," she said. "After all, did we not meet in the dark?"

"Yes, but there is so much I want for you to have, so much that you were cheated of and none of it involves this living nightmare of endless battle between good and evil. I no longer want to use the tools, face the nightmares, or make the compromises. I don't have the power or the strength left."

"Certainly, you will do no more tonight," she said, "a bath and then bed."

Again, the wan smile. "You Japanese think a warm bath fixes all ills. But I will take mine in the morning, I'm exhausted."

"Very well," she said with a touch of disapproval. Then she pulled him against her, to where his face was against her neck. After a second, his arms wound tight around her. They sat that way for a minute. Then, he slowly released her. She sat back, feeling a reluctance to let him go.

"Thank you," he said.

"I will be at your side," she said. "Always."

"That's supposed to be my line," he said making a helpless gesture. "I'm supposed to be protecting you." With a last touch of her hand, he headed for his room, exhaustion and defeat evident in the set of his body. The door closed behind him.

Yukari looked at the closed door to Jeremy's room.

He is beset by enemies, she thought, *both around him and inside him. About the doubt and angers that plague his heart, I can do little.*

Or could I? she wondered. *I am a woman in both body and years. In my own country and time, I would have been married by now. Likely I would have had a child. I am not the little sister that he tries to see me as. I could open that door, go in, and ease this pain and anger.*

But between her and that door lay the valley of her memories. She would have to confront what had happened to her and deal again with the memory of the man that had touched her first. She beat back the memories.

I am good at that, she thought bitterly, *so good that I managed to divide my own soul and live in a fantasy for eighty years. My past buried where I need not see it. I cannot travel that road again.* She sighed. *But I am not ready to travel this new road either. Perhaps I am not so grown up as I pretend.*

Resolution grew in her. *He has taken me into that heart and into his home. I will not let him face these enemies alone. When I was a yurei, neither Debbie nor Jeremy could prevail against me. In truth I used little of my power against either. I could have destroyed them had that been my wish. The Haras would not have lasted an instant, but for my desire to torment them first.*

What was the limit of my powers? As the Dark Yukari, I certainly never found anything that I could not do if it was my will.

Do I have any powers left? When I was dead, I used my powers without conscious volition, just as a living person breathes while asleep. I have no idea how I could even begin to check if I still have power. Who can advise me? Jeremy himself said that ghosts were a mystery to Templars. The order had not believed in their existence. Debbie is supernatural and undead. She is as ignorant of the nature of ghosts as Jeremy. Nor do I want to involve the vampire hussy any more in our lives than I must. She is not proper, and Jeremy deserves much better.

So, who can I turn to? There is this Muzania, but Jeremy does not like her. Still, she is a celestial being and must have great knowledge. It cannot hurt to respectfully ask, and she is the only resource available to me. I must dare Oniichan's disapproval for both our sakes.

She pressed her ear against Jeremy's door but heard nothing and decided that now was the best time for her illicit adventure. Picking up a sweater, she headed toward the front door and the cool of the evening.

Yukari paused on the stoop of their condo. The usual traffic and noises of the city seemed muted, as if the world was more distant now. She looked at the figure lounging below. Where Jeremy saw Muzania as a woman in a severe business suit, Yukari now saw a nine-tailed fox the size of a man seated on the sidewalk. The fox didn't deign to notice her until she walked in front of it.

"*Shitsurei itashimasu, Kami-dono. Kikasete-itadakeru to ureshii no desu ga.*"

"Japanese, really?" the fox said.

"Why not? I am Japanese after all. Though, after all these years as a *yurei* here, I know and can think in English, I still find Japanese more natural."

"What do you want?" the fox asked, with un-Japanese directness.

Yukari bowed. *Kitsune*, fox spirits, were often dangerous, especially to women. She must tread carefully. "I am concerned and have questions. This Bob that struck Jeremy, he is powerful, *ne?*"

The fox spirit glanced at her sidewise out of its golden eyes. "Why should I speak to you?"

"You disapprove of me?"

"You're an abomination. You should have died and left space-time."

"Yet, I was allowed to stay."

"I cannot fathom why."

"Perhaps it was to help Jeremy."

"That is my task."

"Perhaps he needs additional help."

The fox blew air out its nose. "The fool rejects my help. He has never met a rule he could follow."

"He has done much good and will do more, but now is a difficult time for him."

"And you think you can take my place?"

"*Kami-dono*, I do not seek anyone's place, but there is nothing that I will not do to help Jeremy."

"*Ara, ara,* don't you fall in love easily."

Yukari shifted slightly, and the red in her eyes glowed like banked coals. "Oniichan is not that to me. I will not say that he never will be, but he is not that now."

The fox looked directly at her. "Then why? What is he to you?"

Yukari gazed steadily into the golden eyes. "When I died, I was little mourned. In my day, when a man was excited by a woman, the woman was often blamed. My father was falsely accused of what was done to me, but that false accusation stained both our souls.

"Jeremy was deeply moved by what happened to me. Then he had to strike me down to save the innocent. No blame attaches to him; I had no power to stop my dark half from murder. But when he struck me, I felt his grief, his pain. It was a raging torrent that almost washed him away. He mourned my death as no other had. Even my return did not end that grief, for though he struck me down, it was not he who returned me to life. That is what he is to me."

The fox turned away. "You said you had other questions. Ask."

"Without the sword, or you, Jeremy faces the darkness with only Miss Melons for an ally—"

"Miss Melons?" the fox spirits ears pricked up. "Oh, the vampire, Boobzilla."

"I cannot leave the task of helping Jeremy entirely to her. She does not strike me as...reliable. So, I must know, *Kami-dono*, do I still have any of the power of a *yurei*?"

"Can you not tell?"

She shook her head. "No. I search inside but...as best I can put it into words, it is like trying to recapture a dream upon waking."

The yellow eyes that turned back on her were unfriendly, but she did not flinch. "None who return from the valley of death are ever completely human again. Abomination, I called you and this is why. You are neither one thing nor the other, not a live human, and yet not a dead one."

Yukari gazed steadily back at the fox and did not move.

Finally, grudgingly, it spoke. "I cannot fully see you, as you are not a mere human. The powers you had as a *yurei* are powers from death. But death is neither wholly of the light or the dark. It is the gate of space-time and both sides battle over its definition. The greatest power of evil is how it has cloaked the gate in terror. But I can see far enough into the darkness to see that you have power. Your eyes glow with the light of it. More I will not say."

"*Domo arigato gozaimasu, Kami-dono,*" Yukari said with a deep graceful bow that the fox affected not to notice. "I am grateful to know that I may be of use to Oniichan."

"It would be better for you to persuade him to return to the path of righteousness."

"*Gomenasai, Kami-dono* but it is not for me to persuade Oniichan to any path but his own."

The fox turned its face away from her.

"*Dewa kore de shitsurei itashimasu.*" Yukari thanked the Kitsune, bowed, and then returned to the stairs, leaving the fox to its vigil. But she did not care about that, and her step was light.

I have power, she thought. *I can save Oniichan. I am not useless.*

CHAPTER TWENTY-SIX

Cuban military forces appear to have been in combat with an unknown force. While the Cuban government has refused official comment, State Dept Officials deny a "Bay of Pigs" scenario...

In the morning, Jeremy found that a hot bath was waiting for him along with a Yukari who would not take no for an answer. It was Saturday, so he wasn't needed anywhere and succumbed to the bath.

"You have no proper *onsens* here," she said. "Even your tubs can overflow. Well, it is the best we can do." She handed him a towel and shooed him toward the bath. Afterward, they sat on the back deck, he had a croissant and coffee, she had rice with an egg. The weather was mild, the sun bright, so he wore only a t-shirt and jeans. She wore the same with a light sweater. The problems of last night hovered nearby but were pushed away by the sun and moment. They did not speak, enjoying a comfortable silence. It could not last, he knew, but even an hour's peace was valuable to him.

He glanced at Yukari from under his sunglasses, puzzled. She seemed well-satisfied with herself and projected a new degree of confidence. Yukari was by nature, cheerful and bright, one of the things that he prized about her.

"*Nani?*" she asked with a little smile.

"Oh, nothing," he said. "Well, it's just that you're different somehow. I don't know, more grownup, perhaps."

She smiled enigmatically. "Perhaps. Maybe I am merely pleased that it is a quiet morning that we have together."

He nodded and settled back in his chair, determined to enjoy both the quiet and company for as long as he could.

The quiet lasted all morning. He saw no sign of Muzania and did not venture out of the house. It was a lazy day, he felt as if he were floating, caught between one existence and another, waiting for something to put him in motion and incapable of volition on his own. He wondered if this was what the Japanese meant by the floating world. If all of time could be frozen into this sunny quiet day, he would accept that.

They watched an old Bogart movie and spent the day in idle conversation. His only activity was to get his car into the garage before it got ticketed. Toward evening, his phone buzzed. Only Sam and his closest acquaintances had the number to what he referred to as his "bat phone." Business calls came in over his computer, or another iPhone that he'd turned off today. They both stared at it for a few seconds before Jeremy moved to answer it, knowing from the special ring that it was Debbie. The vampire rarely called just to chitchat. It wasn't in the character for a creature that had to live a solitary existence.

He picked up the phone. "Hey."

"Jeremy, honey," Debbie said most traces of her Southern accent gone. "You and I need to have a serious talk and we need to have it now. Meet me at Halston at CPCC; it may be safer than some places."

"What's this about?" he demanded.

"When we meet. There are too many ways to listen in on cell phones." She hung up.

"What is wrong?" Yukari asked.

"I don't know," Jeremy replied, "but it sounds like I need to find out."

"I understand. I plan to practice meditation tonight."

"Meditation?"

"Yes, I feel this desire to look inside myself."

"Likely all you will see will be a bit of cake, or a cookie," he teased.

She stuck out her tongue then walked up to him. "You will come right back after you see Debbie-san?"

"Probably, I don't know what she has found. She sounded pretty spooked."

"Hmmm," she said with a definite undertone of disapproval.

"My plan is to come right back."

"I think you should stick to the plan and at all costs avoid wardrobes, closets, and other enclosed spaces with Miss Melons."

While her tone was light, he was in no doubt that she was serious. He smiled at her, but when she didn't return it, he raised a hand. "When next you see me, there will be no bite marks or other scratches."

"I shall inspect the returned goods," she replied, raising an eyebrow.

"Well, not everywhere surely," he laughed, surprised to find himself blushing.

"I guarantee nothing," Yukari said, folding her arms.

Armed with his promise to retain his chastity, a bemused Jeremy made his way to his Mini, raised the garage door, and backed out. He caught a glimpse of blond hair, but when his head snapped around, there was nothing to be seen. It darkened his mood to think that Muzania might still be in the area, and he wondered if it was safe to leave Yukari here with the angel lurking about. Still, she hadn't shown any interest in or hostility to Yukari. His reaction to her one threat had made clear what would follow any harm to Yukari.

He sighed. Debbie was not the nervous sort, and she wanted his help. He put the car in gear and backed out.

. . .

Yukari watched from the kitchen window over the back deck. When Jeremy's car pulled out and sped up the alley, she returned to the main room and the *kotatsu* he'd bought her to remind her of home. She sat beside the low, wide table with its skirt designed to keep the heat under it and composed herself. Her father had practiced meditation, it wasn't something often taught to girls in her day, but she had watched him, listened to him talk to others about it, while she, the dutiful daughter, served tea and waited on his company.

It seemed so strange now. She lived with a Western man, who not only did not expect her to wait silently on him, but would often try, sometimes ineptly, to wait on her. He sought out her opinions, consulted her wishes. In her day, no man would have been interested in the opinion of a teen female; for that matter, the opinion of a grown woman was of little more account. The word for wife in Japanese could also be translated as "the woman at the back of the house."

Sometimes she found all the newfound freedoms and expectations overwhelming. Jeremy saw himself as her protector, not an unusual role and one she had seen played often enough in *Noh* dramas. But unlike those heroes, Jeremy relied much more readily on females. Samantha was clearly a friend and a fully human one, but Jeremy had told her of Sam's battling beside him against evil things. Apparently, she was good with a very large gun that had been her father's legacy to her.

Then there was Miss Melons. The vampire had great physical strength and other abilities. But she was as much a part of the darkness as many of Jeremy's enemies.

Well, she thought, *I was one of those enemies for a bit, or part of me was. But now he is precious to me. The vampire is an ally, but she remains a vampire and her essential nature is not to be trusted. He must have someone powerful and loyal. I am that person.*

She gazed into herself and tried to settle her wa. *I must reconnect with my yurei self, with my powers. The kitsune said that my powers were not from darkness, though they were from death. If I can reach those powers, perhaps I can become stronger.*

Yukari's breathing slowed, and she dove into her soul.

CHAPTER TWENTY-SEVEN

Charlotte Observer: Pastor Ronald Inkfest unexpectedly retired from the Heights Mega Church after conducting a "going out of business" sale and distributing church funds to the poor. Church leaders denounced the largesse as a "socialistic and liberal misadventure."

A worried Jeremy pulled to the curb and got out of the car, checking carefully in all directions with his newfound caution. Debbie had asked to meet him at Central Piedmont Community College, a well-lit and well-patrolled area. He avoided the parking deck, having developed a healthy dislike for such structures. So, he parked in an open lot and headed for the steps of the Halston Auditorium, where *Little Shop of Horrors* was being presented. Debbie stood in plain sight. She wore a blouse and slacks and ignored the theater-goers, casting sidelong glances at her figure, or perhaps wondering how she was dealing with the abnormal chill.

He trotted up the stairs to where she stood behind the column and under the overhang of a huge Romanesque façade of the theatre. She was looking up at the last rags of fading light reflecting from the clouds to the west.

"No danger?" he asked, hooking a thumb at the banners of color of the sunset.

She glanced at him. "Nope. It tingles some, but I kinda like it. Old Sun and I wink at each other sometimes. We just can't see eye to eye."

"I'm here," he offered.

She stared up at him as if at an unfamiliar person, and in truth she looked different too, somehow older and diminished.

"Let's find a more private spot." She gestured with her head, and they went around the side into an alley behind Halston.

"We have trouble, Jeremy, right here in River City," she began.

"What do you mean?"

"The world has been out of joint for a while. I know that you've been involved in your own little world, but the larger one has been going to hell for months now."

"I know that I haven't been attending my duties—"

"It's not that. The world, Jeremy, the real one beyond the city limits. Wars, rumors of wars, enough strange things to make one think we are living in the End Times."

"Do you actually believe in that?"

"Not as the church has it. No, before last night I would have said that I didn't believe that God is going to ring down the curtain on space-time soon, or probably ever."

"What's changed?"

"I met something, something powerful enough to put a ship in the middle of the desert or cause a river to run backward."

He stared at her in surprise.

"An angel," she continued. "Not one of your sissy-ass guardian angels. This is one of the originals, a worker on space-time itself. One that turned its back on its maker and cast off to make its own way across creation."

"What?" he said, numb with shock. "But, how? Even Shadowheart could only use her powers within strict guidelines. We were taught that the Celestial Realm could not penetrate the Realm of Earth without falling under the rules of time, matter, and energy."

"Time to revise the textbooks then. This is an angel of origin and perhaps the rules of space-time don't apply to something that wrote them. Maybe something is broke somewhere. All I know is that this thing is here. It's been on Earth for a while, and its presence has been disrupting causality. I don't think it's been intentional. I suspect it's just a side effect of the thing it doesn't follow rules and it disrupts merely by its presence. It's an Angel of Chaos."

"What is it doing here?"

"I didn't interrogate the damn thing!"

"Calm down, we have to think."

"Point is that thinking and logic may not be relevant to this thing. I don't know if it was attracted here or is just passing through, but Jeremy, a couple of huge things on the magic scale have hit the register here."

"Yukari," he whispered.

"Maybe. A human returning from death. Yeah, it could call down cosmic attention. She would be the third I have heard of, and honestly, I don't know if Lazarus and Jesus are just stories or not."

"Me neither," he said. "It's all so unreliable. I carry a stone that supposedly touched the Blood, taken away by Joseph of Arimathea. It has power I know, but it comes from so far back in the mists of time, who can say? These are all just stories repeated and handed down. I myself met Hel, a Norse god. What path leads to the truth?"

"I know. I'm a vampire, met demons and worse, but as you have always said, the real players, the real powers have always been off stage. Maybe they are one step closer to what created the universe, but we have only their word for it.

"So, we have a Templar who has split from his angel and refused the great sword," she continued. "We had a ghost, the rarest of all supernatural phenomena, and then there is the reincarnated Yukari, risen literally from the dead. Perhaps it created some sort of vortex that has drawn this thing here. But it's here. I don't think it's a coincidence. And I don't think it's going to leave on its own."

"What are we going to do about it?" Jeremy asked.

She turned and faced him squarely. "We? Have you been hearing me?"

He looked at the vampire-her eyes glimmered in the low light, which with her was a deliberate act. Leaning back against the wall, he drew a deep breath. "I'm listening, Debbie."

"I like you, a lot, yeah, an awful lot. You know that."

"Yes, I do. You've been with me through thick and thin blood."

"And in some tight places," she returned with a half-smile.

"In another one now."

"One that is partly of your own making," she said, in no friendly tone.

"What?"

"You heard me. And you heard Bob in the garage. You were somebody—you had an angel and a magic sword, and nobody considered messing with you if there was somewhere else to be, or some easier place to do it. Now, what are you? What do you have?"

He gave a weak smile. "I thought I had you."

"Are you a god-damned fool, boy?" she demanded, as angry as he'd ever seen her. "I'm the undead: a vampire, the ultimate in selfish. Sure, I've changed some by an act of self-will, but that's my basic nature, and the adventures we've shared have been in our mutual interest. Now, you're looking to me take your side in a battle with something impossible ancient and powerful. Something by its very angelic nature strikes sheer effing terror into me and anything like me. Just as in my bad old days I would have struck terror in the last seconds of my victim's lives.

"And you, you damn fool, have disarmed yourself of your two most powerful weapons just when you need them most!"

"You haven't met the new angel."

"New angel? Hell, I don't want to meet any more damn angels," she replied, a touch of sullenness in her tone.

"This one is a beast, a heartless monster. She's called Muzania, which is too pretty a name for what looks like a corporate shark with a face that could spoil milk. She's nothing like Shadowheart. I can't work with that."

"Can't or won't?"

"May not be a difference there."

"Honey, you have to listen. I want to help you, but I'm only going to back a losing horse so far."

"What's that supposed to mean?"

"What it means is that I am soulless and ungrateful. I may exist for a thousand years if I don't push my luck. That's a lot of days to hazard for a standup fight when my other option is run like hell."

He stared at her.

"Dammit," she said, "don't look at me like I took away your Christmas puppy. You knew what I was when we first met. You knew every time you banged me in some fit of guilt, lust, or whatever. We're something more than friends, maybe even something like lovers, but I ain't no champion of justice. I'm just saying you can't expect me to hang long in this fight with you handicapping us to death."

They stared at each other, hot and angry as never before. Him feeling betrayed, and her angry and surprised that she could still feel guilt. But it was Debbie who turned away first. She walked over to the railing, staring down at the theater crowd, and she just felt old.

Jeremy fought the urge to tell her to go to Hell, knowing there was too much truth in what she was saying. "You were there...you saw what I did what that damned sword."

"I did and, honey, that is the damned point. YOU did it. The sword was just a tool. Putting the blame on a hunk of metal is just stupid and cowardly. You did what you did, and there was a reason for it. Time for you to man up and stop being a boy; even if you are a damn cute one. You need that sword."

Now it was his turn to turn away. "How much longer can I count on you?"

"Until I feel the need to run away," she said quietly. "For old time's sake, I'll hang for a while longer, but Jeremy-love, this old vampire is as scared as she has ever been. We're punching well over our weight here, unless...unless your little Japanese ghost girl is much more than she seems. She was a ghost—the rarest, most powerful, and unpredictable thing in the supernatural world."

"She's a kid, just a teen girl."

"No, honey, she ain't. She's playing seventeen because she understudied, but never got the chance to play the role and she's loving it. Loving it and loving you too, her Oniichan. But she's been dead four times as long as she was alive, and when she was dead, I wasn't near a match for her. She could have destroyed me; she didn't see the need because I wasn't really a threat."

"You think a revived Yukari can do anything against the Chaos Angel?" he asked, aghast.

"I don't know what she can do, and I expect that she doesn't either, but if she can access any of her former power, she may be the strongest of us all."

"Debbie, I swear this, as far as I know, she's just a seventeen-year-old whose eyes occasionally glow. I have seen no other indication of power. I won't put her in danger."

"You may not have that choice. This town is in trouble, and unless you are going to take her and run, we may not have a chance. The only promise I want from you, Jeremy is, if you are going to run, let me know. I don't plan of being in the rear guard."

He stared. "I would never leave you behind."

Debbie sighed all the way down to the place where her soul had been. "Yeah, I suppose you wouldn't and that's the difference between us. You still care. You still have these illusions about good and evil, about doing the right thing, and I'm too much of a coward to try holding on to those. They slipped my fingers a long time ago."

"Whatever you are, Debbie, coward isn't it."

"Ah, you do know how to sweet-talk a girl. You always have." She leaned forward, pulled him to her and kissed him hard, then she spun him around and slapped him on the butt. "Now get you home. Your little geisha is waiting for you. Just think about everything that was said here."

"I will."

"Good night. I'm bound for one of my safe havens to get underground before the Big Yellow shows up. Call me after sunset tomorrow." With that, she slipped away quickly, leaving him alone with his thoughts.

CHAPTER TWENTY-EIGHT

The former Attorney General of the United States shot himself on TV today after apologizing for his sins. He claimed to have been judged by an angel.

Jeremy returned to his condo to find Yukari asleep, or at least with her door closed. He sat on the couch and pondered everything that Debbie had said and that had passed in recent months. Thinking brought him no closer to understanding, and at some point, he drifted into sleep.

When he awoke with a start, it was to find himself under a blanket with his shoes off. The sun was beaming in through the curtains. He remembered it was Sunday, so a sleep-in was not a problem. He sat up feeling oddly light and looked around. Yukari was on the deck. He watched her through the slats of the curtain; she was tending their outdoor garden. The smell of tea and food reached him. She was probably waiting breakfast on him.

He stood, putting the blanket aside. A compulsion settled on him, a desire to move out of reactive mode he'd been forced into. The door to Yukari's room was open; everything inside was perfectly made up in Yukari-fashion, dirt and disorder feared her name. The thought lightened his mood further, giving him the strength to face what he had avoided for months.

Jeremy walked into her room and knelt beside Yukari's bed, took a deep breath, and reached under to pull out a long plastic box. He set aside the top and stared down at the Templar bloodsword. With her usual Japanese fastidiousness, she had wrapped the sword in a length of fabric. He unwrapped it and drew out the cold steel blade with its baleful gem. He had no power to destroy the weapon, or otherwise rid himself of it, but he had hoped never to set a hand to again.

Not knowing better, the girl had stored the weapon in its leather sheath. He could see rust on the blade. He laid it on the floor. The weapon was a standard Templar sword, similar to the type that Hugh had borne on the walls of Acre, or Bernard had fought his way into Jerusalem with. Its simple design came from a time when men warred with blades and was a testament to military efficiency. Forty inches of double-edged cold steel over a hand and a half of wire-wrapped leather hilt.

But there was an essential difference to this weapon that took it out of the realms of knight of old and into high magic. A stone sat in the pommel, appearing like an immense ruby wrapped in metal. Merely a gem now, it glowed with fire when his heart and the sword's power were aligned. This had not happened since he struck Yukari with it, even looking at the blade made him feel sick. He had always had an uneasy alliance with the sword, sometimes doubting the purpose for which the two of them had been joined. More than that, he doubted that the gem had been touched by the blood of a carpenter two thousand years ago.

Who was that man, he wondered, *a mere carpenter with delusions that he could make the world a less brutal place? Was he just a magical being of some sort, or most absurdly could he have been some fragment of something that had created space-time? Will I never have any certainty about what I am doing and for whom? I have met beings who call themselves angels and demons and yet still I have doubts. I fight in the war for men's souls and yet doubt the existence of my own. I have stood on the floor of Hell yet doubt there is a Heaven.*

I am again at that crisis of faith and worse off than before. The vision of Yukari's shocked face as the sword cut through her came to him. He heard her anguished cry, *Doshte,* as if it was happening again. His breath came fast and shallow and sweat ran down his back.

If only Shadowheart was here, he thought. His relationship with the angel had been far stronger than his relationship with the sword. He was hard-pressed to say what lay between them. From the beginning, they had fought, quarreled, and debated, his eternal questioning, his doubts. Yet, he had never doubted that Shadowheart would stand by him. There had been an affinity between them that could not be denied.

With Muzania, he'd felt an immediate revulsion, and that had not improved on further exposure, hate at first sight.

Is it Muzania's fault, he wondered? *Haven't I broken every rule of a monastic order of warrior monks? They'd have killed me back in the old days for a heretic.* Only the fact that, for reasons no human knew, an angel had settled on him as a partner, had saved him from expulsion. Yet, for all his questions, for all his lack of faith, he had routed great evils. Jeremy counted his victories more in lives saved than in demons or other minions destroyed. Now something that was powerful, but defying definitions of good or evil menaced his world.

"What do I do?" he asked looking down at the lifeless blade. "I'm asking this time. Asking for a sign. Asking for direction, for some certainty for once in my life."

Silence lay heavy and dense across the room. There was no answer, no revelation; God would not speak to him.

"No flower's petals fall but that God notices," he said, mouth twisting into a bitter smile, "but you have no time and no truth to share with me. Perhaps I am less than the petals of a flower to you after all."

"Jeremy," Yukari's voice came through the door. "Are you alright?" Her quick footsteps sounded behind him. The idea of him, the sword and Yukari all together was suddenly too much. He dropped the sword back into the plastic box and spurned it with his foot back under the bed. As he wobbled to his feet, he drew a hand across his face. "Yes, of course, come on in."

The door swung open slowly and Yukari slipped in, beautiful and slender in a modest skirt and blouse. A patterned scarf was about her neck, and her hair flowed over her shoulders. Her face held its usual serene expression, so unusual for her apparent age. From somewhere, he managed to pull out a smile for her.

She stood next to him, her hands resting on her skirt. "Jeremy, why did the vampire call? There is some terrible danger, isn't there?"

The planned reassurance evaporated as he stared into her faintly glowing red eyes.

"Oniichan," she scolded, "only the truth between us. Remember that I am not a child."

He sighed. "Yes Yukari, only the truth between us, ever. You're right. We are in trouble. The whole city, maybe the whole world, is in danger."

In a few minutes, he relayed the story Debbie had told him the night before. She listened intent but calm.

"The Chaos Angel is an enemy beyond anything that has ever been faced in the Realm of Earth. At my best, and I am so far from that right now, I might have mattered very little in such a contest.

"Now, as I am, all I feel is helpless. Debbie Middleton may flee at any moment. Shadowheart is gone. No other ally can be reached. Even Bob doesn't have enough firepower to handle this. Hell, I think he's looking to me for help. He wanted me to take up the sword again and maybe even the angel."

"Jeremy-kun," she said, in her delicate voice. "You are not alone. For so long as I exist, you will never face anything alone."

Now the smile on his face was genuine though sad. "Again, that is supposed to be my line to you."

"Jeremy, I am not a little girl for all my appearance. I love that you treat me as such, but I was a *yurei* for decades, the most powerful of all human-originated supernatural manifestations."

"But—"

"I did not return as a human, Jeremy. I am something more, I returned with powers."

"What do you mean, Yukari? What powers?"

"I do not know for certain as I have not tested them. I have enjoyed playing a teenager too much. But I am certain that I have some of the powers of the Dark Yukari. She is, after all, the real me—"

"You," he insisted, "are the real you. She was your anger; you are more."

She laid a hand on his arm.

"I still feel this is an enemy beyond me."

"As you are now," she agreed, startling him.

They stared at each other for a few seconds. Then she turned knelt and pulled the box with the sword out. She lifted the unsheathed sword out, her lips tightly compressed, and held it out to him.

"You must take up the sword again," Yukari said.

"Yukari," he whispered, "I can't take the sword from you."

"No, Jeremy-kun. I am the only one you *can* take the sword from."

The images flashed in his eyes, the blade cutting through her. He heard the anguished, cry as she dissolved into rags in the wind and his guts clenched.

"Had you destroyed me," she said, "I would still have been grateful. If you hadn't acted, Hell would surely have embraced me after I burned the Hara family alive. But you did not destroy me, and I believe that is because you had such sympathy and feeling for me from the instant we met, that it drew me back from death.

"As I told you when you took me up in your arms, you did not fail me then. There is no reason for you to feel—"

"Your face...when I...when I struck..."

She held out the naked sword. "For me, for all who need your help, take up the sword."

He stared down at the weapon, his face white and tense, then he lifted it from her hands.

"Blade's tarnished," he said.

She put her hands around his.

"There's more, isn't there?"

"There is," she said. "You must make enough peace with Muzania to gain her aid. I know that she only reminds you of the one who is gone, but she is a power. We need her to survive, to be able to live our lives together."

Jeremy felt a flash of warmth and a little surprise at her choice of words. Perhaps she was surprised as well, as a blush shaded her cheeks.

"Thank you," he said. "I feel like I have been wandering in darkness for a long time and you are the light by the door."

She laid her head against his shoulder, the scent of her hair sweet and warm. They stood that way for a while.

"Yukari," he finally said, "would you wait here, please."

"I will go make some tea," she said. "It will be ready when you come back in."

He picked up the scabbard and left with the sword. It needed maintenance but that would come later. Down the stairs, he sheathed the sword at the bottom, then went out the front door. The cool of the approaching summer thunderstorm was welcome, clearing the last cobwebs from his brain. Cars whipped by, but as usual there were few pedestrians out. He reversed his grip on the sword so it was behind his left shoulder and not visible to the casual observer.

Muzania stood at the foot of his stairs, whether others could see her, or she had just popped into existence he had no way to know. She wore the usual dark-gray business suit and turned her perpetually sour face toward him. He thought he saw a flicker of something, surprise or relief, when her sharp eyes picked up the sword over his left shoulder. He paused a few steps away from her.

"That sword has seen better days and better hands," she began in her flinty voice.

He stared at her for as long as ten seconds, then, "I don't like you either, harridan. You and I are not now or ever going to be a team of anything."

Her face hardened, and she gave a short, sharp shrug.

"Winston Churchill," Jeremy said, "observed that the only thing worse than having allies, was not having them. This world faces a menace, something from your world."

"Not mine," she said, looking away. "It's outside of all the fucking laws."

"I'm willing to work with you," he replied, "to protect the realm of Earth."

"You are only interested in your whore friend and that," Muzania noticeably paused a second before saying, "ghost girl."

"Does it matter?"

"So now I, who date from the beginning of this crapfest, need to take note of whims of a human, a matchstick that burns for a moment before being extinguished."

"Seems like pride has gone before the fall of angels again," he said.

Her eyes blazed and Jeremy snapped the sword, still sheathed, out from behind him wondering if his battle with the supernatural would explode on his doorstep.

"You know nothing," she hissed.

"Or did my shot in the dark, hit home, Muzania?" he replied evenly. "Can it be that you once followed a prideful angel, supported him, but bowed, perhaps reluctantly, to orders before it was too late to turn back?"

The fire in the angel's eyes subsided, but she said nothing.

"So, what is it to be, angel?" he asked, as he slowly put the sword back behind his shoulder. "Do we put aside our personal antipathy and cooperate for the greater good? Or do we both fail?"

She turned her back to him and looked up at the thunder clouds beginning to build overhead. "Unlike the Mad One, the agent of Chaos, I am constrained by the Law within the Realm of Earth. Only a small part of my power is in this universe."

"It may make the difference," he said. "We are gathering all of the supernatural powers we can persuade to this fight."

She gave a derisive snort. "What? More of your dubious friends: vampires, demons, and God knows what else?"

"Yes," he said.

She shook her head. "You were right before. We will never like or trust each other."

"Do you ever watch old movies when you're sitting on the clouds up there?"

She simply stared at him.

"Old Charlton Heston film," he continued, "called *Major Dundee*. Two enemies serve in the same force, sworn to a truce until an enemy greater than either was taken or destroyed."

"Very well, then," Muzania replied, her eyes filled with frank dislike, "until the enemy is taken or destroyed, but no longer."

"Good enough," he replied. "Yukari is making tea and we need to make plans. Come into the house. And watch your language."

Muzania followed Jeremy back into his townhouse. They found Yukari waiting just inside the door. She must have been watching from the window.

She greeted the angel with a tranquil expression, seeming less concerned than Jeremy was. There was a mature regard to her gaze, and she did not look like a teenager.

"I see we have a guest," Yukari said with a bow. "I have everything ready."

She gestured at them to follow her into the living room where the kotatsu sat in the middle of the floor and bore a small, dark-blue tea service that he had purchased in their first days together. A pink vase held a sprig of green and some small white flowers that he did not know the name of. A plate of cookies rested next to it. "Please be seated."

Jeremy had noticed that when Yukari was immersed in something of her culture, her Japanese accent strengthened. It was particularly strong just now. He seated himself cross-legged on the floor, sliding his knees under the *kotatsu's* skirt. The heater was set on low and felt good on his legs.

Muzania slid under the opposite side. The angel's perpetually sour face had not changed, but something about her indicated a less bellicose mood. She met no one's eyes and merely glanced at the table, seeming to study the flowers.

Yukari knelt next to the *kotatsu*, midway between them, then placed two small plates with tiny sugar cubes. He remembered that Japanese did not put sugar in tea but in their mouths. Yukari picked up the teapot and carefully poured into the delicate deep-blue cups. Notably, she did not pour for herself.

It's like a peace treaty, he thought. *Yukari's the mediator. We're the enemies.*

He picked up a cube of sugar, put it in his mouth, and drank the tea. Opposite him, Muzania did the same. But still the atmosphere was not right to speak. Yukari refilled the cups twice more before the atmosphere lightened appreciable.

"I would have preferred sake," Muzania finally ventured.

Jeremy gave a tiny breath out, and Muzania ducked her head as if to conceal a smile. The tension receded further.

"Can you," he began slowly, "give us any information on our mutual enemy, this, well, we call it the Chaos Angel."

"There is no relevance to its name," Muzania replied with equal care. "The true names of all angels are very long in human terms. The short ones we use with humans are a mere convenience. Chaos Angel will do as well as any other.

"I can give you little information that you would find relevant. The Chaos Angel is ancient, even by the standards of angels. It was one of the originals, created before space-time to bring space-time itself into being. You have no reference for that frame of time and indeed the entire concept of time is irrelevant to the Chaos Angel, as it among those that created time. I exist as a conscious being only in one Realm at a time and am reduced by penetrating into the Realm of Earth, but not all of what I am, is here. You might think of the rest of me as being in storage. It was the same for Shadowheart. This Chaos Angel exists in many Realms at once. Not all of it would fit it into the Realm of Earth; indeed, parts of it could never do so, as they have no analog in space-time. Much of what it appears to be doing is only your sensory interpretation of its effect on space-time. Merely by passing through it, this angel twists the warp and weft of the fabric of the universe as, in one sense, the universe seeks to expel something that cannot and should not exist here."

"Then why does it?"

Muzania's mouth gave a bitter twist, "That I cannot say. It is a 'higher matter' beyond what I am allowed to know, or even ask. In that regard an angel is not different from a human in knowing the mind of that which created all. All angels are not created equal. We have our functions, rank, and our charges. If I could ask, or know that answer, there is no likelihood that I would be allowed to tell it to you, or that you would have the capacity to understand it if I did.

"The best piece of information that I can give you is that, in some respects, it may be even more confined than I am because I was made to enter space-time, even if in a vastly reduced existence, and it was not. The universe corrupts around it and then tries to heal itself by expelling it. It is vastly powerful in some temporal respects and limited in others."

Jeremy contemplated the entity, if that was even the right word for it. It was terrifying.

"So," he said, "if it is here, it loosely conforms to the laws of physics. At least for the part of it that is here. We don't have to fight, if that is what it comes to, all of it. Just that part that has reached Earth. It will be made of matter—"

"Yes," Muzania said, narrow-eyed, "but that matter is strengthened by a will that can bend your physics, possibly destroy them. If it comes to battle, we can only try and overload the corporeal matter that holds it together to form a presence here."

"Can we reason with it?" he asked.

"Even I cannot say what it will find reasonable, or whether that concept itself has any meaning to it."

"One cannot help but express dismay at how poorly the Heavens govern things," he said tightly.

Muzania's eyes flared. "Who are you to say?"

"The one who may have to fight a monster from beyond time," he shot back.

Yukari raised the teapot and refilled their cups in a silent rebuke.

"Can you find it?" he asked, forcing himself to calmness.

"Not it," Muzania said, ignoring the tea, "some of its effects and only then if it doesn't choose to conceal itself. It will be something like mediation and may take considerable time."

He tried to keep the thought that her leaving would be a pleasure from his face. "Then perhaps we should leave that task to you. I will see what can be done in the human world—if it is indeed coming here and if it wants something from us."

"Do not pick up the housing," Muzania said, pointing at the golden pendant in its place of honor in its étagère. "I am not Shadowheart, and that link will not work for us." She reached into her pocket and cast a cross on the table; it rang with an odd sound as it hit the table-top. "Hold that and invoke my name if you must summon me before I return on my own."

He looked at the cross but did not pick it up, confined himself to a nod.

Muzania was simply not there the next moment.

Yukari sighed for the lack of manners and reached across and picked up the abandoned cup. She sipped it. "The tea is good, *ne?*"

"It is, as is everything else you make," he replied, drinking his. "I appreciate all you do."

"Ah." She smiled. "Such appreciation makes it all light work."

CHAPTER TWENTY-NINE

Snow unexpectedly struck Atlanta today—the first such event in recorded history in summer.

J eremy waited in the shadows outside of a massage parlor in the Dilworth neighborhood. It was bright afternoon, the least favorite time of all things of evil and darkness. He expected Bob would exit under the shady canopy in the back over what was nearly a sunken lane. It was safe from prying eyes or so he hoped.

Bob, dressed in a tracksuit, opened the door. "Hey, babe, great time. I'll see you next week?"

The demon let the door close and walked right into Jeremy's straight right. His head snapped back. Jeremy's foot caught him in the middle of his gut. It jarred Jeremy and knocked Bob back a step. Before the demon could recover, he whipped out the bloodsword and held its point at Bob's breast.

The demon rubbed his chin, more surprised than injured by either blow. He looked at the sword, then at Jeremy.

"That's for the old man that died," he growled at the demon.

"Okay," Bob said, eyeing the sword. "Collateral damage and necessary, but I can appreciate that you find that a bit tough to swallow."

"What are you on about?" Jeremy growled.

"You're really not all that bright," Bob said with a world-weary tone. "I'm on your side, idiot."

Jeremy barked a laugh. "Oh Bob, please. You're embarrassing yourself. You can come up with something better than that."

The demon held his eye. "Think about it, Templar. When you had the bloodsword and the angel, the town ran well. Bad guys avoided Charlotte and the area around it after you put down most of the local mad, bad, and dangerous to know.

"Me, I ran things, but I kept them from being meaty and bloody. You found it convenient to leave me alone. We even cooperated on mutual threats. Plenty of purple-people eaters out there for you to clip, why bother with a guy whose evil is mostly financial? Fuck, I'm no more evil than the prick you idiots elected president in 2016, maybe not as bad."

"My side is happy to get some use out of a place with a Templar in it. Your side is happy Evil Inc isn't collecting lives and souls out of here.

"Then you—you get yourself and your guardian angel all up in Hell's grill and almost bring on the Apocalypse. She gets recalled to Heavenly carpet. Next you get yourself so fucked up with guilt over this Yukari that you put down the bloodsword!

"You think that was a great victory for Evil Inc? Well, not so much for my part of it. All of a sudden, it's not so dangerous for the mad, bad, and dangerous. They know they can come back to Charlotte because our Templar...ain't."

"Yeah," Jeremy replied. "I remember how vividly you pointed that out to me in the garage."

"What are you, delicate? Okay, I knocked you around some. I was trying to get your head out of your asshole. I told you that you weren't anybody without the angel and the sword and that you needed to walk small or pick up the damn sword. And if you walked small, kid, you weren't going to walk for long."

"I remember," Jeremy said, tight-lipped but his anger was beginning to fade. The demon was making too much sense.

"So here we are kid. You went off the reservation and the bad guys started coming. I have been blocking and tackling for a while—"

"You're a regular humanitarian—"

"Can it, dick. I'm not the one who went AWOL."

Jeremy felt a stab of irritation but controlled the twitch in his hand.

"I don't care about humans any more than it is profitable for me do. But I like the good life. That means fine wine, good food, opera, museums, and I don't cook, sing, or stomp my own grapes."

The pair stared at each other as the seconds ticked on. "So do we get out of here, have an espresso like gentlemen, or what?" Bob demanded.

Jeremy slowly backed up and slid the sword back into its sheath in his coat. Bob rubbed his jaw, glared at Jeremy then snorted a laugh. Jeremy then slid out of the coat; it was too warm for even light leather.

"Say I believe you," Jeremy said. "What now?"

"You have the bloodsword," Bob said. "Do you have, and it hurts my mouth to say it, the angel?"

Jeremy grimaced. "Shadowheart hasn't returned. Worse yet, they have sent a replacement, a miserable hag named Muzania."

"Yeah, I heard something about her. A bundle of joy by anybody's standard."

"You don't know the half of it," he growled. "She's kind-of a cross between a female warden and a psychopathic nun. There is no bond between us as there was between Shadowheart and me."

Bob sighed theatrically. "Still the bitch is an angel, right? She's on the side of Light."

"I'm never sure that means what you'd think."

"Consider mending fences with her for the nonce," Bob said.

"The nonce?" Jeremy said, eyebrows rising.

"Cute, kid, cute. Remember how long I've been around."

"We're not without resources even without the angel," Jeremy added. "You have your... people, and I have Debbie. As for the angel— you probably know better than I how loath they are to meddle in their

Lord and Master's space-time. Even with Shadowheart, aid was minimal unless your side broke some celestial rule."

"Yeah, but this isn't the usual situation. What's moving in our town is an unaffiliated fallen angel, one from the original downfall."

"You know already?"

"Been tracking it across the grid as it moves over the Earth, hoping it didn't come this way. Evil Inc has been suffering more than humanity. Some of the dumber on my side can't control their combative nature or abide the proximity of an angel of any sort. No one has heard from anybody that fucked with the, what did you call it?"

"Chaos Angel," he shrugged.

"Good a name as any," he said.

They looked at each other.

"So," Bob said. "Coffee? And no Starbucks shit."

He nodded slowly.

Bob's eyes narrowed. "Are you back? Really back?"

"Do I have a choice?" he said.

"No more than I do," Bob replied. "Nobody asked me if I wanted to be created evil."

CHAPTER THIRTY

"Odd things happen in a battle, and the human heart has strange and gruesome depths and the human brain still stranger shallows."

With Bob dealt with, and several espressos later, he headed home, driving in early evening traffic, deep in thought. Jeremy felt intact in a way he had not since Shadowheart had been drawn back to the Celestial Realm. The bloodsword rode in its accustomed spot in his duster—though this was the lighter duster made from microfiber, a concession to the season. While he would have traded almost anything to be again paired with Shadowheart—he could at least count on the help of an angelic being, from duty if not out of love. Duty would be enough for them both in this fight. Debbie and even Bob were allies. With Bob came a legion of minions that the demon kept sequestered in and mostly below Charlotte. They were cannon, or rather, angel-fodder, and if they were largely eliminated in what was to come that could only be a good thing. Though, he reflected ruefully Bob would likely be thinking similar thoughts about his side.

This left only one variable on his side, Yukari. Muzania believed the confluence of events that culminated in her resurrection might consciously or unconsciously be attracting the angel to them.

Muzania said this is one of the original beings who worked on space-time itself, for all that it seems to disrupt it while passing through it, he thought. *Maybe that accounts for it, my own intrusion into Hell, the ghost, and the resurrection are surely among the greatest of noncausal events. We may be acting like a whirlpool for it. All interesting but it doesn't help me with how to get rid of it.*

Yukari was wrapped up in noncausality. Does she have the powers she thinks she might?

He frankly did not know what to hope for. Jeremy wanted a normal and peaceful life for her, all the things she had been cheated of by Shoji Hara, who he fervently hoped was burning in some Hell somewhere. But first they had to survive. He doubted that the Chaos Angel's intentions for them were benign and was not in any event going to submit Yukari to its whims. As he pulled up before his building, he wondered how long they had before thing slipped control entirely.

Circumstances didn't wait on Muzania. The Chaos Angel was not long in making its presence felt and that turned out to be Bob's fault. In a rundown section of northwest Charlotte stood a warehouse Bob used. It was a transshipment point for magical devices and supplies and other things that would not be healthy for humans to know of. No humans used the facility or had ever willingly stepped into it.

Bob's security was based around threats from the forces of darkness. During the day, a small detail of goblins sufficed. At night, when the forces of darkness were in their ascendancy, he brought out one of his most powerful of minions. Minotaurs were mountains of hooves, horns, and muscle and mercifully rare. This one was powerful and ancient and even more bad-tempered than usual. With the setting of the sun, it made its way through the tunnels that men and other things had dug beneath the Queen City. The Minotaur had been fed before being released, but the goblins wasted no time in reaching their own separate exit.

The Great Beast strode in, snorting at the warehouse and the scent of goblin. It stared at the walls that confined it, but these were bespelled to keep it within the environs of the building. This was nothing new. The Minotaur had been caged in one structure or another for most of its existence. Lesser spells kept it from damaging, or investigating, the mystical contents of the building, not that this was likely; the beast had a limited intellect based mainly on anger and territoriality.

So, when a beautiful and delicate creature, with barely seen gossamer wings, appeared in the building, the Minotaur did not wonder how it had made its way through the banks of spells that kept the building innocuous and guarded. It bellowed at the chance to exercise its obscene lusts before gorging on the flesh of so helpless a victim. Nor did it wonder why the creature did not flee its onrushing charge, nor scream and why the only expression that drifted across the serene face was one of mere annoyance.

The blast was partly contained by Bob's spells but still leveled everything for a thousand yards in any direction. Casualties were small for the dreadful explosion. Some security guards in nearby structures, a dozen or so homeless, some petty criminals lairing in the area and a few unfortunate drivers who had chanced on the wrong spot at the wrong time.

Charlotte woke up to the flash and the dull building rumble that surpassed any thunderstorm to rattle windows, then doors and finally buildings themselves. Glass sheets in the downtown skyscrapers shivered and split. People tumbled out of beds wondering about terrorists and nuclear attacks. Fireman and policeman raced for vehicles. Politicians wondered what the hell had happened. News people grabbed their equipment, sensing that something huge had struck the Queen City in the biggest story in decades. They had no idea how right they were.

. . .

Like thousands of others, Jeremy and Yukari tumbled out of their beds, raced out of their bedrooms to meet downstairs.

"What was that?" Yukari asked, eyes wide. She had thrown on a kimono before coming down. He fortunately had gotten a robe, remembering at the last second before he opened his bedroom door that she was there.

"I don't know. A plane crash maybe? I haven't felt anything remotely like that since they blew down the Old Hornets Arena."

"Alexa," he called, "WFAE, local news."

They listened for a few minutes but learned nothing. There had been an explosion, authorities were urging calm and police, fire, and medic were enroute to the area.

"Can it be an attack?" Yukari wondered.

"No, not like Pearl Harbor, if that is what you mean," Jeremy said. "Terrorists possibly, or an industrial accident, but no one would launch a conventional attack on the US these days. And if they were going to, I doubt Charlotte would be a significant target. Outside of shopping and chain restaurants there's nothing here."

Jeremy's phone buzzed. He stared at it. The number was another seldom used one, Bob Diablesse's. He picked it up. "Leclerc."

"Yeah, we've had a bit of a problem at our end."

"Let me guess, it involved a huge fucking blast."

"Yep. I just lost a warehouse full of irreplaceable treasures and one of my strongest fighters. Looks like your theory about it being attracted by the volume of magical shit around here was right. I had some good stuff there, things I thought we could use against this Chaos Angel if it comes to a fight. Gone now."

Jeremy, who had not known of the warehouse, felt a wave of chagrin. What else had Bob been hiding in Charlotte while Jeremy kept the rest of the forces of evil at bay?

"What happened?"

"Minotaur was starting his watch when the Chaos Angel appeared in the warehouse. Don't ask me how it got in, but it did. Unfortunately Hoof and Horn was not the brightest of the bright and charged it. Our friend appeared to have an objection to being raped and gored —a big one."

"How do you know all this?"

"Jeez, Leclerc ever heard of CCTV? Not a lot of film footage before everything went white but enough to figure it out. My staff is loading it into a file for you on Dropbox if you want to see it.

"In any event, this thing is here and now. We seem to have woken it out of its daydream stage."

"Yes," Jeremy said. "Whether it was just attracted to the emanations of your warehouse, or if it planned a preemptive strike is irrelevant. It's hit us first and hard. Any idea where it has gone?"

"No. I have all my stations and people on alert. But I suspect that the first we will know is when one of them goes dark. Anything at your end? Does ghosty-girl have a clue?"

He glanced at Yukari, who shook her head, apparently, surprised to be asked.

"I will try and reach Muzania," he said. "Meanwhile keep your head down and try and keep your side from provoking it again, or we may not have a city to protect."

"Got it. Check back in later. And get some sleep, human. I think it will be hard to come by after tonight."

Whether it was a disturbance in the other Realms, or the lack of affinity between Jeremy and Muzania, he did not succeed in reaching the angel despite holding her cross. Too wound up to sleep, Jeremy and Yukari listened to the radio as the tale of the disaster unfolded. He called Debbie, even had the vampire not been a night creature, she would be awake by now.

"Debbie are you okay?"

"Yes, though I was wondering if vamps could live through Atom-bombs."

"Nothing lives through atom-bombs," he replied.

"That's where I came out too."

He filled her in on the warehouse.

"Fuck, fuck, fuck," she responded. "Now what?"

"I don't know," he replied. "Bob's got his forces watching, but he mostly expects them to act as tripwires and die."

"Sounds like Bob."

"I can't reach Muzania."

"That's worrisome."

"She may just be ignoring me because she doesn't know anything more. There is no way to tell. With Shadowheart, I would know if something happened to her. With this…angel, I can't tell you."

"Yukari?"

"Knows nothing," he said with an edge to his voice. "What about you? Are you out and about?"

"Fuck no. I am underground in a hidey-hole I prepared for bad times. The only reason you can reach me is I had an antenna rigged for cell phones. Unless you are coming out with me, I am staying down."

He considered.

"Oniichan," Yukari's voice was very firm. "If you are going out to confront this, I am coming with you."

"Then we are staying in for tonight," Jeremy decided. "I am not through playing defense. Let's see what develops when the sun comes up. Stay in touch."

"Alright baby, but if it comes time to run…"

"I have only violated my sworn word once," Jeremy said, ignoring Yukari's small gasp, "and I will die before doing it again. We won't run without you."

"I believe you, honey. You know that I do, right?"

He struggled to find his voice.

"You know it, right?"

"Yes, I do."

"Okay, check in later."

He leaned back to find Yukari looking anxiously at him. "It's okay."

They listened some more to the reports, but to their mutual surprise, at some point, both fell asleep, with Yukari's head pillowed on his lap. There was some awkward laughing and blushing when they woke to the sun's rays cut through the window.

When the morning dawned, the sky was blood red and remained that way. Electronic communications became intermittent. Traffic control went to hell. Jeremy's business appointments canceled because of the bizarre weather, savage gusts of wind, followed sudden blasts of heat and then bone-chilling cold. Those local TV stations that could get on the air were filled with images of weather reporters pointing at the sky. People headed for shelters and churches, staring warily at the sky. Yukari's year-round school was canceled. Even the terrible blast began to be eclipsed by the news of the strangeness enfolding the city.

Jeremy and Yukari stood on their back deck staring up into the ominous sky.

"It's beginning, isn't it?" she said.

"Yes," he replied, dread making his voice flat. "I don't know if it is part of a deliberate plan, or if it's merely the side effect of its presence. It distorts reality and maybe this is just how our senses interpret the side effects."

"Then it could be worse," she said. "Our senses could interpret it as a storm of fangs and talons."

He gave her a sidelong glance. "Yes, that would be worse."

"But how do we end this?" she said.

He shook his head. "I don't know. If we drive it off, then this effect will just occur elsewhere. Some of the manifestations have been benign, some have been horrible, and all are disruptive. This is a world hovering on the edge of war in so many places. What could this start and where might it end? There is no safe place in the Realm of Earth for such a dangerous being."

"It is not here to battle us," she said, almost as if to herself, "but it was drawn here, in all the world, possibly by you and me."

He nodded reluctantly. "Like a person might be drawn to a sound in a forest. I am afraid that my and Shadowheart's adventures in Hell and perhaps even more so, your return from death are vibrations on the web of this particular spider."

"Then a challenge by us might draw it into battle at a place of our choosing," she said.

"How would it even hear us? Unless it, or we, stumble across each other..."

"It is an angel," Yukari asked. "Perhaps Muzania could reach it."

"Lovely," he replied, but the makings of a plan were beginning to resonate for him. "First, I have to make sure of our allies. I hate to take Samantha with us; she has no supernatural power, but she keeps a level head in a fight, and she may be safer with us than not."

"Nor is it likely," Yukari said, "that she would remain behind unless you tie her up."

While Jeremy made his calls and preparations, Yukari heard her phone buzz. She picked it up, seeing Trice's photo appear on it.

"*Mooshi, mooshi,*" she said.

"Yukari are you alright?" Trice demanded.

"Yes, we are safe here. Are you?"

"For the moment, but it seems like everything is going to hell around here. I'm planning on bugging out. Amy is here with me. We're going to take my bike and head for her parent's place in the mountains. They are already up there from last week."

"Listen to me," Yukari said, quietly but with force. "That is not safe. You would go directly into what is surrounding Charlotte with uncertain results. Stay in town, find a secure place, and remain in hiding. The danger here will be more from other humans and lawlessness."

A long silence followed. "You know," Trice finally said, "something about what is going on. Don't you?"

"Yes," she said, throwing caution to the winds for the sake of her new friends. Jeremy would simply have to accept that she could not do otherwise. "Enough to know that the greater danger is on the road. Shelter in place is what they taught us at school, *ne?*"

She listened to the other girl's frightened breathing for a few seconds. "Who are you, Yukari, really? I've always known there was something different about you."

"I am one who knows," she replied earnestly. "I cannot tell you more now, nor would you be able to believe it if I did. But Trice, you are an important friend to me, as are Amy and Linh. I will not risk harm to any of you. Things are being done to stop what is happening, and I am part of those things. Await outcomes and trust in what I say."

"Are you—?"

"It is not safe for you to be more involved than you are now. It could be that I am a dangerous acquaintance, through no desire of my own. But know that I will not accept your being harmed if it is within my power to stop it. Tell me that you will do what I have asked."

She could hear her talking to Amy and could only wait.

"Okay," Trice said in a calmer tone. "Amy says we should listen to you and, irony of ironies, I am listening to her. She wants to know if we can come to where you are?"

"No," Yukari said with regret. "That is least safe of all. We will be moving and…there may be fighting."

"Fighting…fighting what?"

"I cannot—"

"Tell us. Okay, we get that."

"*Gomen*, I would if I could."

"All right. We are heading for the basement in my apartment then. I have a storage unit down there and we'll bring food, water, and anything else we can find."

"I will call you when it is safe," Yukari said. *If it is ever safe again and if I live to do it.*

"Listen," Trice demanded. "Whatever happens, don't get yourself killed. We will talk again on the other side of this."

"*Hai*," Yukari replied, because she was one of the few humans to know there was another side, her voice carried a ring of conviction.

CHAPTER THIRTY-ONE

"This is WFAE broadcasting as part of the emergency broadcast system. The mayor and city authorities urge calm and that all citizens remain in their homes. Contrary to rumors, martial law has not been declared, but remains a possibility.

"What is presently known is that some form of interference, being called a storm by the authorities, has sealed the City of Charlotte away from all external contact beyond a radius of 15 miles from Center City. There is no radio, television, cell, or other form of communication with the outside world and the circular wall of clouds goes down to ground level. Vehicles and personnel going into the storm cloud, experience disorientation and find themselves back inside the perimeter of Charlotte.

"Authorities have pointed out that there has been no attack, no casualties inside Charlotte that are not due to panic or accidents. All police, fire, National Guard, and military units have been activated, any and all military and emergency personnel transiting Charlotte are ordered to report to the nearest unit of their type..."

J eremy turned off the radio and turned to Yukari. "Looks like we won't be running anywhere."

"No," Yukari said softly. "No running away for us."

"This thing is warping reality. Whether it's part of some plan, or just due to its nature, I don't know, but we are cut off from the rest of the world. For all we know, we may no longer even be on Earth. A city like this cannot last in these conditions. There will be food riots within days. I have no idea how long water and power will last, or even why it's still on."

"That last is hopeful," Yukari said. "It must be that we are connected to the world to some degree, or I cannot imagine that there would be power."

At times like this, Jeremy was reminded that Yukari, for all her youthful appearance was not seventeen. No normal girl her age would likely be so calm. Despite all he had been through, he had to fight a rising sense of dread and panic.

"We must deal with this now and in this place," Yukari said. "Time is not our friend."

"Nor will the authorities be," Jeremy nodded, looking out the window at the mess of traffic and pedestrians milling about outside. "We will not be able to make them understand the nature of this threat. Any rational person will dismiss us as insane until it is too late."

She nodded. "Which means it falls to us. We must gather our forces together shortly after sunset and pick a location for our battle, preferably one where there will be fewer normal humans about."

"Well put." He gave a weak grin. "You would make a fine general."

"Less than you think, for I have no idea what we will do once we gather."

"As for a place," he said, wiping his hand across his face, "I think Bob's HQ downtown will be best. Even now, few people live downtown. That tower of his is partly a fortress, and who knows how far underground it goes. It will be the best defended supernatural location here.

"I'll text Debbie. She won't be able to move until near sunset anyway. I'm glad Sam came in on her own. She was almost here when I called her."

He nodded, drew a deep breath, and drew the cross from his jean pockets, then concentrated on it with all his power. "Muzania."

A moment later the angel appeared, her pinched face marked with its perpetual disapproval.

"We're moving," he said, not letting his relief at her late appearance show. "When in doubt use the basic military principles of mass. We'll make our stand with everyone at Bob's HQ in downtown Charlotte, try and draw it to us there."

"A fucking demon's haunt?" she said, aghast.

"The most defensible place, and Bob has more assets than the rest of us put together."

"You're shitting me," she said.

"I'm dead earnest. Trust me that Bob's side will be as horrified about an angel within their walls as you are. He's almost as fond of rules as you. The Chaos Angel threatens Bob's carefully ordered little universe and his regular deliveries of Cuban cigars. You'll be safe enough."

"Safe?" she scorned. "I fear no damned demon in the Realm of Earth."

"Then, Muzania-dono," Yukari said, entering the room with a bag, "take pity on us lesser beings who need greater protection."

Muzania grimaced but did not look at Yukari; something about the ghost girl always seemed to unsettle the angel. "I will come when you call for me," she said, but her eyes met Jeremy's, "until the enemy is taken or destroyed."

He nodded. "Until then."

She disappeared

"Sam," Jeremy called. "We're moving."

"Okay," she called down. "Give a girl a minute to get her accessories in order. I'm finishing cutting crosses into some ammo." Sam appeared at the base of the stairs a minute later in her usual jeans and a sweater shirt. A .357 S+W was holstered under one arm but came down to her hip and looked like a bazooka on her small frame. She held a field coat in one hand, its pockets probably stuffed with bullets, crosses, and small bottles of holy water.

Jeremy tucked his Walther in the back of his own jeans and picked up the black leather duster with its hidden scabbard for the blood-sword. Yukari put on her jacket and, more practical than most, picked up her overnight bag. He suspected there was a change of clothes for him in it as well.

They slipped out the back of his apartment, ignoring neighbors who were talking on their patio decks or in the alleyway. A few steps had them in his Mini, Sam and the bags in the back, and pulling out into a side street. Fire engines and police sirens clamored in the night, as did the sound of distant shouting.

"Had to get a two-door foreign matchbox," Sam grumbled from the back. "Why don't you buy a nice American car like a Toyota Camry?"

Jeremy grinned as he pulled the nimble Mini into traffic. "I think I'll wait until I get married for one of those." He violated about five traffic laws in the first five hundred yards. Traffic was miserable and the driving in Charlotte verged on terrorism most of the time.

A National Guard convoy of Humvees pulled out, heading for downtown, and Jeremy latched on to the last Humvee's tail. Most of the traffic was heading out of downtown, and everyone yielded to the big, ominous, sand-colored Humvees with their grim soldiers looking out the windows and top hatches.

The convoy got them most of the way before they reached a road-block that admitted the Guard but waved them off.

Jeremy cut right into an underground parking garage.

"We're in luck," he said. "Downtown is a connected by a lot of pedestrian skyways and underground passages. We can make it to the Bank of Stone from here without getting out in the street among the cops and soldiers."

They parked the Mini by a staircase, and unwilling to trust to elevators, made their way upward. From there, they took a small skybridge over Trade Street. Cutting through underground halls, they passed closed shops of every variety before reaching another skybridge. This one took them near the bank, though they first had to skirt a collection of people gathered around one man preaching in overly loud Protestant fervency. Overt religion grated on Jeremy at all times, and he gave a curt response to the entreaty to join them in praying for the end times. Sam, a born-again pagan, simply ignored them. Yukari stopped and apologized on their behalf and pled that an urgent matter would not allow them to accept the kind invitation.

"Get right with Him before the end," the man called after them.

"Let him get right with me," Jeremy muttered. "I'm always protecting his creation for some reason."

Sam glanced at him reproachfully. While she didn't believe, she had been raised "proper," and blaspheming in public was poor manners. He grimaced at her, to be rewarded with a chuckle.

They came out into a huge, vaulted space, roofed in glass, from which descended long strands of plastic, like so much lighted vermicelli.

"Jeremy-kun," Yukari said, her voice serious. "At the far end, by the escalators, there are unhumans."

They advanced slowly to the base of the escalator. At the top stood a half-dozen beings. To a normal person, they would have seemed human but between training, exposure, and nature, the three saw clearly through to warted skin and squinty black eyes below the glamour. These were something like the orcs of the Tolkien movies, dangerous enough in their own way. They wore security uniforms and held a mix of human weapons and crooked scimitars and maces. They lifted their weapons on Jeremy's approach, but the largest and ugliest of them grunted and waved the others back.

"These are expected," he said, in a voice like gravel in a tin can.

"Yeah, me too," came a twangy Southern voice behind them. Debbie Middleton took the escalator stairs two at a time to join them at the top. She wore plain cowboy boots with a low heel, jeans, and a black sweater. A leather jacket replaced her usual rhinestone and denim one and her bright blond hair was almost out of sight under a hat.

"All you forgot was the face-camo," Sam cracked.

"Quiet, little girl," Debbie growled, pointed teeth resting on her lower lip. "I've been scurrying from one patch of shadow to another for two hours, and occasionally starting to burn when I cut it too close. I am in no mood for smart-mouthing."

"Debbie-san," Yukari said with a small bow. "Thank you for coming. We are most pleased and grateful to have you with us."

"Yep," Debbie said, "now them's good manners. Some people could take a page from Yukari's book."

"Which was written in 1932," Sam said, rolling her eyes.

"Take the road show up to the boss," the lead orc said. "Last elevator on bank four, top floor. He's waiting for you, and he doesn't like to wait."

"He should learn patience," Muzania announced, popping into existence next to the orc.

Several things occurred at the same time. The orcs took one look at the angel, shrieked and fled, dropping their weapons to run faster. Debbie yelped and prepared to do the same, but Jeremy grabbed her arm, she then dodged behind him.

"Was that necessary?" Jeremy asked, exasperated.

"Oh hell," Muzania said with a dismissive wave of her hand. "They're useless cannon fodder anyway. If my appearance causes them to flee, what use will they be with the Chaos Angel in sight?"

Her eyes fastened on Debbie, who gave a squeak and pressed against Jeremy's back.

"Allies, remember," Jeremy said.

Muzania ignored them and marched toward the elevator back and perforce they followed, Debbie bringing up the rear. When they reached the elevator, Jeremy pushed the button and the doors opened.

"I'll take the next one," Debbie said.

"Just get in the damn elevator," Muzania growled, "before I fill your D-cups with vampire ashes."

"You'll be fine," Jeremy assured, glaring at the unaffected Muzania. "I guarantee your safety."

"Who guarantees yours?" Debbie whispered from behind him.

"I do," Yukari said. Her eyes glowed bright with inner fire and her hair rippled. The surrounding temperature plunged. Everyone's breath misted in the chilled air. She seemed to almost crackle with suppressed energy.

Muzania's expression took on a worried cast, and she said nothing more, just moved to the back of the elevator as far from Yukari as possible. The rest piled in, Yukari standing next to Jeremy. He reached to pat her shoulder, half-expecting that his hand would pass through her as she now so resembled her former ghostly self, but she was solid, if cool under his hand.

He pushed the button for the top floor; the ride up was long, silent, and cold. The doors finally opened onto a wide and opulent reception area. Only Bob awaited them. As usual, he wore a fine Italian suit, silk tie, and gleaming shoes, and looked more prepared for a hostile takeover than a battle to the death.

"Well, well, Jeremy Leclerc and the whole harem," he said, flashing an insincere smile. "Do you even have any male friends? What do you do on Super Bowl Sunday?"

"Opera, you would like it." Jeremy shot back. "Where are all the troops?"

"Underground, below the parking deck," he said eyeing Muzania. "Not many of them could abide the presence of an angel."

"I know how they feel," Debbie muttered.

"I am no happier in the company of demons, vampires, and this so-called Templar monk," Muzania snapped.

Bob turned to Jeremy. "Monk? Boy, she really missed the briefing on you. Didn't she?"

"Enough," Jeremy said. "We don't have to love each other, but we are all the supernatural power there is in Charlotte. We're the only chance this town has against the Chaos Angel."

Bob nodded and gestured for them to follow. They moved down a hallway lined with original artwork and statuary toward lights and the hum of machinery and voices. The doors slid open at their approach, and they climbed up a spiraling ramp to the next level entering what looked like the combat-information-center of an aircraft carrier. A large screen, overlaid with a map of Charlotte, dominated the room, and there were feeds from CCTV cameras around the building.

"Human staff," Bob said, as he glanced over the scurrying minions. "They don't care much about angels, more about paychecks."

A young attractive brunette strode up to Bob. "Sir."

"Yes, Tamica? Any news?"

"Nothing on the supernatural detection grid," she said with a South African accent. "But the Hobgoblins on Central Avenue haven't reported in. They're overdue by an hour."

"Huh," Bob said, looking up at the map. "The trolls I had in the old Eastland Mall area went dark earlier. I wonder if it's moving through the north of town. Anything on the human stations?"

She shrugged. "The authorities are dealing with unrest and some rioting in the poorer areas of the city. It's worsening quickly. That does include the north, it may be stirring things up to weaken and divert the city authorities."

"You're thinking conventionally," Muzania sneered, "the Chaos Angel follows no law other than its own. It's not concerned about police, guns, or other physicality, or about revealing its existence."

"Yeah," Bob groused. "The damn thing might want Charlotte now and in ten minutes decide to do something else. I hate Chaotic Evil."

"Evil needs a fucking purpose?" Muzania asked, seeming amused.

"Yes," Bob said. "What's the point of evil if it isn't the quickest and easiest way to the best wines, cigars, the finest suits, the nimblest—"

"Language," Jeremy rapped out.

Muzania and Bob both rolled their eyes.

"He's been like this since he brought the little ghost girl back," Muzania sighed.

"Tell me about it," Bob said with feeling.

Yukari walked past the two, past the monitors and the staring human staff to face the huge glass windows that circled the center. Her eyes glowing like the coals of a campfire, reflected back from the glass.

"It is coming this way," she said. "From the north. It's not yet close."

"You can track it?" Bob demanded.

"No," Yukari said over her shoulder, "it is more a matter of feeling. I feel...randomness, power, and a great ennui. I may be feeling it because it is thinking of us. It knows we are here."

"Damn," Bob said.

"You believe this child," Muzania said, "who claims to sense what neither you nor I can?"

"With respect," Yukari said, turning to face the angel. "You are not properly of this world, Muzania-dono. You, Bob-san, are perhaps too much of it, a demon, mere animated base matter of the world without a soul."

Bob opened his mouth, then noted Jeremy's level unblinking stare and closed it.

"Your point?" Debbie said.

"I am of this world, born human, and yet I am a ghost, the rarest of the supernatural beings that humans can become. I stand with a foot in space-time and another in eternity, the place after, reserved for my kind after death takes us. I see more clearly into both worlds than either of you."

"But do you have powers from both worlds?" Sam asked. "There's something ancient and powerful coming."

"Yeah," Debbie added, "I doubt I can bite it or hit it hard enough for it to notice. Frankly, if there was a way out of this town, I would be gone already. What can a vamp do against an angel?

"Sam's a mere human—" she continued.

"Smile when you say that," Sam interjected.

Debbie ignored her. "Jeremy is too, but he bears that damn sword with its magic jewel so maybe he can do something. As for you two, angel and demon, you both were afraid to take this thing on singly; maybe together you can do something. But the X-factor here, the big unknown is Yukari. So, ghost-girl, can you do anything?"

"We shall see, Debbie-san," Yukari returned, unperturbed. "We shall see."

"Ok, enough yakking," Bob said. "We need more info on where this thing is specifically. I got thousands of goblins, trolls, and the like below. I want to hit this thing with everything we got at the same time. A vague feeling of where it is, won't do.

"So, Vamp, you got a relationship with bats, right?"

"Bats," Debbie said. "What am I, sixteen? I haven't played with bats in a hundred years."

"Well regress and send some out," Bob snapped. "We need eyes on the baddie, and we need them now."

"Can't do it from in here," she said.

"Next level is roof access, up the spiral staircase. Tamica," he turned to his aide, "we'll be on the roof. Call me if we learn anything."

"Yes, sir."

CHAPTER THIRTY-TWO

"And yet we shouldn't need the cataclysm to love life today. It would have been enough to think that we are humans, and that death may come this evening."

They trooped up to the door that opened onto the roof. Around them rose the metal projections that crowned the building, but they were exposed to the night air and the wind that howled around the building. They quickly moved into the lee of a large air conditioning unit. Even from this height, they could hear the wail of sirens. Toward Central Avenue, fires could be seen burning.

Just as they reached that shelter, most of the lights in sight flickered and died.

"Crap," Bob said, "that can't be good. We've got a generator, but there will be no information coming in. We're blind now."

He turned to Debbie. "Make with the bats, honey, we are running out of time."

Debbie walked away from them and stood nearer the edge arms raised, head thrown back. Meanwhile Jeremy studied the cloud wall that embraced the city. Only directly above them could a few stars still be seen and a sliver of moon.

"Ever been in a hurricane? It looks like this." Bob's eyes drifted upward, and he sighed. "At least we have the stars and a crescent of moon."

Jeremy glanced in surprise at the demon.

"What, you think my side doesn't appreciate beauty? I like French wine, Italian tailoring, Corinthian leather, and most other beautiful things."

Jeremy nodded, unsure of what to say.

A rustle of wings made them both turn. A cloud of bats circled Debbie, occasionally blocking all sight of the buxom vampire. Then they dispersed, winging into the darkness.

She came back to them. "I can focus on one at a time and see what it sees, or they can report back to me physically. Gimme some quiet while I concentrate." For the next fifteen minutes, Debbie stood motionless as only the undead could. Occasionally a bat would return and light on her shoulder for a few seconds before departing.

"Aha!" Deb said. "Gotcha. I see it at Pecan and Central. Ouch!" She jumped. "God damn it."

"What happened?" Sam asked.

"It probably fried the bat," Bob said.

"Yeah," Debbie swore, "and I felt it across the link."

"We got bats to spare," Bob said.

That turned out not to be true. As soon as one bat reached the area, it winked out of existence. Each time, it stung Debbie like a hornet. Still, it allowed them to track the angel's approach as it marched, apparently at a leisurely pace toward downtown.

"Dammit, that's enough," Debbie said, jumping again. "We gotta find another way to do this."

Muzania's lip curled. "It's playing with us. It's coming straight here."

"We need eyes on," Bob insisted. "It's close to one of the underground entrances. I can send out my troops."

"Send the blond hussy," Debbie said, stung out of all caution. "Doesn't she have wings under that jacket?"

"Hussy!" Muzania snarled. "Pot calling the kettle black!"

Yukari waved them all to silence. "Your army will be of no use. The angel has lifted into the air. I feel it, it is coming. You were right. It was playing with Debbie."

"And you cannot see it?" Jeremy asked of Muzania, while drawing his sword. Behind him, Sam unlimbered her revolver.

"No," she answered reluctantly, as if loath to admit Yukari had some power she did not. "It is far older than I am, maybe far more powerful. I cannot see its mind."

"But it can see yours," Yukari said, in a remote voice. "It is amused by us. We break its everlasting ennui. It's actually grateful for the distraction."

"It is coming," she added, looking into the sky. "It is almost here."

Yukari came back to stand next to Jeremy. Samantha was on his other side. Muzania and Bob took position to the left and right and Debbie fell back to stand between them and Bob.

Then it was there, looking down at them. It floated near the edge of the building, tattered gossamer wings spread wide behind it, glowing softly. It had a ruined beauty to it, Jeremy thought, like a great actress past her prime. There was something indistinct in the apparition, as if it stood partly in this world and partly in another.

It drifted closer, eyes considering, measuring, and dismissing each of them in turn. "Angel, demon, vampire, Templar, human..." Its eyes rested on Yukari, who stood facing it, straight and slim, the breeze stirring the skirt she wore and tugging at her hair. Its expression grew clouded, like a young child's. "And what are you?"

Yukari, her hands knotted together, contemplated the angel with a calmness Jeremy could not emulate. She did not speak but maintained that faintly smiling Japanese face she reserved for when she wanted to keep her thoughts to herself. She simply bowed to acknowledge the angel.

"Human," the Chaos Angel said, "of the Realm of Earth but not... How can this be?"

"What do you want?" Jeremy demanded, concerned over its focus on Yukari.

It turned to face him and he, who had more experience of angels than any living man, felt the hair on the back of his head rise. This was no gentle guardian; this was something raw and powerful, deadly dangerous. He was like a grain of sand on a beach under that searching regard. Coldness infiltrated his blood, his bones, and his soul.

"I have decided to make this place mine," it replied, waving an indolent hand at the city below.

"For what purpose?" he managed, sliding his hand over the hilt of the bloodsword. He fancied that warmth spread from the gem, easing the numbness in his hand, seeping through his body. Perhaps it was a reminder that somehow, he was not merely a grain of sand, that he had a place in the immensity of the universe.

"Purpose?" the Chaos Angel echoed, seeming genuinely puzzled. "My will is its own purpose. I need no other."

"Why are you here?" he demanded again. "There is more to it than that."

The angel regarded him. "It is an interesting place. Causality, that most tedious of all music—flat, bland, and repetitive—is weakened here. So much that is chaos borders this place."

"The people of this city are not playthings for you," he challenged.

"This does not concern me," it replied, its eyes sliding off him in disinterest.

Muzania stepped forward. "Disobedient angel, have you not disturbed The Plan enough in your vainglory?"

A cold smile came over the Chaos Angel's face. "Stupid child, do not speak so to your elders. I walked the corridors of eternity when you were discordant ether. The warp and weft of space-time were my instrument. I sang before the light came."

"She ain't alone," Bob chimed in. "Though, I'll grant that I never thought the day would come when I would say that."

"Ah, this is wearying. Imbecile children and animated dust fatigue me with their nonsense. I, who made some of the superstructure of space-time itself."

"You lack modesty and humility," Yukari said into the spreading silence. "It is unbecoming in one who claims greatness."

The Chaos Angel turned its curious regard on her but did not speak.

"Enough talk," Muzania said. "You know the Law as do I; our powers are limited for the Realm of Earth."

"You will find," the Chaos Angel said, and now there was no mistaking a malicious edge to its voice, "that even what limited powers I bring here are far more than enough. I have tarried here and favored you with my attention more than you merit."

"Big talk," Bob said. The emanations from the angels had disrupted his appearance. Horns sprouted from his head and a tail whipped around his Luisaviaroma suit.

The Chaos Angel laughed, a bell-like sound that reverberated in the air.

Everything happened at once. Power roiled in Muzania's hands, flashing like lighting, but an instant later the angel was filling a massive dent in the huge a/c unit behind them. Jeremy hadn't even seen her be flung back. He more felt that heard that sound of the impact.

Bob dashed forward on the right, Debbie on the left, both moving faster than humans could. As Jeremy raised his sword, he could hear the pitiful bark of Sam's revolver behind him.

But as quickly as the attack began, it ended. Bob got off his shot, a ball of red power the angel deflected with a delicate wave of its hand. It returned a bolt of blue that flung Bob spinning off the building, into the night, without even a cry.

What smashed Debbie into the concrete parapet was invisible and not as hard as what struck Muzania, as if she was not worth the effort. The vampire's bones made a horrible sound as they shattered. She lay still, blood leaking from her body.

The angel's face turned to Jeremy, and it held every horror that man dreaded in it. His felt his will sapped, his courage blown away and his strength fail. He stumbled to his knees. Behind him he could see Sam face down and still. They were dust, mere ephemera in eternity. How dare they oppose a creator of the universe?

He turned an anguished face to Yukari, hoping she was not destroyed.

But the ghost girl stood tall, hair now whipping and rising around, her. Yukari's face was resolute and her eyes glowed coal-red.

How was she standing? The awful presence of the Chaos Angel had driven him to his knees despite the bloodsword. As he looked up at her, the terrible pressure on him eased. The angel's attention had shifted to Yukari. Its form was now less distinct, and it seemed the sketch of an angelic figure on a billowing darkness, a half-glimpsed horror of a winged shape.

"Fall," it demanded.

Yukari staggered and stepped back, but she did not fall, or turn from her enemy.

Jeremy tried to rise but could not find the strength. "Run, Yukari, run!"

"I will not abandon you, Oniichan," she said. "You did not abandon me. Nor will I leave our friends unprotected.

"You," she shouted at the angel, her eyes standing out like beacons in the darkness enveloping the tower. "You have no place here. Release your hold on the world and return to the outer dark."

"Do not bid me stay or go," the voice intoned, deep now and menacing. "Die now."

"I will not listen to you," Yukari shot back. Her face had become that of the Dark Yukari of before: grim, resolute, and powerful.

"I am an angel of origin," it said. "You are nothing in my sight."

"I am human," Yukari said. "I am all that humanity is and can be, its lows, its failures, its loves. I stand here in the place ordained for my kind. It is you who offend the Wa of the world. You do not command me, Angel. You were not given dominion over this world."

"Not given dominion," Jeremy repeated. It raced around in his mind. "Not given dominion. This is our place, ours!" Strength began to return to his body. The gem in his sword hilt glowed, but not its usual sullen red, this was a yellow glow like sunrise over fields. He fought to his feet and staggered to Yukari's side. They stood together and he felt additional strength flow into him, not from the sword, but from the girl at his side.

She could only spare him a moment's glance, but it held such feeling that it shattered the last of his enemy's hold on him. Now they were shoulder to shoulder, his sword before him not as a blade, but reversed, gem up, glowing to hold away the darkness that whirled around them.

He looked around at the fallen Muzania, her face hidden beneath her hair, unmoving in the massive dent of the aluminum wall, Debbie, who lay still by the wall where Bob had vanished.

"It's on us," he said.

"Yes, Oniichan," Yukari said. "This is our world. We are not the toys of this spoiled child, descended to a lesser being by its own choice."

"Die," the Chaos Angel shrieked. The crushing weight of its will drove them backward. Around them concrete cracked and metal began to twist and shriek. Jeremy cast a panicked glance at Sam, face down a yard behind them.

"Jeremy," Yukari said. "We must hold. Samantha cannot survive this if we are driven past her. We must stand together."

Her hands wrapped over his own on the sword and both pressed their full wills into the glowing gem. The stone's yellow light waxed brighter. The pressure receded. Darkness fell back before the light.

"Demons and angels fall before me," the darkness hissed, its wings flapping. "You cannot withstand me. I am unique. I make my own music. I sing my own songs. I am not a mere handyman to do the work of others."

"Ungrateful child," Yukari scolded. "Who gave you your music? Did you create yourself, that you should be so proud? Like us, you were created by that which was before."

"Where is it now?" the Chaos Angel taunted. "Why does it not defend you from me?"

"Because this is our world, we define ourselves in it," Yukari said. "I am who I decide I am."

"Fool," it said. "I will show you what you really are. I will strip the glamour of life you pretend to have from you. Let your companion see what you really are."

An awful stench of death and decay rolled over Jeremy. He looked at Yukari and gasped, falling back from the tottering corpse of rotted flesh, exposed bone, matted hair, and ragged clothing.

"No," he managed. "No. You came back. You were alive."

"Jeremy," the stick figure of bone and rags said. "Believe. Believe in me. Not in the words of this spiteful monster." Her eyes were still hers, glowing in the ruined face. They held the same shock, the same betrayal as when he had struck her down with the bloodsword.

"Why don't you believe?"

He wanted to look away but couldn't.

"*Doshte?*" she cried.

The word hung in the air as if it had physical existence, falling in slow motion to the ground between them.

Doshte, he thought. *Why don't you believe? You heard this once before. You vowed to yourself that there would never again be such a failure. Death first.*

Fury overtook him and displaced everything else.

"How dare you?" he screamed. "How dare you do this to Yukari?"

The sword gem blazed as it had never before. He cared nothing if it consumed him in the process so long as he struck his enemy down first. Yellow sunrise enveloped him. He moved and pulled Yukari to him, reckoning nothing of sight or scent. The cleansing yellow glow fell on her, and she was Yukari again. Her eyes glowed, but yellow as if the stone's power was suffusing her. He could see the tear tracks on her face, and his anger turned to icy, remorseless, determination.

"I'm sorry," he said, touching her face. "I believe in you. I've believed in you from the first moments I met you."

Her smile was all the answer he needed.

"Unjust Angel, uncaring monster," he swore. "You have no dominion here." He advanced, the sword a flaming torch before him.

Yukari her hands level, with force rippling about her, advanced along-side him.

"You have no dominion here," they chanted as they advanced. The Chaos Angel began to back from them.

"Yukari," he whispered. "I don't have the strength to block and attack. We can't let it get away."

"It cannot abide me," she said. "Throw the power of the gem behind it and follow me."

He leaned forward into the impeding will of the angel and forced himself to concentrate, imagining a wall of golden light behind the twisting darkness. It built, defining and holding the darkness. Yukari, as if advancing into a great wind, leaned forward, gaining each step with terrible effort, but the angel gave way, shrieking and battering at the wall that arched up and over it, as it retreated from Yukari.

"I will yield," it cried. "Give me leave to go, and I will flee."

"You have hurt many and for what but your vanity?" Jeremy grated. "But worst of all, you made Yukari taste death a second time. This, I can never forgive!"

With the last of his will, he brought the yellow wall in to envelope the Chaos Angel. The golden glow wrapped like a blanket around the struggling angel, and in a last convulsion both disappeared into the void. Air shrieked into the wound in space-time. They were thrown from their feet as thunder blasted them.

AFTERMATH

Consciousness came back to Jeremy slowly; he was lying on the rooftop, a light rain falling on him. He fought to hang on to awareness as his vision swam. He turned to where the angel had been ripped into the void, but there was nothing there. The sword lay under his hand next to him, its gem cracked and lifeless, the blade was burned. Sound came back, wind and the patter of rain.

Yukari, where is Yukari?

He saw her form lying yards away face down and still.

"No," he demanded, willing his body forward into a crawl. "No. I believe, Yukari. I believe. I believe." He reached her, forced himself up to sitting and pulled her into his lap. He pressed her to him, and kissed her, tears flowing down his face. He sat rocking her in his arms as the rain fell on them.

"Oniichan," came the whisper, "you must not cry."

His head snapped up. "Yukari," he said, brushing wet hair from her face.

"Yes," she replied, eyes barely open, but the tiniest of smiles curved her lips. "I live."

He ran his hands over her, searching for broken bones, bleeding, anything amiss.

"Oniichan," she said, embarrassed. "What will people think?"

He laughed, though it came out as something between a laugh and a sob. He held her to him and buried his face in her hair. "I don't care what anyone thinks. I only care that you're alive."

"You believed in me," she said, when he sat back.

"Yes. For the first time in my life, I completely believed in something, and it came true. For the first time."

"I am glad," she replied. "I think I can stand, if you help me."

They struggled to their feet and staggered over to Sam, but she was already sitting up, shivering in the wet and looking like someone glad to escape a horrible dream.

"Are you both all right?" she asked, as they helped the smaller woman up. "What happened?"

"Exhausted," Jeremy said, "but not more." Though he cast another anxious look at Yukari, who simply shook her head and smiled.

"I am well," Yukari said. "Perhaps more than you, Onii. I feel my connection with the world even more now. I will tend to Sam-chan."

He nodded and headed for Debbie. The vampire lay where she had been hurled. The puddle spreading around was tinged with her blood.

"Is she," Sam called, "is she...dead? Well, more dead than usual. That kind of not moving around, not talking, dead?"

Jeremy knelt beside Debbie, whose eyes slitted open. "Did you get it?"

"Yeah," he nodded. "It's gone. But what of you?"

"I'm a bag of broken bones, boy. It slammed me into the wall but good. I can't die unless the Big Yellow comes up, or my head comes off, but I never hurt like this before. I'm going to be a long time healing. I need a safe place to rest."

"We'll get you home," he promised.

"No, Jeremy. I need a place I can be guarded. I won't be able to protect myself for months."

"Okay, my place then, but what do we do—"

"For blood?" she managed though it was clearly hard to speak. "I've prepared for a day like this. Remember this number." She gave him an

888 number. "They'll deliver what I need to survive. May need an occasional sip of your high-test, baby."

"Can we move you?"

"Gonna have to. Sun gets me otherwise. Thought I was in trouble when your gem turned yellow, but it didn't hurt me. Find some of Bob's minions, they'll be used to moving bodies and they ain't gonna screw with you, especially with Bob gone."

"Okay," Jeremy said, wiping the drizzle from her face. The rain had slackened and the clouds above were thinning and breaking up. Dawn would come soon.

He turned to Yukari, who was supporting Sam, then looked past them to the a/c unit. He could see the dent into which Muzania had been slammed, but the angel was gone.

"Until the enemy is taken or destroyed," he murmured, "but not a second longer. So be it." He drew his Walther, scooped up the scorched bloodsword with its broken gem, and set off in search of minions.

They fled back to Jeremy's home, aided by the fact that power, light, and communications had returned to Charlotte. The radio blasted the good news that the rest of the world was still there. State police, troops, and all the apparatus of a modern state flooded in. Some, still panicked by the freak storm, clogged the outbound roads, fearful of its return.

In the chaos of the reviving city's morning hours, they made their way back to his condo. While Yukari seemed none the worse for wear, her eyes still glowed with their inner fire. He hoped it would fade soon or he would need to find sunglasses for her at least. Sam, utterly exhausted, fell into Jeremy's bed and was asleep in seconds. He removed her shoes, relieved her of the .357, then covered her in a blanket and went downstairs.

A van pulled up behind the house. He raised the garage door to see four of Bob's human, or nearly human, minions holding a casket. With a glance to see that none of the neighbors were watching, he ushered them in, then up to the small loft at the top of the stairs that he'd never found any use for before today. The minions left silently. Jeremy opened the casket and looked inside at Debbie, who didn't react. An IV was already attached to her, and he set up the small stand for it. Fortunately, the yucky details of attending to a human in such a state didn't apply. A vampire was the ultimate closed system, blood in and nothing out.

A scent of food reached him. Yukari was keeping house again; normalcy was returning to the world. With a last check of the quiescent Debbie, he decided to check in again at Sam before continuing downstairs. He sat next to his friend for a moment as a wave of fatigue settled on him.

Jeremy woke with a start. He realized he was face down on the bed next to Sam. *Should have put Sam in Yukari's room,* he thought fuzzily. He must have fallen asleep for a few minutes while checking on her. He carefully slipped off the bed, leaving Sam undisturbed. He heard Yukari's voice and wondered who she was speaking to. There was something in the tone of Yukari's voice that banished the last of sleepiness from him.

"Not Muzania," he muttered, "anything but that." Worry struck him anew and he sped down only to freeze at the bottom of the stairs.

Yukari sat on the edge of the couch, her hands clasped, staring wide-eyed at the girl opposite her.

Shadowheart, in her blond, teenage manifestation, sat in the stuffed chair opposite Yukari. She wore Daisy Duke shorts and a halter top over a belly well-rounded in pregnancy. She was chewing bubblegum and giving Yukari a cool regard.

Both women spotted him at the same instant. Yukari's eyes blazed red as Shadowheart stood bolt-upright and pointed a finger at him.

"You did this to me!" she shrilled.

"Oniichan!" Yukari demanded, clearly scandalized.

Jeremy couldn't move or speak. The cosmological dimensions of the disaster facing him were too great.

Suddenly Shadowheart blew a bubble and snapped it. In the same instant, her belly went taut and flat.

"Just funning you," she said with an evil grin.

Jeremy folded down on the stairs, unable to stand. Yukari stared open-mouthed in a very un-Japanese fashion.

"Hey, I'm back," Shadowheart said brightly. "Didja miss me?"

The End